# Death of a Busybody

# Death
## of a
# Busybody

**DELL SHANNON**

MYSTERY GUILD
Doubleday Book & Music Clubs, Inc.
Garden City, New York

ISBN 1-56865-082-5

He who pries into every cloud may be stricken with a thunderbolt.

Old Proverb

# 1

"Nice big lots," said Alison, "two hundred by three hundred. And all the trees left. On Jovenita Canyon Road. *No*, Sheba!" She rescued her clean stockings and began to put them on.

"I refuse," said Mendoza from the bathroom, "to live on a street called Little Woman Canyon."

"Well, I know, but— Get *down*, Nefertite, *not* my earrings. There were some on Appian Way too." Silence from the bathroom, except for splashing, was not encouraging. "I didn't like the one on Elusive Drive," she said hastily. "Too hilly. And Lulu Glen is too far up."

"*¡Por mi vida!*" said Mendoza. "Who names these places?"

"I can't imagine," said Alison, removing Bast from her dress on the bed and starting to get into it. Emerging in the middle of a sentence, she added, "—On account of the cats. Because almost anywhere else it's illegal to keep more than three, of course. It wouldn't be too much of a drive for you, would it, darling? There were two others at the end of a street called Haslam Terrace—"

"Possible," said Mendoza. He came out of the bathroom, shirtless, and surveyed her with approval. "I don't know why we're going to build a house. And don't say because I didn't like any of those already built."

"Because you can't bring up children in an apartment."

"All right, all right. Two. No more. If I had had any idea you harbored these medieval notions—"

"But you can afford more. Not like most people. Oh, damn. Come and fasten this, Luis."

"As if that had anything to do with it." He came and fastened it. They both looked at Alison in the mirror and were pleased, from their reflected expressions. Mendoza bent and kissed the back of her neck.

"So we'll go and look at the lots on Haslam Terrace tomorrow." He went to get a clean shirt.

"Yes, I thought so. Where are you taking Art?"

"As it happens, nowhere but the office. Something more showed up on a case."

"Oh," said Alison, spraying cologne. "Well, buy him a drink or something afterward—better not let him go until at least eleven. These hen-parties—Luis, you left the closet door open."

It was too late. El Señor had noticed before she had. Six ties lay in a heap on the floor while El Señor reached for the seventh, delicately.

"*¡Señor Molestio!*" said Mendoza. "*¡Salga de acqui*—bad cat!*" He began to pick up the ties. El Señor stalked across the room, floated lightly up to the bureau-top and fixed a cold stare on his mother Bast, who was industriously washing his sister Sheba. Mendoza put on shirt, tie, and jacket. Alison picked up her short coat and bag; in the living-room collected a large gift-wrapped box. The cats sat in a row across the living-room floor and watched them.

"Did you latch the record-cabinet, *novia?*"

"It doesn't matter," said Alison, "he's found out how to unlatch it, I meant to tell you."

"That cat. I tell you, it's reincarnation. He was a sorcerer or a high priest in Egypt."

El Señor slitted his green eyes and yawned at them. El Señor looked like the negative of a Siamese cat; he was mostly black with blond touches on face, ears, paws and tail-tip. He stared at them and moved his tail once, contemptuously.

"*No me tome el palo,*" said Mendoza, "you know, but you won't tell!" He shut the door behind them and they went out to the garage. "Be careful now, *querida*. Lock both doors on your way home—"

"Don't fuss, I've lived in a big city quite awhile and survived. You too . . . Here, wait a minute, you're all over lipstick— Have a nice time with your murderer, darling."

He watched her back out the Facel-Vega Excellence before opening the driver's door of the big black Ferrari. He thought, sliding under the wheel, the trouble was he didn't think they could get Benson on a murder charge. Quite likely only plain manslaughter. Moral certainty was not evidence; it was annoying.

Alison drove toward Highland Park sedately, on her way to a shower for Mrs. Arthur Hackett who was expecting a baby in September. She thought amusedly about Luis. Two only, he said in horror. Am I merely a stud animal? Well, as to that— The fact was, of course, that many more than two (and of course she *was* thirty-three next November, a horrid thought) and people would think, oh, well, Mendoza, naturally. Like that. When he hadn't set foot in a church for twenty-five years. Men.

Indeed, men. This car—and that Ferrari. They said it could go a hundred and sixty-three miles an hour, and he never drove over sixty. Not often, anyway. *Eighteen* thousand dollars. And insisting on getting her the Facel-Vega, when she'd preferred that nice little Mercedes sports-car. "Those little things are dangerous in traffic. No." "Well, if you like the Facel-Vega so much, why don't you have one too, instead of that ridiculous Martian-looking racing car? After all—" "Unpleasant associations," he'd said. He'd smashed up a Facel-Vega last year, chasing after Alison and a murderer. Well, it was a nice car to handle . . .

She went out Los Feliz, took the Golden State Freeway down to Figueroa and got onto the Pasadena Freeway. The quickest way, really. Followed that up into Highland Park, got off it and drove up to Spring-vale Street where Sergeant Hackett and his Angel had lived in an almost-new house since January.

She didn't anticipate enjoying the evening greatly. Angel, as involuntary hostess (it was a surprise shower) wouldn't be able to chat with individuals much; the woman who had called Alison had been a stranger, a Mrs. Larkin, and doubtless most of the guests would be too —people Angel had known before she knew Alison Weir Mendoza, people she knew from the job she'd briefly held before she married Art.

There were people already there. Cars crowded along the curb, both sides; perhaps other people along here were having parties tonight. Alison parked the car halfway down the block and walked back. Angel, looking pretty and flushed in a very smart navy maternity-smock, kissed her at the door; said all the expected things and in a whisper, "Thanks for letting me know!" Because Alison, having some common sense, had: knowing how Angel would hate being "surprised" with a party the night she had planned to wash her hair or give herself a facial. These hearty extroverts.

She filed her gift-parcel with the others, was introduced to eight or ten other women. She had met only one of them before, Roberta Silverman—an overtall, dark girl about twenty-eight, with a careless drawl and lovely dark eyes, an interesting face. As a painter, Alison saw faces a little differently than other people. Most people wouldn't call Roberta Silverman goodlooking; Alison would. An interesting face, flat-planed, and that mobile wide mouth. And she remembered liking her, too. Unfortunately, she was at once shunted into a small group of strangers. A Miss Chadwick, Margaret Chadwick. A Joy Chester or Chesterton. A Mrs. Larkin, the one who had called her.

Everyone was social and gay; ashtrays filled, were emptied. Margaret Chadwick, beside Alison on the couch, talked to her more than anyone else, in a thin discontented voice. Margaret Chadwick hadn't much to say of good cheer; the burden of her talk was largely complaints about rude salespeople, garage-mechanics who overcharged, and the awful weather. Tiring of Margaret rather soon, Alison made several polite attempts to change her seat but was foiled each time; it was a smallish room, and crowded. Once she intercepted a sympathetic glance from Roberta Silverman; and about ten minutes later, turning to stub out a cigarette, she saw Roberta Silverman's eyes fixed on Miss Chadwick with something very like hatred. The next moment the dark eyes dropped, and Alison wondered if she was imagining things. A dull person, yes, a dreary girl, but that was not enough for hate, merely dislike.

Angel's bright little living-room (those curtains had been a bargain, so right for the room, and wasn't that a new lamp table?) was filled with unfortunately high-pitched female chatter. Everyone was having a fine time. Presently there came the high moment of gift-unwrapping, and Angel was properly and prettily grateful and admiring over everything, from the inevitably duplicated bootees to the eminently practical packages of diapers. And shortly after that Alison found herself in the kitchen helping Angel set out plates—open sandwiches, cake and coffee.

"How I loathe these affairs, *which* is ungrateful," said Angel. "But you know. It's so nice of all of you, I appreciate it. But—" she glanced sideways at Alison over a poised slice of cake— "in the middle of a hen-party, I really don't like women very much at all."

"How well I know what you mean," said Alison. "I told Luis to keep Art busy until at least eleven, but that's only another hour or so. Be bloody, bold and resolute, stick it out and eventually we'll be at peace alone with our men."

"So much more restful," said Angel, and having served the last piece of cake, licked frosting off the knife. "Thank God you warned me . . . You rather got stuck with Margaret Chadwick, I'm sorry."

Alison knew what she meant there too. "Where's she date from, school or later?"

"Oh, school," said Angel rather vaguely. Angel had had a childhood, a young-girlhood, she didn't much enjoy looking back on. "You could say. We were at Merriam's Academy together. I expect it was Rose Larkin—included her tonight. She's all right, but—"

And then someone came in eagerly offering to help serve. The serving was accomplished. The bright female chatter continued as everyone settled again, ate sandwiches and cake and drank coffee.

Alison had ended up back in her original place, there being none other empty. She sat beside Margaret Chadwick, who had not offered to help serve plates. She longed to tell Margaret Chadwick that that fussy powder-blue dress with its lace-trimmed collar was all wrong for her.

"You just have to watch these people like a hawk or something, you know. They'll shortchange you every time if they think they can get away with it." Margaret Chadwick was about twenty-eight (Angel's age). She hadn't a bad figure, a rather good one for very plain, tailored things—which meant, face it, almost no figure. She was tall and thin, rather bony; she had a narrow face with quite regular features, but she'd thinned her eyebrows too drastically and her lipstick was too pale—these newly fashionable "muted" shades; she needed a good deep-toned pink lipstick, with her dark brown hair and fair skin. Her eyes were an unfortunately pale blue and she wore a perpetual expression of faint disapproval. Of, apparently, everything.

"Such shoddy materials," she was saying now, looking at the pile of presents on the coffee-table. "I said to the clerk, Is that the best you have? And such outrageous prices too. People trying to do you out of money, any way at all . . . That's a very pretty ring, Mrs.—Mendoza? Is it a real emerald, may I ask?"

"Well, yes," said Alison, and thought she sounded apologetic for no good reason.

"And your earrings and bracelet. How nice. I'm afraid I'm terribly old-fashioned, I never feel quite respectable wearing rings when I have on colored polish. Of course, I don't wear it as a rule. It gets chipped so easily, doesn't it? Have you known dear Angel long, Mrs. Mendoza?"

Alison said equably, "Just a couple of years." The delicate implication there put over very nicely: *I* have had a socially better bringing-up—such vulgar display, jewels *and* colored polish—and, faintly, the inevitable prejudice: Mexicans-and-people-like-that. "My husband and Angel's husband work together—Lieutenant Mendoza."

"Oh, yes. Such a—an unusual job, a police officer." And then the phone rang, and Angel went into the little hall to answer it, came back and said it was someone who wanted Miss Chadwick. And Margaret Chadwick went out, and after a short time came back, smiling. By then Alison had succeeded in finding a seat near Roberta Silverman.

Between ten-thirty and eleven the hen-party broke up. Margaret Chadwick was one of the first to leave. Others drifted off after her, saying all the indicated things. Alison murmured, "Dishes?" to Angel.

"Don't bother, it's nothing. I'll stack them and Art can help me in the morning . . . Thanks, Alison."

Alison thought a little regretfully, no casual, Regards to Luis, etcetera. Luis and Angel didn't appreciate each other. Funny, when I like Art, thought Alison vaguely. It was ten past eleven when she left. Dutifully she locked both doors of the car. Drove down to the Pasadena Freeway, followed it back to the Golden State, turned right there. Scarcely any traffic at this hour. She turned on Fletcher Drive, up to Rowena, and up past there to dead-end St. John Place. She slid the Facel-Vega into her garage-slot. The space next it was empty, though it was ten to twelve. She'd expected him to be home before her.

Three of the cats were asleep in a neat huddle on the couch. El Señor sat before the record-cabinet, which was open, contemplating the photograph of Harry Belafonte on the album dragged onto the floor.

"¡Señor Demonio!" said Alison, put the album back, shut the cabinet, went into the bedroom and did some worrying as she undressed.

They had gone out to arrest somebody, and he'd had a gun, and Luis was in the morgue and Art in the General Hospital. He'd got in the way of a drunk driver on his way home. There had been—

When he came in she was sitting up in bed smoking, surrounded by cats. "You're in the morgue and I've been shopping for black dresses," she told him.

"¡Que atrocidad, mi corazon! Only more paper-work at the office . . . New nightgown. Very nice. Did you have fun at your hen-party?"

"No. Angel and I both agree, females en masse can be horribly boring . . . Look out, don't sit on Sheba."

Mendoza laughed. "But who wants them en masse? Much more fun in the singular . . ."

"Mmh," said Alison presently, "and also, I suppose—I just thought of that—because of the red hair."

"What because of what?"

"You. About children. Because it's quite likely that at least half of them would have, isn't it? And it would be rather funny at that—red-haired Mendozas."

"Are you back to that again? *¡Frene—ay de hijos todos!* Let go of me, let me get undressed. I've been up since six and working on this damned Benson thing, and then when I do get home you nag at me—"

"Yes, dear. And not so young as you were either, I know—you need your sleep. Would you like some hot milk?" asked Alison solicitously.

*"Impudente,"* said Mendoza.

"Well, tomorrow *is* Sunday. Do you have to rush right downtown after the Benson thing, whatever it is? I want you to see those lots, so we can decide."

"And then there'll be an architect, and too much money paid out, and new furniture— Of course, one thing, it'll keep you occupied and take your mind off this hypothetical family awhile . . . All right, all right. You take me to see the lots tomorrow." Mendoza lifted an armful of cats off the bed, deposited them in the nearest chair, and reached for the lamp-switch.

But he did not get taken to see the lots next morning. Because at six o'clock next morning an employee of the Southern Pacific on his way to work noticed something lying up against the high fence which separates North Broadway from the S. P. main freight-yards, and stopped to investigate. After which he called the police. It was, of course, in the headquarters area, so some men came straight out from headquarters.

It was a dead woman lying there; she had been dead some time; she had been strangled. The police didn't have any trouble finding out who she was: her handbag was lying right there beside her. All the bills (if there had been any) had been taken out of her wallet, but apparently nothing else, and the I.D. card and driver's license identified her as a Miss Margaret Chadwick of 6704 Franklin Avenue, Hollywood.

# 2

Mendoza contemplated the array of objects on his desk. It was an old subject for jokes to a lot of people: the junk in a female's handbag. To a homicide officer, it was more apt to have the connotation, possessions of deceased.

There was the handbag, a smart black patent-leather one. It had a rough abrasion on one side; otherwise it looked brand-new, and the lining was not stained with powder. There was a gold loose-powder compact, a clean powder puff, and two lipsticks. One was "Coral Pastel," and the other "Pink Pastel." There was a used handkerchief, white with an embroidered M in one corner, and a clean folded handkerchief, blue-and-rose printed. There was a wallet, feminine version, of tan ostrichskin. In the wallet's coin-pocket was ninety-seven cents in change; in the wallet's little plastic slots were a filled-out identity card, a driver's license recently renewed, a candid snapshot of a youngish man, a library-card, a membership-card of a West Hollywood women's club for the present year, and that was all. No Social Security card. After the wallet came a checkbook in a leather folder stamped with her name. It held seven blank checks, which were also printed with her name. There was a small address-book of red leather. An automatic pencil, silver and black: a famous brand. A fountain pen ditto. A little folder of tear-off memo-notes. A leather key-case with three keys in it. A pair of glasses in a silk case. The glasses were of exaggerated Harlequin shape, blue set with rhinestones; the silk case was blue, embroidered in white. There was a small ingenious gadget, a pocket calculator for doing quick sums. There was a green leather case containing a pair of manicure scissors and a nail-file. There was a crayon-like object which, by its label, when moistened halted runs in stockings. There was a dollar-bill which had been tucked, folded small, out of sight in an inner pocket of the hand-bag. There was a little gold box studded with blue stones, which con-tained three aspirins. There was a long, flat, polished gold cigarette-case, made to hold a full pack; left in it were four Marlboros. There was a gold lighter. There was one full book of matches, and one half-used. There was an unopened pack of Marlboro cigarettes.

"*Ver y creer*," said Mendoza, "seeing is believing. Wasn't she careful and foresighted, though! Very unfeminine—or is it?"

"What?" Hackett looked up from the map spread out before him.

"Everything she might need. Several things she'd need only in vari-ous kinds of emergency. A second handkerchief. A second lipstick. Just going out on an evening party, her address book. None of these keys are car-keys—I'd say two house-keys and a key to a safety-vault. So she kept her car-keys in a separate case. So careful. A handy little calculator—to check up on salesclerks? A manicure set in case she broke a fingernail. This thing to stop a run in her stocking if one got started. A dollar tucked away in case she lost her wallet. Aspirin in case she had a head-ache. A fresh pack of cigarettes in case she finished all those in the case. A lighter—which works," and he snapped it, "but also matches—just in case. A pen and also a pencil, and a memo-pad, in case she needed to write somebody a note. Her checkbook, in case she needed to write a check. She didn't need glasses for driving, so her license says—so, just for reading, maybe. Yet she brings them along to the party."

"So?"

"So, wasn't she the careful, efficient one, our Margaret, looking ahead? No Social Security card—the set-up looks like money, yes. What a waste—she'd have made somebody an inhumanly good secretary." Mendoza went on staring at the array.

Hackett looked at him. "Don't," he said. "Don't, Luis, try to turn it all complicated just for a hunch. It's run of the mill. She was driving home alone from a party, about eleven o'clock. Her best way was down the Pasadena Freeway to the Golden State, and then up Rowena or one of the through streets there to reach Franklin. O.K. Somewhere on the Pasadena Freeway or at the exchange-point, she ran into trouble. Stopped for some reason, and somebody jumped into the car. Or some-thing. Anyway, she picked up a passenger. Who forced her into some dark side-street down there, killed her, robbed her, tossed the body and the bag out, and drove off in the car. The place where Riverside—the Golden State—joins the Pasadena Freeway is about ten blocks away from the freight yards. North Broadway's deserted and dark as hell, that hour. He wouldn't even have to stop. Slow down, shove her out. No sidewalks, so she rolled up against the fence. That's all."

"No," said Mendoza, shaking his head. "Don't try to cover it up, Arturo. You did it. She'd been inciting Angel to leave you, telling her a lot of nasty lies. So you lurked until she came out, followed her, stopped her and killed her. And of course your wife will give you a false alibi. What did you do with the car?"

"These labored jokes," said Hackett, annoyed. "So it is a little— unusual—that she'd been at my wife's party. That Angel knew her— that Alison knew her." Because that was one of the first things they'd heard. Sergeant Lake, calling Hackett at home to invite him to Sunday work, had reported the identity, and Angel, of course, had told him of Margaret's presence at the shower. "All kinds of people get themselves knocked off. Now listen, Luis—" He was exasperated: Luis was wearing that familiar look.

"That's what we were meant to think," said Mendoza. "The random pro thing. But this was a private kill, I can smell it."

Hackett shut his eyes. But he had known it when Mendoza had gone on hanging around. Ordinarily, a thing like this on a Sunday morning, he'd come in for half an hour to set the ball rolling, leave it with Hackett or one of the other sergeants. On this one, he'd hung around. Had a look at the corpse: pored over everything they had, which wasn't much yet. Now he pulled the outside phone toward him and dialed.

"Look, *querida*, I'm stuck here for awhile, I'm sorry—"

Hackett heard Alison's outraged wail from where he sat, and said aloud, "That's a lie. It's a perfectly straightforward—"

"Yes, I know, *novia*, but . . . I'll be home by three, I promise, we can go then . . . Well, it's a very funny thing, but you happen to be a witness in the case and I'll have to come home to pick your brains sometime . . . Margaret Chadwick, you met her at that affair last night. Murdered. Immediately afterward . . . Oh? *¿Parece mentira?* That's interesting. Yes, I want to hear all about it—later. Three o'clock . . . No, I am not heartless . . . No . . . Three o'clock," said Mendoza firmly, and replaced the receiver. "Alison says that after talking with Miss Chadwick for an hour or so, she's not surprised that someone murdered her. The girl was a dead bore, she says."

"Yes, we're always running across people who kill people because they're so boring. I've known you to have some offbeat hunches, and a few of them paid off, but— Just give me one good reason, on this."

Mendoza pointed at the array on the desk. "That cigarette-case is fourteen-karat. So is the lighter. Why didn't this random killer take them? He went through her bag—he had to, to get the wallet, which ten to one was in the bottom under other things, being one of the heaviest items. Also, why was he so helpful as to toss the bag after her? Containing evidence of her identity? The quicker we know who she was, the quicker we know she was driving and put out a call on her car. Which I trust has been done."

Hackett nodded. "Nineteen-sixty Buick hardtop coupé, light blue."

"Oh, really. All this adds up to money. The cigarette-case—Franklin Avenue—I wonder how much cash was in that wallet. But that's just what it was meant to look like, the random theft and murder. Victim might have been anybody, sure. So we don't look at her, we go chasing off after him."

"Look," said Hackett. "So it was maybe a punk kid, his first time at something big. So it was a hophead using just half a mind. They make mistakes or we wouldn't catch so many."

"And she was on freeways all the way, except for—give me that map —except for ten or fifteen blocks between your house and the nearest entrance to the Pasadena Freeway. No sidewalks on freeways, no traffic-lights. Why did she stop? Presumably she had a little sense. No woman driving alone at night would stop for a hitch-hiker or any lone male waving at her. Where do we get that kind of thing, a man jumping a car with a single person in it, late at night? On main drags where traffic-lights are still operating to stop the car for him. And not as much of it as there used to be, at that."

"We don't know that she was on either freeway," said Hackett. "Some people are afraid of them, avoid them. No, there wouldn't be the traffic, even on Saturday night, at that hour. But people who avoid the freeways do it automatically." He took back the map. "If she did, she'd probably come straight out Figueroa. She'd have to take the Golden State because right there where Figueroa runs into Riverside, it's the only place there's an overpass over the river-bed, for a long way. Unless she turned up Cypress off Figueroa and went way up to get onto San Fernando Road and cross the river by Fletcher Drive. And who would? It's miles out of her way, halfway to Glendale. But all right, say she came back Figueroa instead of the Pasadena Freeway. That's just the street for it. Traffic-lights still on, but not many cars or people around. She stops for a light, this fellow jumps her."

Mendoza got out a cigarette and tapped it on the desk, lit it, still looking at the contents of the handbag. "And he was either hopped up, or just in a hurry and a little nervous, so he missed the gold case and lighter, and also her wrist-watch, only good piece of jewelry she had on, and it didn't occur to him that handing us her identity by way of the purse would put us onto the stolen car quicker. But he did carefully wipe the purse all over to destroy any prints."

"I—" said Hackett. "Well. That's so. No prints on it at all. Where there should have been some of hers. That patent leather takes prints just dandy, too. Maybe she did that. It looks as if she was the neat, persnickety kind—like you."

"If she did," said Mendoza, "it would have been as she left for the party. So she'd have put some prints on it during the evening."

"I'll give you that," admitted Hackett.

"It's very funny that there wasn't a distracted set of parents knocking at Missing Persons at about two A.M. This was a girl from a—mmh—socially good home, a moneyed home—guarded, well brought up. Yet apparently nobody has yet realized she didn't come home last night." He looked at the clock; it was eleven-thirty. "Well, they do now. Dwyer'll be telling them now. I should have gone myself, damn it—first reactions sometimes revealing." Suddenly Mendoza swept all the articles together, put them back into the bag and set the bag at one side of his desk. He emptied the brass ashtray, brushed off ash-flakes and to-bacco-crumbs, and aligned the blotter and desk-tray nicely.

"So why, do you suppose? If it was a private kill? Which I don't yet see altogether."

"¿Quien sabe? We don't know much about her. About her family and friends. And, possibly, enemies. We'll find out. The doctor said between ten and one, probably nearer midnight. Did Angel remember what time she left?"

"She was evidently one of the first to leave—between ten-thirty and a quarter to eleven."

"Mmh." Mendoza spread out the map again. "She was about eleven miles from home in a straight line, but a good sixteen any way she went, freeways or main streets. If the doctor's wrong about the time of death, that doesn't give us any more evidence to back up my hunch. But if she was killed around midnight, give or take fifteen minutes, that's another little point. Because, look. From your place down to, roughly, the area where she might have been jumped—somewhere around the place where both Figueroa and the Pasadena Freeway meet Riverside Drive—is about six to six-and-a-half miles. We're saying she acquired a passenger around there because the killer wouldn't want to drive around with the body long, he'd get rid of it at the nearest safe place—which turned out to be the freight-yards. Whichever way she came, even if she was a slow driver, if she left your place as late as ten-forty-five, she couldn't have taken any more than fifteen or twenty minutes to get there. If she was doing the average, say thirty-five an hour—and not much traffic to slow her up—she'd have been down there by around eleven. Even call it eleven-ten. And then gets jumped by a hophead and rides around with him for three quarters of an hour before he kills and robs her? If she'd been raped—but she wasn't. If it was that kind of thing, Art, well, it usually goes very damn fast, doesn't it? Yank the unlocked door open, dive in, show a gun to the driver—keep it fast, so the driver hasn't time to think, plan. Get the car into the nearest dark side-street, grab the purse if it's a woman, grab the billfold—get out and run. We used to have quite a little of it. And a few times the driver—always a man—showed some fight and got shot or bludgeoned for it. Not often. But—If she'd been raped, I'd buy the random killer," said Mendoza. He looked at the bag. "This one had her head screwed on tight, you see. If that had happened, a man jumping into the car, putting a gun on her, I think our Margaret would have been smart enough to sit still, let herself be robbed, and watch him run. She wouldn't—few women would—put up any resistance, unless he assaulted her. *¿Como no*, are you with me?"

"I'm with you that far."

"So O.K. Except for getting dirty from the street, her clothes are all right, nothing torn. There wasn't a mark on her that looks as if she'd had a struggle with anyone. The scratches on her face and arm—right side—were post mortem, made when she was rolled out of the car. It's a very little point, but if she'd been tense, scared, with a stranger holding a gun on her, she'd have been expecting personal attack, ready to struggle. But if she was taken unawares—well, strangling doesn't take long. But I just don't see the car-jumping purse-snatcher making her drive round the better part of forty-five minutes before robbing her. Unless he intended to assault her. And why should he kill her at all, if she didn't put up a struggle?"

"This is all up in the air," said Hackett patiently. "You don't know she didn't. You don't know she didn't have a drink on the way home, stop for a malt, so she didn't get that far until forty-five minutes later. It's too early to dream up stories, we don't know enough."

"*De veras*. But I like my dream better," said Mendoza.

"How does the tune go?"

"She was with somebody she knew." Mendoza put out his cigarette and swiveled half-round to stare out his office-window. "She went somewhere else after she left the party. On impulse or by appointment. There, by chance or arrangement she met somebody. And she didn't think she was in any danger. Somebody—in her car or elsewhere— maybe pretending to make love to her?—put his hands round her throat. If you know just where to find the carotid artery, pressure there can cause unconsciousness within fifteen seconds. *Terminar*."

Hackett sighed and said, "Maybe. Maybe." Sergeant Lake looked in and said that Bert was back, with the father.

"So let's start to ask questions," said Mendoza, and got up. "Get a definite identification from him first."

Charles Chadwick was about fifty, a big goodlooking man: not fat but solid, chesty. He had kept his hair, thick iron-gray hair; his pleasant face looked as if it was normally ruddy. Now it looked drawn and his blue eyes held shock.

But he did not lose control. Looking at the body, he said quietly, "Yes, that is Margaret. My daughter Margaret." Chadwick was a man to keep emotions largely to himself, feeling, perhaps, that it was rude, undignified, to exhibit emotion. On the way back to the headquarters building he was silent, volunteering nothing.

In Mendoza's office he answered questions courteously, dully, as they were asked. Margaret Chadwick had been twenty-eight, unmarried, living at home. Not officially engaged, no, but she had been going about with one young man and it was "understood" that they were to be married, though no definite date had been set. George Arden. Chadwick was not sure of the address, somewhere in Hollywood; no, Mr. Arden did not work; he and his mother lived on inherited income. Chadwick realized that it must look odd, that no one had missed Margaret last night. Not until this morning was it discovered that she hadn't come home; they had, after checking with several of her closest friends, been just about to call the police when Sergeant Dwyer arrived.

"My wife and I were out last night ourselves," said Chadwick. "And our elder daughter Laura." He had accepted a cigarette, but only held it burning, seldom putting it to his mouth. "My wife and I attended a rather formal dinner—the home of a business friend." Chadwick operated a C.P.A. business on Wilshire Boulevard—tax-experts, etcetera. Judging from his clothes and his daughter's possessions, a large and flourishing business. "We didn't get home until after midnight, and you see, we knew Margaret had expected to be home earlier—she said probably about eleven. We—assumed she had come in and gone to bed, her door was closed . . . Well, no, I'm afraid we wouldn't necessarily notice, about her car. You see, we have a two-car garage, and it's generally understood that my car and my wife's are to occupy it. Both Laura and Margaret park around the corner or in the drive. If I noticed that Margaret's car wasn't in the drive, I suppose I thought it was around on the side-street . . . Yes, Laura had been out too—with her fiancé. I heard her come in shortly after we had, but she did not—that is, of course it was late, she came up and—retired—without disturbing us. Then this morning, when Margaret hadn't come down by nine-thirty— we thought perhaps she was ill, and investigated, and—"

"Yes, I understand, Mr. Chadwick. Do you know whether your daughter intended to go on somewhere else from this—party?"

Chadwick shook his head. "I shouldn't think so, Lieutenant. She didn't say, but then—I wasn't exactly sure where she was going. I just knew, to a party somewhere. Perhaps her sister knew—"

"I see. Miss Chadwick was—mmh—usually reserved about her plans? Even casual plans? Didn't always mention exactly where she was going?"

Chadwick didn't answer for a moment. He leaned forward and pressed out his cigarette in the ashtray on the desk. He put a hand to his temple as if his head ached. "They—we all have—had our own—interests," he said with difficulty. "Looking back now, it's easy to think I— we—were careless. But it isn't as if she was a child. Or Laura. With the difference in their ages, they had different circles of friends, different concerns. My wife is active in several clubs. It wasn't—I don't want to give the impression—that we weren't—concerned. But after all the girls are grown up. Responsible. Both of them might often be away most of the day, or in the evening, and I—wouldn't be exactly sure where. It might, you see, be several different places. Of course, they would say if either of them planned to be out for dinner—things like that. Of course, in the evening Laura would usually be with her fiancé."

"Tell me, Mr. Chadwick, do you approve of your daughter's fiancé?"

Chadwick looked very surprised. "Why, what has that to— Of Kenny Lord? Yes, certainly, a very nice young fellow."

"Excuse me, I misled you— I mean of your daughter Margaret's fiancé?"

"I don't think—it was quite as definite as that, to say fiancé," said Chadwick. "I—we didn't like him quite as well as Kenny Lord, but if Margaret—well, that is, he was Margaret's—it was her affair. Excuse me, Lieutenant, why do you ask? I—this terrible thing, it was most probably a—hold-up, one of these drug-addicts or—? She was usually careful about locking the doors of the car at night, but—"

"We don't know, Mr. Chadwick," said Mendoza noncommittally. "Not yet. We'll find out." The outside telephone rang and he picked it up. "Mendoza speaking."

"Oh—" said Angel. "Hello. I just—"

"D'you want Art? He's right here."

"It doesn't matter. I just remembered and thought I'd better tell you. She had a phone-call last evening, while she was here. The nearest I can place it, it was ten o'clock or a bit after."

"You don't tell me," said Mendoza. "Interesting. I take it you answered the phone?"

"Yes. It was a man's voice—he just said, 'Miss Chadwick?' and I said just a minute and went and told her."

"Mmh. Was it a long call?"

"I don't think so. Of course we were all talking, I wasn't noticing particularly, but I don't think it was more than three or four minutes, five at the outside, before she came back to the living-room."

"Well. What kind of voice? Bass, tenor?"

Angel considered. "In between's the best I can do, I'm afraid. Ordinary. Only two words—"

"Yes, never mind. That's suggestive. Thanks very much." Mendoza put the phone down and stared at it thoughtfully. Then he looked up to Chadwick. "We don't like to annoy people more than we have to, Mr. Chadwick, on a thing like this. But of course you realize there are questions we have to ask. I'd like to see your wife and elder daughter. Sergeant Dwyer brought you down, didn't he?— Yes, well, if I drive you home now, perhaps it would be convenient for me to see Mrs. and Miss Chadwick?"

"Yes, certainly." Chadwick sounded numb.

"If you'd wait for us in the hall, just a moment." Mendoza stood up, watched him out. "Art, put some men on that address-book. Find out her closest friends. And start somebody locating Arden. A long shot we might try is the general area—did anybody see anything? And—"

"*Pues sí,*" said Hackett. "Why do they pick Saturday nights? I haven't had a clear Sunday off in a month. Don't forget you promised to be home by three."

"As a public servant—" said Mendoza, and Hackett laughed rudely and said a redheaded wife could give him more grief than the Chief ever could.

# 3

"**Y**ou don't," said Alison, "think it was just at random. You think someone killed her as—as Margaret Chadwick, not just a woman alone in a car. Well, of course I'd never met her before, but I can see that she might have been. She—belittled."

"*¿Qué tal?* How?"

"Next turn to the right. *Desgracia sabre desgracia,*" said Alison, "like that. Nothing the way it should be for Margaret. Salespeople always tried to cheat her, shops never stocked what she wanted to buy, the man at the filling-station overcharged her."

"Oh. Like that. Yes, that kind always looking for trouble, aren't they? She found it."

"The suspicious vinegary spinster in the making."

"No. She had an attached male. Of what quality I can't say yet. Is this the place?" Mendoza slowed the Ferrari. The lots were fairly level, uncleared as yet. The nearest house was two hundred yards down the hill; the newly subdivided wilderness bore a sign, For Sale, Lots 200 X 300, drainage, Cox Realty. Mendoza stopped the car and looked.

"Trees," said Alison hopefully. "And level. A nice view to the southeast."

Mendoza shook his head. "And you've lived in California awhile, too. Look at that cliff behind—all loose soil, nothing but a few bushes. The first good rain, you'd get half the hill and a flood of water right through the whole house. And a retaining wall would cost a fortune. Not worth it. But if you're set on something up here, let's cruise around and see what else there is."

"Finding fault!" said Alison as he turned the car. "You sound just like Margaret . . . She had a boy-friend?"

"Apparently—and that's a vulgar term." Mendoza got back onto Sunset Plaza and presently turned on a recently-blacktopped road as yet, evidently, nameless. This was a newly-opened section above Sunset Boulevard—many short winding streets, steep and narrow for the most part. They passed Lechero Street. *"¡Caray!"* he said. "But who *is* responsible? Do they toss a coin, or has the real-estate dealer first choice? Milkman Street, I ask you." They came to Trueno Lane and then to Granizada Avenue—unpaved alleys wandering off to the right.

"Whoever it is, they don't know any Spanish," agreed Alison. "It just sounds right for California, and most Spanish words are—you know—mellifluous, whatever they mean. Compared to English. I think it'd be rather fun to live on Thunder Lane or Hailstorm Street. Come to think of it, there's no comparing the most ordinary phrases, just from the point of how they sound. What's *winding road*—" they had just passed the sign—"compared to *camino sinuoso?* I suppose somebody hears the words and thinks, that'd be a pretty name for a street, and—"

The Ferrari stopped dead. *"¡Porvida, abran paso!"* exclaimed Mendoza in awed rapture. "Here we build a house! I want to live on Great Thunderbolt Avenue. I'll be satisfied with no less."

*"How* absurd," said Alison, peering at the neat black sign which read *Rayo Grande.*

"I mean it, *chica.* I really mean it. Are there lots for sale? There must be!" He turned down the narrow road. A hopeful sign promised *Paving by Woodes Bros.,* but didn't say when. There were a few dispirited scrub-oaks, a lot of wild mustard and rocks. "There, you see?" Another sign—Lots for sale, 75 X 130, Cox Realty.

"Luis, *mi amante solamente!* No! Look at it! No sewage connection—"

"There will be eventually, you can see the whole section's building up fast. Look at the nice view." If it hadn't been unusually smoggy this July, there would have been a view over the city; as it was, this gray day, only the Capitol Record building and Prudential Insurance peered vaguely through the murk. "Just as many trees, and no cliffs."

"Liar!" said Alison. "The cliff just goes down instead of up. *Amado mio, por favor*—be sensible—you've had your joke—"

"Nice level lots," said Mendoza, "see? We'd better have two, to have plenty of room and no neighbors jostling us. I build a house on Great Thunderbolt Avenue or nowhere." He started to turn the Ferrari around. As the street was fifteen feet wide and the Ferrari nearly fifteen feet long, this involved some maneuvering. Dust rose.

"They're impossible lots! For heaven's *sake*, Luis— Darling, Hailstorm Street is just as funny—please, *por favor*, dearest Luis, I'll never ask for another thing—"

"Now you're acting female," said Mendoza. "A good architect will solve all problems."

"You don't know the realty people's address—"

"It was on the sign, 5210 Sunset. *¡No tiene motivo para quejarse—* don't be contrary! You want to buy a lot and build a house. I'm going to buy you two lots. I'm an indulgent husband—"

"*¡Tu mentiroso infame!*" said Alison bitterly. "You're a damned autocrat. And I like to think I've domesticated you, but it's only a fond dream. Why was I such a fool to marry you? Two dominant characters—"

"You want a lecture, *niña?*" He braked violently, angled across the road, and reached for her.

"No, you idiot—*Si, no lo niego—¡eso basta,* that will do! Luis, you fool . . . All right, I admit it, I love you—*y esta no tiene remedia,* no cure for it, more's the pity . . . Let me go for heaven's sake, there's a car coming . . . But," added Alison as he released the brake, and that was to herself a little ruefully, "you're *not* domesticated, my darling. Maybe you walked alone too long."

By five o'clock Mendoza had purchased two lots on Rayo Grande Avenue. The fact that he could have written a number of checks for eight thousand five hundred dollars did not prevent him from haggling with Mr. Letter of Cox Realty, and eventually getting the two lots for seven thousand flat.

"Now," he said to Alison, "you go and find the tame architect. It's your house—you tell him what you want, don't let him bully you."

"No price-limit?" asked Alison only half-lightly. He wasn't really much interested.

He looked at her, absurdly hurt and astonished, stopping there in the middle of the sidewalk. "*Gatita*—do I ever? Anything you—"

"Oh, Luis, I didn't mean—! Of course not, darling. Let's go home. I'll show you some rough plans I've drawn up, just ideas—and there's steak—"

"*Si, bien.* But I'll run down to the office afterward. This thing— Yes, and I want to hear in detail what you remember about that affair last night."

And so in the end she had to tell him about Roberta Silverman. Which was a very little thing; and while she liked Roberta Silverman, and hadn't particularly liked Margaret Chadwick, she had to tell him for what it was worth. How Roberta Silverman's lovely dark eyes had held brief hatred, resting on Margaret Chadwick.

"But I think she left after the Chadwick girl. Angel might remember. And anyway, even if—it couldn't have been a woman?"

"No telling. A man's more likely, but a strong woman . . . Our Margaret, five-eight, but only a hundred and fifteen. Not a big strong girl. What's the Silverman woman do?"

"I don't know. I'd met her before, at the housewarming party in January for Angel and Art. I liked her," said Alison. "She's—down to earth."

"Well," said Mendoza mildly, "we don't persecute people just for pleasure." Getting her feeling, the nuance, as he often did, even as she felt it herself. "We'll see."

"Have you any idea yet? I mean, if it *was* a personal motive?"

"Ideas come plural in a homicide case," said Mendoza. He smiled, and his unremarkable regular features, with the heavy brows and neat line of moustache and widow's peak for punctuation, flashed into sudden charm. "Tell you one thing I did, after I saw the family this afternoon. I attached a tail to Mr. Charles Chadwick."

Alison stared at him. "Her father? Why on earth? I don't—"

"You have not," said Mendoza, "met Mrs. Myra Chadwick."

She was a tall, pale, fair woman, sitting there in the straight-backed chair opposite him, withstanding invasion. That was the atmosphere. The invasion of death; of its intrusion on her planned, tidy life; and of anything so crude as police-officers—especially when one of them bore a Foreign Name. She was, he thought, older than Chadwick. A thin angular woman, in the phrase well-preserved; everything about her studied, precise.

She was well-dressed. A plain beige sheath dress, high-heeled tan sandals, copper jewelry. Her hair was beautifully maintained at something, probably, near its original shade—ash-blonde. Which most men might not have known; but Luis Mendoza knew a good deal about women, from both professional and personal experience. Her hands gave away her age—manicured hands, rose-colored polish, but the blue veins standing out on their backs. Wedding-band, big solitaire diamond; on the right one, a square topaz.

"This terrible thing," she said in a thin remote voice. She did not look at him, but at Hackett. (Hackett, with a good American name.) "Anything we can tell you to help, of course," she said, fiddling with her bracelet.

"Oh, of *course,*" said Laura Chadwick eagerly, tearfully, earnestly.

Charles Chadwick sat a little apart, saying nothing, doing nothing.

These big houses on Franklin were relics of another era. Moneyed people didn't buy them, live in them, now; they went to more newly fashionable sections, in the valley or toward the beach. So maybe this tall Mediterranean house with its balcony and grilles, its wide sweep of terraced lawn, had been "in the family," retained for convenience, of disdain for the new rich who headed for Pacific Palisades, Beverly Hills . . . It was a depressing room, this living-room. Large, rich, and sombre. Heavy, good, no-period furniture. A subdued seascape over the mantel, in a wide gold frame (he wondered what Alison would say of it. Alison who was, in his poor lay opinion, a very good painter indeed). Most of all, it was extremely neat and clean. And Mendoza, whose passion for order bordered on the neurotic, yet felt this particular kind of tidiness to be inhuman—unnatural.

There was not an ashtray in the room, nor a magazine, nor a book. The ancient Douglas pine in the front yard shadowed the two windows, making the room dark even at noon of a very warm day in July.

And they got little except a look at the family. Although the family was duly cooperative.

Looking at Laura Chadwick, Mendoza thought it was odd that none of Mrs. Chadwick's svelte smartness had descended to her daughters. Well, a thing inborn maybe. Even dead and disarranged, Margaret had been slightly dowdy—if the dress, the nylon lingerie, bore the Saks label. Laura was prettier than her sister had been: fair like the mother, blonder than the mother ever had been. Softer features than Margaret's, but she just missed being goodlooking. Shallow blue-green eyes, a mouth too small wearing too dark a shade of lipstick, brows plucked too thin and penciled too dark. She wore her blonde-rinsed hair a little too long, and she liked bracelets that dangled—there were two of them on her left arm. He put her down as thirty or a bit more. Despite a slender figure, she wore clothes badly, and like many tall women, held herself awkwardly, stooping a little.

"Anything—" she said. She had a trick of punctuating what she said with little nervous gasps.

Mendoza said yes, of course, and asked questions. They got very little more. Laura and her fiancé—she dragged the word in, timidly proud—had gone to dinner together, leaving at eight o'clock. "I mean, Ken picked me up here then." To Frascati's. They had gone on from there to the Club Afrique on the Strip—well, on the edge of the Strip. And somewhere else later, she didn't remember the name but she could ask Kenny. And he'd brought her home about, well, maybe twelve-thirty or a quarter of one, around there. She'd never thought but what Margaret was home and asleep— No, she hadn't looked for Margaret's car. She'd thought— And these awful *men* who did such things, it just wouldn't bear thinking—

From Mrs. Chadwick they got what they'd had from Chadwick. Formal dinner and bridge at the home of Mr. and Mrs. James Porter in Beverly Hills.

And no ashtrays.

Mendoza came out with Hackett to the big black Ferrari at the curb. (Chadwick had looked surprised, confused, at the Ferrari.) He got out a cigarette, gave one to Hackett, lit both. "You know, Arturo," he said, "those fellows who drew up the Declaration of Independence. Mr. Jefferson."

"Um?" said Hackett.

"I'm with them all the way. But they made a little grammatical error. Men deserve equal opportunity, sure. But they aren't born equal. Some of us—among other things—do have a little rudimentary feeling for other people. Consideration. Empathy." He stood on the curb smoking, rocking slightly heel to toe, back and forth.

"So we do," said Hackett. He sounded subtly amused. "Empathy. You got a message there? So did I. But I'm surprised at you, boy. Picture crooked on the wall, you'd crawl over on two broken legs to straighten it out. What bothered you?"

"*Todo tiene sus limitas,*" said Mendoza, "a limit to everything. So nobody must smoke in her nice clean conventional living-room. And in the order of nature policemen rank pretty near the bottom. Though she liked you a little better, you've got a nice Anglo-Saxon name. You're a

virtuous young man, with nothing approaching my knowledge of females—"

"Are you telling me?"

"But I never knew a woman who was so much concerned with the
tangibilities—such as the lack of dust on the coffee-table and the precise
arrangement of the artificial roses on the mantel—who was also at all
interested in—mmh—the life-urge on a somewhat lower level."

"How prettily you put it," said Hackett. "These days, I forget how I
wangled a B.A. as a psychology major. Could you mean that Mrs. C.
doesn't let him beyond her boudoir any more? And never did very often
—or very nice and willing?"

"You're just a big dumb cop," said Mendoza. "Sure. He's a virile-
looking specimen. Younger than she is."

"Is that so? You're the specialist on females."

"At least five years—maybe ten. He's the kind looks older than he is.
She's a good sixty, or edging it. And he's feeling guilty about something.
Maybe just that he didn't have more concern for his daughter. But all
the same, Art, a male specimen. And a goodlooking fellow—kept his
figure, his hair. And money. You follow me?"

"No," said Hackett. He got into the Ferrari after Mendoza. "Why?
So what? It's his daughter in a tray in the morgue. So he's got a playmate—a couple of playmates. He's not a queer—our Margaret wouldn't
enter in. Why?"

Mendoza eased the twelve-cylinder engine into high. "Just extraneous information. Let's find out things. About all of them—all the people
around her. And our Margaret herself—just in case. Put a tail on Chadwick, as of now. And look up past history."

"Why, for God's sake? I don't see—"

"Well, for people who've just lost a daughter, a sister, unexpectedly,
they didn't show very much grief and shock, did they? Not even the
aggressive kind— Find the villain, kill him! Of course it is Sunday.
Maybe Laura and Mrs. Chadwick had already taken such pains over
their clothes and jewelry before they heard about Margaret. So that isn't
evidence. But somehow I got the message that they're more upset at
how Margaret was killed, the crude violence—bringing policemen and
reporters down on them—than grieving over the fact that Margaret's
dead." He shot over into the left lane, the Ferrari's uncanny accelera-
tion-power surprising a new Pontiac behind.

"You're reading too much into upper-class reserve, because you want suspects for your hunch that it was a private motive. We just agreed that Mrs. C. is a cold proposition. The daughter's like her, maybe—all surface convention. Anyway, people like that, it's like *noblesse oblige*—not good form to show emotion in public, to inferiors. I thought Chadwick was feeling it more—something real to his shock."

Mendoza agreed. "Nevertheless, we'll take a look at all of them. And the office-boys should have turned up George Arden by now, you go and take a long look at him."

"O.K. It's after two, you'd better get on home or Alison'll start acting like Mrs. C."

"That'll be the day," said Mendoza abstractedly.

Information was starting to come in from several directions by now. A number of men had begun the ordinary routine on any homicide, and the fact that it was Sunday slowed them up only a little. On Mendoza's orders, other men were busy at more unusual routine. Tomorrow everything would be a little easier.

Most of the women present at the shower had been interviewed. Collective information from Laura Chadwick, her mother, and Rose Larkin indicated that Margaret's closest friends had been Rose Larkin, Betty-Lou Cole, Esther MacRae. All of whom were simply prostrated or just couldn't *believe* it, at hearing the terrible news, officer. Miss MacRae and Mrs. Larkin were also members of the women's club Margaret had belonged to. A service club, said Mrs. Larkin: they found out about Needy People and provided clothes, baskets of groceries. They also Visited the Sick. A kind of private, voluntary social service.

The club, and occasional bridge-parties, seemed to have been Margaret's only hobbies. And, of course (probably) shopping. Tomorrow, they would go through her possessions, have a look for anything significant.

Mr. and Mrs. James Porter agreed that Mr. and Mrs. Chadwick had left their Beverly Hills home at almost exactly midnight. They had spent the evening, with the Porters and two other couples, playing bridge.

Miss Roberta Silverman said that she had left the party just after Margaret Chadwick—oh, perhaps two or three minutes. Her car was parked a space away from Miss Chadwick's and she had started down Springvale Street immediately after the blue Buick. Had, in fact, followed the Buick all the way down to Figueroa and along Figueroa until she reached York Boulevard. As Miss Silverman lived in South Pasadena, she had turned left on York and lost sight of the Buick. How fast was the Buick traveling? Oh—moderate, said Miss Silverman. Thirty, thirty-five, sometimes forty. Obviously, she had been traveling at about the same speed. Could she guess what time it might have been when she turned off Figueroa? Heavens, no; you didn't keep looking at your watch while you were driving. But it was only, what, about ten or twelve blocks from Springvale Street, and if it had been about ten-forty-five when they both drove off, it couldn't have been more than, say, five to eleven. Or six or seven minutes to eleven; there hadn't been much traffic.

Several men, without much hope that they'd get anything, were tramping Figueroa between Avenue 40 and Avenue 22, finding out what places had still been open after eleven, about possible late newsboys and so on. It was a very long chance, but somebody might have seen something: might have seen a man walk into the street, open the door of a car halted for a traffic-light, get in. And thought nothing of it.

Detective-Sergeant (third grade) John Palliser, who had achieved his rank only three months ago, thought for an excited moment that he had got something, on this tiresome job. He had also been the man to interview Miss Roberta Silverman, and like Alison he had an eye for an unusual type of good looks; he'd liked Miss Silverman, kind of a girl he could go for—liked her enough so that he was thinking he'd ask around, whether it was against some unwritten rule to contact a casual witness, well, privately. Taking advantage of that kind of introduction. And also wondering whether it would be any use; Miss Silverman, who taught fourth grade in a South Pasadena public school, might not be exactly flattered to have a detective-sergeant (third grade) pestering her . . .

Now he was helping out, at six o'clock of this hot afternoon, tramping the streets asking silly questions. Or were they?

Because here was this fat woman exclaiming excitedly, "I did! I saw something like that, honest to God, officer!" The fat woman and her husband, whose name was Spriesterbach, had a delicatessen, and they stayed open late on Saturday nights. "It was when I stepped out to the street, just before we shut, see—breath of air, it was kind of stuffy in the store—I saw this man, the light at the corner was red, see, and a couple cars stopped for it, I see this man walk out and get into one—"

For a minute there Palliser was excited. He had a little vision of himself bringing in this important evidence, and the lieutenant—the great Mendoza himself, with such a reputation—patting him on the back and saying this boy would go far, keep an eye on him. He got out his notebook and asked questions.

"Aw, Greta, use sense!" said Mr. Spriesterbach disgustedly. "You just wanna see your pitcher in the papers. Don't pay no notion, officer, all she saw was Jack Waters, he works swing-shift at that little assembly plant round the corner, see. He gets off every night at eleven and his wife picks him up on her way home, she's a dance-hostess at one of those Arthur Murray places. Greta, you damn fool. Six nights a week you see Mrs. Waters pick up Jack at the corner, eleven-ten, around there."

"Oh," said Palliser. "Well, anyway we'll check it. To see if it was. What was the approximate time? Can you describe the man you saw?"

"It was Jack Waters," said Spriesterbach.

Palliser got a vague description, found Waters, and found that in all probability it had been Jack Waters, getting picked up by his wife.

He'd worked overtime on that, so then he reported in, wondering why the hell he'd ever joined the force. But there in the sergeants' room was senior Sergeant Hackett, looking tired, picking up an outside telephone; so it wasn't just low ranks worked overtime. Had to. There wasn't any have-to about it, Palliser figured, you just got interested, and one thing led to another. He waited to report to Hackett; and started thinking again about Roberta Silverman. Hell of a nice girl, and a smart girl too—you didn't have to talk down to her, and she didn't giggle or put on an act of any kind, as so many girls did. He wondered—

"About this Arden, Luis," Hackett was saying.

# 4

George Arden's address was on McCadden Place. It was a narrow street of old, rather shabby houses and rental-units—middle-class to lower-middle-class. The address, when he got there in the middle of the afternoon, surprised Hackett. No connection with the substantial old-fashioned solvency of Franklin Avenue. Could it be that George Arden had been cultivating Margaret for what she had—potentially had?

It was a house, not an apartment. An old frame California bungalow, painted white and needing paint. The strip of lawn each side of the front walk was brownish: not enough water. An experienced house-holder of seven months, Hackett knew that in summer you had to pour the water on daily to keep grass green. A damn fool idea, trying to keep lawns in California. Much smarter to do as the Spanish had (they'd understood the country)—walled patios, greenery in pots, and let it go.

There was a driveway at the left side, and standing in it a shabby ten-year-old gray Chevvy. As Hackett turned up the front walk, a man came down the drive with a pail and rags, toward the car. It wasn't hard to recognize the original of the candid snapshot in Margaret Chadwick's billfold. Hackett swerved across the lawn.

"Mr. George Arden?"

"I—yes, that's me." Arden was perhaps thirty, or a year or two younger. About five-nine, a head and a half shorter than Hackett anyway. He wasn't fat, but he was stockily built and looked soft. Not bad-looking, but—immature. He had very thick, shiny dark-brown hair with a natural curl in it; his face was squarish, with a suggestion of jowls, and he had a cleft in his chin. His eyes, under thick straight brows, were deep blue. He had on a short-sleeved shirt, and his arms were hairless, untanned.

Hackett started to reach for his identification.

"You're a police-officer," said Arden. He had a pleasant light baritone voice, and articulated his words carefully, like an actor. "About Margaret. Margaret—oh, God!" He set down the pail of water, dropped the rags. "Aren't you?"

"Yes, Mr. Arden. Just a few—"

"Oh, God!" said Arden again. "Laura—her sister—phoned to tell me, this morning. Of course neither of her parents would—they didn't approve. Approve! I couldn't believe it—a thing like that—Margaret! She was always careful about locking the doors, if she was alone at night —I remember her saying that. I've been—I've been—" He looked away from Hackett, vaguely, to the pail and the heap of rags. "I was going to wash the car," he said. "Do you think that's—funny? Take my mind off —and, sort of, get away from Mother. She loved Margaret, you see— she was so looking forward to our—our getting— That's ungrateful, beastly of me, because Mother—but I couldn't stand hearing her talk about Margaret. *Do* you think it's funny?"

"Well, now," said Hackett, "people have different ways of—meeting grief, Mr. Arden. You needn't think we're not hunting, every way there is, for the one responsible . . . A terrible thing, yes . . . Would you mind telling me where you were last night, between eleven and one A.M.? Just for the record."

Arden stared at him, wetting his full lips. "Eleven and one? I don't— But what do *I*—I mean, from what Laura s-said, it was some dope-fiend, some real criminal, a robber —somehow got in her car. I don't—"

"That's probably the way it was," agreed Hackett. "But we like to check everywhere, just to be sure, Mr. Arden. It's just routine. If you don't mind."

"Oh," said Arden. "Oh, I see. No, I don't mind—of course, anything I can do to help you—only I don't see how that could, but— It's made a setback for Mother. She has arthritis, you see, and heart-trouble. It was —bad, breaking it to her, after Laura called. She was very fond of Margaret. I was—" he made a vague unfinished gesture. "Well, it's been hard on her. She *felt* it, you know, that the Chadwicks didn't seem to think I was good enough for Margaret. Because I haven't got a job or much money. I—I write. Or try to. It's not easy to get started, just at first, you know—and Mother sees that, as long as we do have a settled income, even a small one, to live on—well, it's much more sensible to give all my time to my own work, instead of getting a nine-to-five job somewhere. Once you've managed to break in, it's a different story, of course. But it's a sort of monopoly, publishers just won't touch unknown writers, you really have to have pull to get them even to read your stuff. Especially when you don't write the fashionable, popular things, all sex and sarcasm—it's hard, but—" He stopped himself. "You don't want to hear all that, I'm sorry. Anything I can do to help—such a terrible, incredible thing—"

"Yes. Just where you were last night, Mr. Arden."

Arden seemed to have dried up, temporarily. He licked his lips, hesitating, and his blue eyes were vague, unfocused. Then he said, "I went to the Hollywood Bowl with a friend of mine, that's all. It—it was a pop-concert night, Gershwin—it usually is, Saturday nights. I suppose we got there about eight-fifteen, it starts at eight-thirty. I don't know exactly what time it finished, I suppose you could find out. Quarter to eleven, around there. And you know what the parking-lot's like. It was quite a jam—we were slow getting out. I guess it might have been half an hour before we did get out, onto Highland, and then we went to a place on Hollywood Boulevard and had a drink before we came home."

"A friend. Man or woman? And may I have the—"

"What d'you mean? What the hell, why shouldn't I—" And, as suddenly as his temper flared, Arden calmed. "I'm sorry, I'm just so shocked and upset, I don't know what I'm— Well, after all, Margaret and I— It was Michael Darrell I was with, I guess you could say he's my closest friend. We're interested in the same things, you know. His address? But why— Oh, well, it's 924 Detroit Avenue. Hollywood, sure. But what—I mean, it was just some dope out on a sleigh-ride—"

Hackett was noting down Darrell's address, and his pencil never hesitated; but he was a smart cop with eleven years' experience behind him. "Thanks very much, Mr. Arden," he said. "Just routine. Yes, it's a bad thing. Big cities—you get violence of this kind." Anywhere, you got violence: the violent ones. Only in a city, more of it.

"—Ought to be killed!" said Arden breathlessly. "Killing people. Girls. I couldn't believe it at first, when Laura— And Margaret was always careful, she knew the dangers, but it must be just once she forgot. I hardly knew how to tell Mother. Even after I'd—grasped it myself. Such an incredible thing. But I think I've got her settled down to her nap now, I hope you won't have to disturb her."

Hackett said no. He thanked Arden again, and swerved back across the brownish lawn to his car. As he turned the Ford into the street, he saw Arden still standing there, looking after him.

He started for Detroit Avenue, to see Michael Darrell.

"Darrell?" said Mendoza, and added, not to Hackett, "*Not* my tie, Nefertite, no!"

"Darrell is, believe it or not, a kind of stand-in. Yes, they're still making movies. Of a sort. Darrell does long-distance dub-ins, where the insurance people say the star mustn't jump out a second-storey window or take a pratfall. Not a real stunt-man. He also does extra work. I'd suppose, pretty good pay. He has a fair-to-middling classy apartment. He's taking an extension course at U.S.C., in advanced sculpture. Lots of muscles. A Samson . . . Yes . . . No. About thirty. Goodlooking —in a sort of primitive way. Muscles, like I say, and curly blond hair. Incidentally, belligerent—what the hell do the cops want now, sniffing around? Yes, he said *now*— direct quote. Just like Arden came out with that *sleigh-ride*, the casual pro slang. Sure to God Darrell went to the Bowl with his pal Arden last night—funny as it might sound to a dumb cop, some men did like to listen to good music . . . *Segura mente qué sí*, I read headlines just like you . . . That I've already done. Yes. Now can I go home to my wife? . . . All right, I'll bear it in mind." Hackett put the phone down and turned, to find Palliser waiting. He uttered a groan. "Make it short."

"—And a studio attached to the garage," said Alison, "like this. If we have maid's quarters, they could go the other side of the garage. Should we? Do they want it nowadays? Isn't it—"

"You'd better," said Mendoza, "ask Bertha."

Alison shut her eyes. "Luis, it makes me feel like Judas. Just thinking about it. She even dusts the tops of doors and the backs of pictures. And she's been a fixture here for Lord knows how long . . . If they gave wild parties, or kept the T.V. on full-volume all day, I wouldn't mind. But they're all such nice people—Mrs. Bryson and Mrs. Carter so obliging, looking after the cats, before we were married—and since then, well, nice. And we're plotting to steal Bertha. Permanently. Bribing her with a—a three-room apartment, or whatever."

"Don't be silly," said Mendoza. "In this life, you have to think of your own concerns first. Consider art."

"Art? What has he to—"

"Art," said Mendoza, "your art. Creativity. You have to waste your time dusting furniture and washing dishes, you never have the leisure to paint masterpieces. So, Bertha."

"¡Mi marido adulador!" said Alison. "Flatter me—I love it. But I still feel guilty. What should I offer her? Three-fifty without maid's quarters? Two-fifty with? The architect—"

"Ask her what she wants," said Mendoza simply. And absently. "She's a prize, I know. Just ask her. Whatever she settles for, to come to us permanently and singly, is O.K. So you needn't worry about dirty windows and dishes. So I don't come home to an exhausted wife moaning about housework. And so you can paint masterpieces."

"Like Judas," said Alison. "Everyone depends on her so! You can—unlike most of them. I'd love to have her, but the Carters and Brysons will never speak to us again."

Mendoza had lost interest in Bertha and the tentative house plans. "Tell me—this phone-call Margaret had, at the party. Angel says about ten o'clock. Is that right?"

"I suppose so, approximately. You aren't noticing the time every five minutes, in a crowd."

"No. She'd been sitting beside you, and when she came back—"

"It wasn't a long call. Three or four minutes."

"Yes. When she came back, how did she look? As if it had been good news, bad news? Pleased—excited?"

"Heavens, I didn't know her well enough to say—and I wasn't interested enough to notice, much. She had rather a poker face, you know. I do remember she was smiling just a little. But when you think about it, isn't it—"

"A little funny to get a phone-call at someone else's house—just a casual call. If she'd been one of Angel's best friends, in and out of the house, yes, somebody else who knew her well might have tried to reach her at home and then thought, she might be at the Hacketts'—sure. But I gather she wasn't."

"No. Not by any means. And that seems to me," said Alison, "to suggest that the phone-call wasn't so casual. Because nobody would call a stranger's house in the middle of a party, to ask for one of the guests, just to say, Oh, I've been meaning to call you, let's meet for lunch tomorrow. Would they? It sounds more on the order of, Jane's just had her baby, or Aunt Mary's sinking fast."

"You're getting a complex about babies. Yes, it does, doesn't it? So who knew she was at the party? Her father didn't know where the party was. I wonder. I do wonder if it was someone relaying urgent news, whether true or false, and adding, Please meet me here as soon as possible." He considered this idea, rather like (Alison thought) a cat stalking all round a strange object, cautiously. He was lying back on the couch, El Señor draped artistically across his stomach with brooding eyes fixed on Mendoza's bare throat. "I like that. Because it's a little awkward to lay an ambush for somebody driving a car. Short of setting up a road-block. So much simpler just to arrange a meeting-place. I suppose she didn't say anything about the phone-call?" Alison shook her head. "And she didn't make some excuse and leave at once—she didn't leave until at least half an hour later." He ruminated awhile on that, and then said, reaching up to smooth El Señor's elegant jawline, "This Silverman girl. She's a schoolteacher, by the way, she's taught fourth grade for four years at the same school that hired her when she was first qualified. So they must like her. You said you liked her."

"I did. She's—interesting looking, and she hasn't any affectations. 'Sensible' is the wrong word—you know what I mean, quiet, reserved, but a subtle sense of humor and—an attractive person."

"Mmh. Did she like you? You can usually tell."

"Yes, I think so. I think basically we're rather alike."

"Excuse me, *Señor Imperioso*," said Mendoza, removing El Señor and sitting up. "Let's call and see if Miss Silverman's home and will receive us. I think if she will, Miss Silverman might have a few significant little things to say about Margaret. And if she likes you, and you introduce me nicely, impressing on her that as an honorable high-minded fellow I'm a seeker after truth—well, she might part. I'll look up the number . . ." He went into the bedroom, where the phone was, and in a few moments she heard his voice registering conscious charm.

Alison massaged Sheba's stomach thoughtfully. When he came back he said, "She'll be expecting us. A little surprised to hear that you're connected to the arm of the law, but polite. Up. It's only a quarter of eight, but it's a little drive."

Alison got up obediently and deposited Sheba on top of El Señor. El Señor was mildly in love with his sister and devoted a good deal of time to washing her; he started in again now. "You don't think she could have been the one? It sounded rather far-fetched at the time—"

"Superfluous cars," said Mendoza. "Awkward to chase somebody, stop the car, do a murder like that. You'd be stuck with two cars. Have to drive off in the first one, dispose of it somewhere, and then get back to your own. At that time of night, very few buses still running, and cabdrivers have an unfortunate habit of remembering fares. No. What I think— Well, we'll treat Miss Silverman kindly and maybe she'll give me a little evidence to back up a hunch."

# 5

**R**oberta Silverman lived in a fairly new apartment on a quiet South Pasadena street. The living-room was a little like its owner— reserved, neat, tailored and characterful. No flowers, a good many books, discreet color. Again Alison thought what an attractive person she was, a tall slender woman with short dark hair, matte-white skin as contrast to those dark eyes: an oddly angular, wide-jawed face. She found herself remembering that maxim—"There is no excellent beauty which hath not some strangeness in its proportion"—was that it?

And how well Luis did this kind of thing—quite blatantly laying out his personal charm, but so reassuringly formal, so openly sincere. Alison smiled at him amusedly without realizing it; and if she had known, it was that which reassured Roberta Silverman more than his deep smooth voice.

"Cards on the table," he was saying. "No sleight of hand. I'm subject to hunches, Miss Silverman, and while this thing looks like a random homicide—the victim chosen by chance—I don't think it was. I think there may have been a private motive, that it was someone who knew her. Had some personal motive to want her—out of the way."

"Oh—" said Roberta Silverman. She tipped ash off her cigarette, looking at him steadily.

Alison put in, "They laugh at him sometimes, but quite a lot of the time his hunches work out."

"So I'm psychic. But this kind of thing, a long tiresome job—routine looking, questioning. Now—I'm frank with you—Alison says to me, she saw you looking at Margaret Chadwick as if—mmh—you weren't loving her very much. And—"

"And you thought, Aha, first suspect?" Roberta had a light, pleasant voice. "I'd never take you for a police-officer, somehow . . . Yes, well, so you're checking up. Did you suppose that if I had a motive to murder her, I'd obligingly tell you all about it? I thought you went prying around at the suspect's friends, asking suggestive questions."

"I don't think," said Mendoza, "that you could have killed her, Miss Silverman, whether you wanted to or not. Because of how it was done. But I have a couple of ideas in my head about our Margaret, and I hoped you'd give me a little evidence to back them up. You see, one of the difficulties about investigating a deliberate homicide is that when somebody's dead, nobody wants to be frank about the corpse. As a general rule, anybody who gets himself murdered has done a little something to provoke it. But dead, he acquires a halo."

Roberta Silverman uttered a short laugh and put out her cigarette. "I see what you mean. Well, I may be putting my head in a noose—no, it's the gas-chamber in California, isn't it?—but I'll come clean, Lieutenant. If for no other reason than that several people know about it—what she did to me, I mean—and you'd get the story easily enough. I'd prefer to tell you my version." She didn't, immediately; she sat back, crossed her long legs the other way (and very nice legs they were) and lit a fresh cigarette. "I've known Margaret casually since we were at school together. The way you do know people casually. I neither liked nor disliked her—just someone I knew, not a close friend. But as it happened, we went to the same college for the first two years—U.C.L.A. At that time, she had some idea of being a teacher too, but she dropped out. Of course, she didn't need to—that is, I gather there's plenty of money. Well, it was then I started to find out a little more about—what made Margaret tick.

"I don't pretend to explain people like that. The psychological jargon—" she gestured with her cigarette— "you know. Maybe it's just that it makes them feel important, knowing things? Little things. Such as how much you pay for stockings. She—"

"She was a snob," said Alison. "I got that."

"Oh, yes. Brought up that way. But also, she—pried. She probed. She liked to find out things about people. Just out of pure inquisitiveness. Just to know. She was never very—popular, which is a word I don't like —I don't particularly like these life-of-the-party girls, usually nitwits, and in that sense I never was either. But—" Roberta was talking mostly to Alison now— "you see what I mean. Lots of girls who are a lot plainer than Margaret still have the—personality to seem attractive, get asked for dates and so on. She didn't. She was—how shall I put it—stiff. And she was always full of good advice. Like a patent dispensing machine, you know— Now, dear, what you want to do is this, just listen to me and I'll tell you how."

"Oh, dear," said Alison.

"Well, maybe it was compensation, because she felt left out socially. Maybe she was just like that, I don't know. Anyway, she was—inquisitive. And always, inevitably, she put the worst interpretation on anything she knew."

"I told him that," said Alison, nodding. "She—belittled."

"Yes. Well, don't they say some people get a great kick out of misfortune, tragedy, happening to other people? Maybe that's the answer. But she could build more on some innocent little fact than—than a Hollywood scriptwriter. There was Marian Vogel, in our class. Margaret somehow found out that she'd bought a pair of used evening slippers at a Junior League rummage-sale. Right away, wasn't it awful, hadn't you heard, poor Marian, her father had lost all his money and she was having to quit college and get a job."

"Oh," said Alison, "she talked about these things. Round and about."

"Talked! My God!" said Roberta violently. Suddenly, with unconscious theatricalism, she passed a hand flat across her wide forehead. "I suppose she'd have said—well, she did say—she didn't mean any harm. Maybe not. All I can say is, *I* felt she meant harm. She got a kick out of —of seeing other people in trouble, any kind of trouble—so she jumped to conclusions, wanting them to *be* in trouble—and passed on the conclusions."

"She meddled," said Mendoza sleepily, "in other words. The catalyst. Taking the effect of stirring up all elements, without suffering any disturbance herself. Like that?"

"That's a good word, catalyst. Say it again," said Roberta. "I knew of a couple of other cases like Marian's. In a minor way, it was a—a byword, about Margaret. Among those of us who knew her. You can find other people to back me up, now. Of course, mostly it was just annoying. Marian could laugh and deny it, and anyway there's nothing scandalous about losing money. But in other cases— Well, there was me, for instance." She leaned forward to put out her cigarette. "It's no good saying I wasn't damned mad about it—I still am, as several people could tell you. With good reason. It's a very short, simple story. Last October my brother's wife came down with polio. They live in Phoenix,

Jim's got an insurance business there. Well, there are three kids under eight, and while he's solvent, it *is* a new business, there isn't much money to spare, and the hospital bills were piling up. Both our parents are dead—there isn't any family except me. So I explained to Mrs. Vanssitart, the principal, and got leave of absence—indefinite. Just one of those things. I went to Phoenix at the end of October, and I was there until May, keeping house for Jim, looking after the kids—and the last couple of months helping take care of Norah. By the grace of God they pulled her out of it, with good treatment, and she's going to be O.K. But when I came home—" She stopped, reached for another cigarette, lit it carefully.

"Oh," said Alison involuntarily, leaping to feminine conclusions. "I see, of course, the length of time you'd been away—"

Roberta looked at her. "I'd got engaged last year, in August, to a man named Lee Stephens. He's a teacher too, a science teacher at a junior high school. We'd planned to be married this June, after school closed . . . I came home in May, and I saw Mrs. Vanssitart and said I could finish out the year or wait until September. She said, seeing that there was only another month, I might as well wait for the fall term. Which was reasonable. And then she said, 'What's all this about your going away to have a baby?' "

"Of course," said Alison. "Deductions."

"I found it was all over. Almost everybody had heard some rumors. You know how that kind of thing—spreads. As far as I know, the only school contact—loosely speaking—Margaret had was Evelyn Carr, she's another casual acquaintance, and her little girl goes to the school where I teach. That's where it started, of course—with Margaret being artlessly gossipy with Evelyn. I found that out definitely. And that kind of thing's like a snowball. Nine out of ten people who knew me were three-quarters convinced that I'd gone away to—to bear the child of shame, as it were. Lee was all the way convinced," she added abruptly.

Neither of the Mendozas said anything to that.

Roberta looked at her cigarette. "He was—rather frank about it. And you can see what a—viciously silly little story it was. I mean, anybody could have found out without much trouble that it wasn't true. By writing a letter to Jim, calling Phoenix by phone. Only of course people don't. Lee didn't. I started out laughing about it, to him I mean, and then I said, for heaven's sake let's get this cleared up, call Jim and ask him where I've been. But—considering his attitude—I saw it wasn't much use, and eventually I broke our engagement." She gave Mendoza a slow, bitter smile. "Is it any good to say, Lieutenant, that since then I have realized all too well that Lee Stephens wasn't much of a capture, when he had so little trust or faith in me? Very fortunately—because public school teachers are like Caesar's wife, we have to be careful— Mrs. Vanssitart believed me. Knew me. If she hadn't, I might easily have lost my job too. She might very well have said, even after checking and knowing it wasn't so, that the mere fact of the gossip was enough excuse to fire me."

"He wasn't good enough for you," said Alison. "Somebody else will be. It happened to me too, Roberta—don't brood on it."

Roberta smiled at her. "Oh, I'm not. Somebody like Prince Charming? Did that happen to you too?"

"Yes, it did indeed . . . You don't still, after he—just listened, and believed it?"

"No. No, I don't still. I didn't nurse an outsize grudge against Margaret and make up any cunning plot to murder her, because she'd separated me and my true love. I was just damned mad, and then very much relieved that I hadn't lost my job. What I did do was tell her how I felt about it. I said it amounted to slander, and—well, I said quite a few things. Of course she said she never meant any harm, it was just girlish speculation all chatty together with a dear friend, and dear Evelyn really shouldn't have passed it on, and so forth and so forth. There was no profit trying to pin it down to her, make her admit it. The damage was done. I let it go. But you can see why I—didn't love our Margaret . . . No, as time went on, it penetrated that Lee wasn't such a good catch, when he could turn against me so easily. Actually, I think it may have been an escape." She smiled crookedly. "He lives with a widowed mother. Rather doting. He's thirty-eight."

"And even that," said Mendoza pleasedly, "may enter in . . . That Mr. George Arden, yes . . . You're a woman in a million, Miss Silverman. Like my wife, you can be objective. This is very helpful. She meddled. It's in the cards she meddled with a lot of other lives than yours."

"I'll be frank with you, Lieutenant," said Roberta amusedly. "That was the first thought that occurred to me, the minute that nice police-sergeant called this noon, to tell me about it and ask questions. I didn't say so to him, but the thought crossed my mind— She annoyed somebody just a little too much, by her meddling."

"Which was," said Mendoza, standing up, "the little idea I had about our Margaret. That service club she belonged to. Yes—dispensing unasked advice, a thing social workers are usually good at. Right up her street. Thanks very much, Miss Silverman."

"At least I'm learning things. I had no idea the police were so—socially correct, these days. That sergeant—Palliser, his name was. A very polite young man, very grammatical."

"This is a crack police force, Miss Silverman. Or we like to think so. You've been very helpful indeed . . . Alison, we won't keep the lady up, come along."

At the door Roberta said, "Whoever it was, whatever happened, you'll find out. Because in your way, Lieutenant, you're rather like Margaret—inquisitive."

"Jigsaw puzzles," said Mendoza. "All the pieces scattered—very untidy. It's a compulsion, I have to put them in order . . . Thanks again, good night."

In the nature of things, Homicide was always busy. There had been this Benson thing, now just getting cleared up, and six or seven other cases —more or less straightforward, but a good deal of red tape to unwind, demanding the attention of a lot of men. When, at nine-forty on Monday morning, another one came in, there weren't many men available to go and look at it. With some misgivings, Hackett gave it to Detective-Sergeant (third grade) John Palliser. Palliser's record was good, and he was a bright young fellow, Hackett thought. All he needed was experience, and there was only one way to have that.

Palliser had mixed feelings about it; he just hoped he wouldn't do something stupid. He went down with a photographer and the doctor to look at it.

It was not a very pleasant corpse. There was a lot of rebuilding going on these days, in the heart of L.A.—old buildings coming down, bigger new ones going up. Slum areas being cleaned up. Just a few blocks from headquarters, men had come recently and torn down an old red-brick office-building: razed it to the ground. Then had come bulldozers, leveling the rubble and digging a deeper new foundation for the building to go up. The bulldozers were still busy there; and at nine-thirty this morning, the jaws of one bulldozer, biting out a hunk of sandy soil, had come up with something unexpected—a body.

The bulldozer was an unfortunate complication, said the doctor testily; it hadn't done the body much good. It was, Palliser thought, a kind of clever idea at that—bury the body here; only whoever had, hadn't realized that the bulldozers weren't through.

It was the body of a woman. Presently Dr. Bainbridge could tell them more. No handbag. Just a blonde young woman, in a cheap ready-made sundress.

More digging didn't turn up a handbag. They hunted through the rubble diligently, but found nothing else at all. So there was nothing to do but take the body away for more careful examination and hope that something would show up to give them a clue. This was the toughest kind of homicide there was, as even Palliser knew: so damned anonymous, nothing to get hold of. And in this case—always supposing that Missing Persons couldn't give them anything—they couldn't even run a photograph in the papers. The bulldozer—or something—had seen to that.

Palliser said, "We'd like a complete description as soon as possible, Doctor."

"Yes, of course. I'll get that out for you at once, and probably do the autopsy tonight. Nothing much more to do here. She's been dead about forty hours, roughly. Give or take a little. O.K., boys, you can take it away." Bainbridge got up and dusted his trousers. "People leave corpses in the damnedest places."

The ambulance-men hoisted the body to the stretcher, and something dropped from it. Palliser pounced. A handkerchief, and one corner of it knotted over a small object. There were no pockets in the sundress; this had been pushed down inside her bra, for safekeeping. An ordinary single knot, kind anybody might tie. He untied it carefully, and looked at what it had guarded.

A gold disc. Superimposed on it was the raised figure of a cat, cleverly engraved and chased to simulate long silky hair. The cat's head was lifted, even the long whiskers and ear-tufts were indicated, and the eyes were small bright green gems. Below the figure were engraved the words *Silver Boy*, in fine Spencerian script.

Palliser stared at the cat and the cat stared back, anonymous and inarticulate.

# 6

The cat was puzzled and uncomfortable. Again, there was no one there. There had always been someone there, oftenest the one who had been there as long as he could remember. The one with the soft voice, who stroked him and spoke lovingly and let him sleep in her lap in the evening. Sometimes the other one who had also lived here in the house with them. Usually both together, though the other one had not been there for some time now.

There was nothing; nothing was as it should be. His time-sense told him when she should be home, and he would wait for her—on the front porch if outside, at the door if inside. He had his own door to the house, set into the kitchen door. Even that was different, now. For his door was always locked at night, so that he could not use it to go out then. Now it was not locked.

She would come, and open the big white door of the thing that held food, and there would be food on his own plate, and a bowl of milk and a bowl of fresh water. She would speak in a loving voice, and stroke him, and afterwards he would lie curled on her lap, or she would brush his coat with his own brush, which felt very good and untangled the knots his tongue and teeth could not manage.

But she did not come.

The cat's ancestors for many generations had been pampered, carefully-guarded; no experienced tough old alley cat, wise in the ways of men and towns, contributed to the cat's inheritance. But instinct had come to his aid, a little. The first night he had been very hungry, but had not attempted to do anything about it. Food was something dispensed at predictable intervals by humans. But by noon the next day instinct had led him to the nearby garbage-cans. He did not find much edible in them. That afternoon, after many trials, he caught and ate a small sparrow, but that was hardly a mouthful for a cat of his size.

The first night, he had been terrified by the other cats. He had never been outside at night in his three years of life; and a long time ago most of his aggression had been surgically removed. Strange cats he had never seen before had come prowling, challenging, calling strange cries, and he had fled back into the house by his own door.

The next day he had caught three birds, but that only whetted his hunger. Thirst had driven him to range wider than he ever had, until he found a drainage-pipe in a strange back yard where brackish water lay. At intervals, he went to meet her when she should be coming, but she did not come. Nobody came to open the big white door and set out food on a plate; nobody came to stroke him and speak soft words.

That night hunger drove him out again to forage in the garbage-cans, to hunt for possible game; but a strange and terrible black cat of enormous size leaped on him and raked the side of his throat painfully, hissing insults. The cat named Silver Boy fled back to his house, and spent a long while licking the wound.

The day after that he began hunting early, in the back yard of the house. He was gradually growing more adept at it, at stalking and timing his pounces.

By now his long smoke-silver coat was matted and rough, and several foxtails were imbedded in it.

He caught seven birds that day, but that left him hungry.

At intervals he sat in his favorite place on the front porch, waiting. Several people who passed the house noticed him there, and two women said, "Oh, what a beautiful cat!" But the people who most frequently passed down this street were used to seeing the great smoke-silver Persian cat at this house, a pampered pet. They did not attempt to call him, or come close enough to notice his rough staring coat, the blood-matted hair on his neck.

The cat sat there now, near noon of the third day she had not come; he sat with his plumed tail coiled lightly around him, staring down the street. In his mind was the intention presently to find another bird. But above every other feeling—hunger and fear—was the awful puzzled uneasiness. Life had turned into a great dark wrongness. Nothing was as it should be.

When his built-in clock told him it was the time, he would again come to sit here and wait for her. This time, surely she would come; and then everything would be right, as it should be, again.

When Palliser came in to report to Hackett, he found Lieutenant Mendoza there, sitting on a corner of Hackett's desk. It wasn't that Palliser was afraid of Mendoza, who was always fair; it was just, well, the abrupt way he had, and his reputation and so on, you felt you had to be on your toes—and polite. Palliser felt a little awed by the way Hackett coolly interrupted him to say, "Just a minute, Luis, I want to hear about this new one. What's the word, Palliser?"

Palliser gave him the meager facts he'd got. "The doctor thinks about forty hours." He tried to sound confident, concise, with the lieutenant listening in. "She was strangled. No handbag. The only thing—"

"Forty hours," said Mendoza. "That makes it some time Saturday night? Manually strangled?"

"I—guess so, he didn't say, but it'll be in the autopsy report, sir. The only thing there was at all—" Palliser got out the gold disc and gave it to Hackett. "It's been printed. Only two of hers on it. Natural, I guess."

Mendoza took it out of Hackett's hand. "What'd she look like?" He studied the disc while Palliser told him. "Strangled," he said to himself. "On Saturday night."

Hackett said, "*Now* what picture is your crystal ball showing you? Don't tell me, a tie-up. Look, Luis, let's not call every card in the deck wild, for God's sake. There are around six and a half million people in this area, and for our sins a pretty high rate of crime. Just because two women happened to get themselves strangled at more or less the same time—"

"*Se comprende.* But— Have you seen Missing Persons, Palliser?"

"Yes, sir, just now. The doctor'll send a complete description up to them. Offhand, from what I could tell him—general appearance and age, you know— Lieutenant Carey didn't spot her as anybody on their books. But it's early. People don't come in sometimes until somebody's been gone a week or so."

"That's so. You might," said Mendoza, "have a lead here." He tapped the disc. "This is fourteen-karat . . . I said that awhile ago. *Caray*, yes, Margaret's cigarette-case. Yes . . . And the cat's eyes are real emeralds. It's probably custom work."

"Yes, sir, I saw that. But all the jewelry-shops in town—"

"Mmh. Might be a shortcut." Mendoza tore a slip off Hackett's memo-pad and scribbled. "Here, you take this and that thing to Mr. Brian Shanrahan—big jewelry shop, Shanrahan and MacReady, out on Wilshire—and ask him all about it. He might be able to suggest something useful, give you some leads."

"Yes, sir, thank you."

"And," said Mendoza, "I'll be interested in whatever you turn up."

"You and your crystal ball!" said Hackett.

Palliser didn't know that he was at all glad to hear that the lieutenant would be keeping an eye on this, the first case he was working more or less on his own; but he said Yes sir again and he'd do his best.

Mendoza grinned at him. "Don't let it ride you. We all learn the hard way—we all make mistakes. And I don't bite."

Palliser smiled back, feeling easier, and said O.K., he'd get on it. It occurred to him suddenly, going out, that a man in Mendoza's rank didn't achieve his reputation solely on brilliance at the job: a lot of it would be, would have to be, his ability to get along with his men—to get the best out of them without either riding them or being too slack. He decided Mendoza deserved his reputation.

The last thing he heard was Mendoza saying, "Now, about this Arden character—"

It was a very classy establishment indeed, a big glass-and-marble place in a classy block of stores. Palliser felt a little seedy, going in; glass cases full of diamonds, suave formally dressed clerks; but he produced Mendoza's note and asked for Shanrahan firmly.

He had, of course, read the note—mostly out of curiosity. "You money-grubbing robber," said Mendoza's neat script, "tell Sgt. Palliser whatever you can about this clue, or you lose a customer."

Mr. Brian Shanrahan was a stocky, smooth-faced man about fifty. He read the note, crumpled it up, and said bitterly, "Customer! Now the old lady—her, I miss. Jewelry such a good investment. But Mendoza! He did give me a little business when he got married—the wedding-ring, but that was nothing, no stones, and he had one of the emeralds remounted for the engagement-ring. But since? All the stuff cleaned once a year, and once in awhile his watch to be repaired, and that's all. Not even the rubies did I get to sell for him. Naturally, with a red-headed wife, he wouldn't want the rubies, and the old lady had quite a little collection—necklace, two bracelets, four rings and some earrings. An easy forty thousand, and the commission—! But if you'll believe me, he gave them away—to the fat wife of that Illinois policeman, some godforsaken little one-horse town, daresay you remember the case—man gave him some important evidence or something, led to his getting that rape-killer who nearly finished the girl he married. I ask you. A nice gesture, but the commission— Well. Come into my office, we'll have a look at this."

In his tiny, elegantly-appointed office beyond the stockroom with its ceiling-high twin safes, he examined the disc through a *loupe* and with the naked eye, and said, "Well, you can see for yourself what it is. A charm, as they're called, for God knows what reason—meant to be hung on a bracelet. The ring for hanging it's missing."

Palliser followed that. The ring had broken, and she had—being away from home?—knotted it in her handkerchief for safekeeping, until she could have it fixed. "I saw what it was," he said. "Lieutenant Mendoza seemed to think it could be a lead to her identity. She's a new corpse, you see—no make on her at all. And—"

"Oh," said Shanrahan, "I see. Yes, he's quite right. It's a custom piece—in a way."

"How d'you mean?"

For answer, Shanrahan opened a drawer and rummaged. Found a thick catalogue. Opened it, leafed through, and handed it to Palliser. "See for yourself."

The catalogue was labeled Crown Lapidary, Inc. The page to which it was opened bore illustrations of about twenty gold charms. Simulations of monthly calendars, the month-name and year engraved, a stone set in an indicated date. Heart-shaped charms with little figures superimposed —a pair of baby-shoes, wedding-bells, a Cupid bearing a jeweled bow and arrows, the dramatic masks, a telephone, a ballerina, a four-leaf clover. He turned the page. Square and round charms faced him: engraved with such messages as *Mother—Always—Sweet 16*—initials— *My Valentine—Dearest—A Date to Remember.*

"Women have collections of them," said Shanrahan. "Marking special occasions, personal interests, that kind of thing. Almost anything you can think of is available."

"I see," said Palliser. He had already noticed the printing at the page-corner: "Initials included in price—special engraving, 30¢ per letter." "Could you tell me where this might have come from?"

Shanrahan turned it over in his fingers. "A number of places, Sergeant. If you'll look at this—" he found another catalogue—"you'll see what I mean, how these things are made up."

Here was another page of illustrated charms—three basic shapes: round, heart-shaped, four-leaf clover—and perhaps thirty designs which could be superimposed. Tiny ships, babies, cats, dogs, telephones, the horn of plenty, the tree of life, a peacock, a cocktail-glass, a heart with an arrow, a key. The printing said, "Any design may be combined with any charm. Please specify by number of design. Any message engraved, 30¢ per letter."

"Most of the big wholesale firms," said Shanrahan, "do this kind of thing. It's cheaper and easier for both them and us. We get an order, say, for a thing like this—it goes straight to the wholesale manufacturer. And some of these firms—both Regent and Crown, and I believe Best —send out private catalogues. That is, they send catalogues to anyone who requests one—run an ad once in awhile in a few magazines, soliciting private customers—and let those customers take forty or fifty percent off the retail price. There is, I suppose you realize, er, quite a high mark-up on jewelry."

"Yes, I know that," said Palliser. "You mean, whoever bought this would have got it that way, wholesale?"

"It might have been bought anywhere, anyhow," said Shanrahan. "From a jewelry-shop, which would send the order back to the manufacturer. From a catalogue. But there'll be a record—somewhere. I don't envy you the hunt for it. I can think of half a dozen outfits which might have made this. And it just might be, too, that some small shop had this in as part of its stock, and it was bought over the counter, and the engraving done locally. I do seem to remember that Crown had a line of things like this, three or four years ago—made-up charms with designs you could pick from—longhaired cat, shorthaired cat, cocker, terrier, collie, boxer, maybe a horse-head—and you pick the one that looks like your darling Rex or Prince, and maybe have his name engraved on it. You see what I mean. So there'd be a record."

Palliser saw what he meant. A lot of people might have a cat named Tom or Fluffy, a lot of people might have a dog named Butch or Rex; but most such items would be individual. Somewhere, there would be a record of this fourteen-karat charm with its longhaired cat and its engraved *Silver Boy*, saying who had ordered it and when and where. But it would be one hell of a hunt, he thought, as he started taking down names and addresses from Shanrahan. There seemed to be dozens of

wholesale manufacturers—and then, as Shanrahan said, there'd be all
the local jewelry-stores, where the thing might also have been purchased.

He thanked Shanrahan and came out. Wires, he thought, not letters.
Because of how the lieutenant had looked. And Sergeant Hackett saying, maybe tied up to that other case. Or, rather, saying it couldn't be—
when the lieutenant thought maybe it was.

Palliser pinned his faith to reputation, and Mendoza. He sent wires.

"Arden," said Mendoza, and blew smoke at the ceiling. "It makes a
picture. A very pretty picture."

"You're building a lot on a little. He *could* be," said Hackett. "That's
all I can say. Hell, Luis, you know it doesn't always show. The fiction-
writers make people think it does—they want to describe a fag, a fairy,
they show him all girlish and swish and coy. They aren't like that, most
of them. You can't mark them on surface behavior. Quite a few of them
look as hundred percent male as anybody. There was that Lemmon—
my God, he was a pro wrestler."

"Sure," said Mendoza. "Almost anybody might be, you can't go on
looks. But we know about Darrell. He's on record. Picked up twice, in
raids on that place on Fairfax, known hangout of the queers. One
charge, attempted assault on that kid. Nothing on Arden, but are you
saying there's nothing funny?"

"No, I'm not. Who can say, about Arden, except Arden? Whether
Darrell's still in the process of seducing him, whether he's been that way
from a long time back? He could be, that's all I can say—go and look at
him yourself. It's a No Man's Land, this sort of thing. But if you want
to pin me down, I think it could be Darrell's still working on him."

"But what a nice picture," said Mendoza, "if he's not. If Mr. George
Arden has been some time committed to the other side of the fence.
Seduced by Darrell or somebody else a long time ago. Because our
Margaret was a strong-minded girl, Art. Liked to be boss—give good
advice, manage people. And the mother?—I must see the mother—
probably not realizing the truth, thinking darling George ought to have
a nice practical wife. Especially one bringing some money with her, so
George can settle back in comfort to write his masterpieces. Quite
conceivably, the two of them masterminding George into an unwilling
engagement. You follow me?"

"Oh, I see what you're driving at."

"Not very stable, that kind, are they? I can see George—with or without collaboration from Darrell—panicking and getting rid of Margaret the easiest way. Once Margaret's out of the way, he'll be damn careful about getting jockeyed into that situation again—and he's safe to go on being chums with Darrell."

"All right," said Hackett, "how did he do it?"

"¡Imaginativo! Easy. Call her up, say meet him at such-and-such a place. Say, his car's stalled. A nice dark corner."

"All right. And so you think this new corpse also ties in. How?"

"How the hell should I know? No, not if it was George. Probably not, anyway. We'll find out. I think I'll go see Arden."

# 7

The machine of routine went on grinding out information. Quite a lot of it, probably, would turn out to be irrelevant information; but right now they were collecting everything they could.

They heard from Rose Larkin and Esther MacRae that Margaret and her sister Laura didn't get on so well. Oh, no open quarrels, just the difference in their ages, and different interests; Margaret had been a serious-minded girl, and Laura—well—wasn't. All she was interested in was dates and clothes and things like that. All the same, Laura hadn't managed to get engaged until a few months ago. Whereas Margaret, of course— Both women had met George Arden and thought him charming. Such a sensitive, nice-looking young man.

About eight o'clock on Sunday night, Charles Chadwick had left home and driven, in his two-year-old Dodge, to an address on Silver Lake Boulevard. It was a court of rental units: fairly new, fairly good, quiet; middle-bracket rents. Mr. Chadwick had called on a Mrs. Helen Ross, and stayed about two hours. It could be surmised that he had made some excuse of business to his wife. Which seemed unusual to say the least, on the day they had learned that their daughter was violently dead. Perhaps even more unusual that she'd accept it, even with protest.

Mrs. Ross, investigation this morning had revealed, was a legal secretary at the firm of Paddock and Byrnes in Hollywood. About forty; nice-looking; nothing known against her. A widow, for some time back; no children. She lived alone.

Charles Chadwick's parents had originally owned the Franklin Avenue house. His business was flourishing, all right, but not so much as to provide his daughters' cars and clothes. It was Mrs. Chadwick who had the money. Rather a lot of it, since about eight years ago. An old bachelor uncle had died and left her about half a million. Had also left a hundred and fifty thousand to each of the girls, set up in trust-funds administered by a local bank. And that was very interesting and suggestive.

Laura Chadwick's fiancé, Kenneth Lord, worked as a clerk at a big brokerage house on Spring Street. They liked him there, said he was a bright young man. It was the brokerage where Mrs. Chadwick's financial advisor had an office, so probably that was how Lord had met Laura. Lord, who was twenty-nine and good-looking, had apparently come to California from somewhere in the south—Virginia or one of the Carolinas—about six years ago. He hadn't any money, but (this from people at the brokerage, at the apartment-house where he lived) he had such nice manners, rather old-fashioned, you could see he came from a really good old family: probably one of those impoverished Old South families. The Chadwicks liked and approved of him highly. And—considering Laura, who was no beauty and a little older than Lord—so maybe he was latching onto her for the money, but that wasn't illegal, after all.

Mrs. Arden had been widowed when George was a baby. Her husband, who had been very much her senior, had left her a modest capital invested in securities, which brought in about four thousand a year. George had attended public schools and had four years at U.C.L.A., where he had known Rose Larkin's brother; and that was how he had happened to meet Margaret. About a year ago, or a little more. There had started to be talk of an engagement between them about four months ago.

Mrs. Chadwick was a bridge-fiend. She belonged to the West Hollywood Woman's Club, the D.A.R., the Republican Woman's Club, and a small private club for bridge-players. She went out and also entertained a good deal. They had two maids in twice a week to clean, and whenever Mrs. Chadwick entertained the same two came to serve and clean up. Mrs. Chadwick drove a new Pontiac, a two-door hardtop.

The Chadwicks had been married for thirty-two years. He was fifty-one; she was fifty-eight. He was a native Californian; she had come here with her parents as a teenager. They had separate checking-accounts; and, which seemed a little odd, Mrs. Chadwick didn't have her husband figure out her income-tax for her, but employed another firm.

Laura Chadwick had a lot of friends more or less like herself, some married, some not. Rather useless young women, but that was a personal opinion of Higgins, who was taking a look at her, and he didn't include it in his report. All with enough money, the unmarried ones, that they didn't have to hold jobs. They occupied themselves going out to lunch together, shopping, taking in the latest shows. Sometimes double or triple dating. Laura didn't seem to have any special hobbies. Several of her unmarried friends admitted being a little girlishly jealous over Kenny Lord—*so* good-looking and *so* nice, Laura was lucky.

All of this was interesting; some of it might turn out to be important. The machine went on collecting facts.

Palliser was not even collecting facts—at least, useful ones. He was thinking disgustedly about crime-novels. In fiction, it was the complex, bizarre cases, with all sorts of mysterious clues and funny goings-on, that were supposed to be the tough ones. If any of these bigger-than-life brains in those books, like Dr. Fell or Mr. Fortune, really existed, Palliser would sure as hell like to turn them loose on one like this. The really tough kind.

Just a body. A body without a name. Impossible as it might sound, they sometimes got one like that they never could put a name to. If and when you got an identification, it was easier; but that could be (and this looked like being) the hell of a job.

He had sent off wires to all those manufacturing jewelers. But no telling when the charm had been bought; they'd have to dig through back records. Until they had, he decided not to waste men and time checking the thousands of retail jewelry-shops in L. A. County.

The official description came up from the morgue about then, with a carbon for Missing Persons, and he studied it gloomily.

The dead woman had been between twenty-two and twenty-six years old. Five feet four and a half, a hundred and ten pounds. Very little dental work: two old fillings, one new cavity not yet attended to. No scars except that of an appendectomy (about ten years ago), no birthmarks. Not *virgo intacta*, but she had never had a child. Natural blonde but used a blonde rinse on her hair, which was not professionally cared for. She had been killed some time between six o'clock and midnight on Saturday; Bainbridge was sorry not to pin it down tighter, but time had elapsed. She had been manually strangled. At some time subsequent to death, not more than two hours later, her face had been disfigured by several blows from something like the back of a spade or a flatiron. The damage added up to a broken nose, several broken front teeth, a fractured cheekbone, and severe contusions. Bainbridge said definitely, not the bulldozer; it had been done too soon after death. So somebody didn't want her recognized.

She had been wearing a pair of high-heeled white sandals, not new, bought (by the label) at a low-priced chain store. No stockings. A pair of white nylon briefs, which bore the tag of another low-priced chain store, and white lace brassière ditto. A rayon-tricot half-slip, white, with no tag at all. A green-and-orange printed sundress, size 12, with a tag indicating that it had been purchased at The Broadway department store. She had retained one earring, the other probably having been torn off in a struggle or during the disposal of the body. The earring was a cheap one, of white enamel, round. She had also been wearing a cheap gold-and-white-enamel necklace and bracelet; a ring with a fake emerald, value about a dollar and a half, and a wedding-ring. Bainbridge enclosed all the jewelry.

Palliser uttered one descriptive expletive.

Nothing there, but nothing, was usable. Everything from chain stores which had sold thousands of such items over the counter for cash. The wedding-ring ditto, just a plain gold band—about thirty bucks retail.

So where did you go from here?

You handed it to Missing Persons; and you hoped that sometime soon a worried husband or mother would come in to say, Mary hasn't been home since Saturday. And possibly (if you had any luck) to say, She ran away with this guy—or, I knew that husband of hers would kill her someday.

Then, you had a place to look: things to do.

Palliser took the description up to Missing Persons, hoping.


The cat crossed backyards, nervously keeping to shrubs and hedges as much as possible, to where the drainage-pipe was with its shallow stagnant water. He crouched and lapped.

He had missed several birds today and caught only one. Under his long matted coat he was already much thinner.

When he had finished drinking, he remained crouching there a moment, green eyes dull. Then he quickened to attention: a bird, a big mocker, had alighted on the grass ten feet away. The cat crouched lower, flowed silently and smoothly toward the bird, freezing whenever the bird moved. When he was but three feet away, and tensing for his spring, the mocker suddenly rocketed up into the air, jeering raucously.

The cat sat down and moved his tail angrily. After a moment he started back to his own yard.

The wound on his neck was healing, but painful. One of the foxtails, after the way of foxtails, had worked its way through his long coat and was burrowing into his skin. He stopped several times to scratch and bite at it, futilely.

"I think so," said Mendoza pleasedly. "About Arden. I like Arden for it. I don't think we can say that George is an innocent victim, Art—or that Darrell's still working on him. He's too much on the defensive. The way you said he flared up when you asked his pal's name. And the act he's putting on about Margaret, such grief and sorrow, my own true love. Because it emerges—George isn't awfully bright, and he answered that one right away—he's known Darrell, been a close friend, for at least seven years. So he must know about Darrell's record. After all, Darrell got six months for that assault, three years ago. George must know why he was out of circulation. Sure, so Darrell says it's a frame-up—and the other times he was picked up, no charge. But—well, ask yourself—a friend of yours gets convicted on a charge like that, do you believe so easy it's a frame? Feel quite the same about him? Go on being pals?"

"I don't know," said Hackett slowly. "We're on the wrong side to say, Luis. We know this force doesn't manhandle people or frame charges. Other people don't. He might have believed it. Darrell's a cop-hater—most of that kind are—and he's probably influenced Arden that way too. I don't know—but I didn't like the feel of Arden, did you?"

"I did not. Nor of Mama. Poor Mama. She's a nice respectable well-meaning soul, who simply closes her nice respectable not-too-bright mind to anything Not Nice. I suppose she's vaguely aware that there are men described as homosexual—nasty word—but, one, of course such awful people are all just drunks and/or tramps, and, two, nice people just don't think about such things, it's morbid. She's—excuse the repetition—a nice woman. Wrapped up in George and his wonderful talent, if only the money-grubbing publishers would realize it."

"That I could have guessed."

"George was nervous," said Mendoza. "Couldn't understand why the police came asking *him* things. It was some real pro criminal, after all, he was at the Hollywood Bowl." He smiled at his cigarette. "I made him a lot more nervous. I'd take a bet he's run along to Darrell to tell him all about it. Maybe it'll make Darrell nervous too."

"I wouldn't doubt it," said Hackett, "but—" And was interrupted by Sergeant Lake looking in the door.

"Excuse me, Lieutenant, but they've found that car. Traffic just called. The Chadwick girl's car."

"Ah," said Mendoza, "I thought it might turn up some time today. Let's go and have a look."

The blue Buick had been parked neatly on Amador Drive, a short residential street about six blocks away from the S.P. yards where Margaret's body had been left. (Indeed, who named these streets? Lover-Boy Drive!) It had been parked in front of the residence of one Mr. Alfredo Sanchez, and when after almost two days Mr. Sanchez found it still there, he surmised it was a hot car abandoned, and called in.

"You gotta do right thing, all this talk you get, Mexicans all such bad people, thieves and crooks, like that, it's bad—so maybe they print it in the paper, mister, it's a Mexican helps the cops, so maybe people don't think so? I think—"

"Yes, fine," said Mendoza absently, looking at the Buick. Men were going over the Buick carefully for prints, for anything. "*¿Y pues qué?*" he added to himself, "So what?" There wouldn't be anything. This one would have seen to it—

"*You* are *mejicano?* Of the police?" asked Mr. Sanchez incredulously. "They let you in?"

"For my sins," said Mendoza. "There's no law."

"It is unwritten," said Mr. Sanchez, dropping into Spanish. "There are no words for the lack of logic in the minds of North Americans, sir. It is the unreason of it that annoys me. Figure it to yourself, they hold the big parades, the yearly festivals, and so proud they are of California's Spanish heritage, as they call it. They dress themselves in Spanish costume, they name their festivals for the names of great genteel old Spanish families—Carrillo, Verdugo, Del Valle—is it not so? They bandy about the few words of the tongue they may know. And then, when the festival is ended, they are again talking of dirty Mexicans. It is not logical!"

"Few matters to do with human people," said Mendoza, "are logical. The Anglo-Saxon mind, it is true, is less so than others. They will persist in thinking the Latin to be overemotional and volatile, whereas in reality we are the most coldly rational of any people. But I agree with you, it is not logic."

"Even they put the Aztec symbol upon their official city seal," said

Mr. Sanchez, "this pagan feathered serpent. They give pretentious Spanish names to the new fashionable places to live. And my daughter Francesca, she has three years' study at the university, she applies for a job and they say, so sorry, we do not hire Mexicans. It is not logical. We are not dirty, there is a modern bathroom in my house. I did not know they admitted Mexicans to the police."

"Well, the force is always shorthanded," said Mendoza. "We take what we can get. One has to make allowance for human nature."

"Indeed that is so," agreed Mr. Sanchez. "But it is annoying. I had thought perhaps, if this should be in the newspapers, a Mexican gentleman who aids the police—"

"I will see it is mentioned," said Mendoza. "But strange ideas are not easily changed."

"You are only too correct, sir," said Mr. Sanchez.

The Buick, of course, was absolutely clean. The wheel had been polished of all prints; likewise the dashboard. Elsewhere there were a few, which would probably prove to belong to Margaret or one of the family. The glove-compartment held only expectable things, maps, cleaning-rags, a whisk-broom. Nothing extraneous at all.

"But you know," said Mendoza, "the car says a little something, Art."

"Like what?"

"Just as I said about that Silverman woman. The superfluous car. So awkward to ambush somebody driving, and even more so if you're driving too. What the set-up says to me is, two people. Look at it. There had to be two cars. Margaret's, and the killer's. So all right, he calls and says, meet me at such-and-such a place. He meets her, and kills her. Drops the body. He had to leave his car where he picked her up, if he was alone. Then he has to leave Margaret's car here, and somehow get back to his own. Well, even in a place like New York, where people use cabs a lot, you can trace cab-fares. Here, how much easier. Nine out of ten people in the L.A. area have a car available, we don't use taxis much —reason fares are so steep, isn't it? So, fares are all the easier checked. He wouldn't use a cab. He could have walked, but would he?"

"You're telling the story."

"No. In all probability, there was a time-element there. He wouldn't want it remembered afterward that he'd got in very late that night, even when he was hoping we'd take it as a random kill. It would waste time, walking any distance. But how much easier all this would be, with two people. One to drive the second car. Two people like, say, George and Darrell."

"Which is very pretty deducting," said Hackett, "but how the hell can we ever find out for sure? The Hollywood Bowl, my God!"

"Yes, I know. We'll send out inquiries to the cab-companies, just in case. But I think the odds are that it was two."

"The *Bowl*," said Hackett. "I ask you. A nice balmy summer evening, and a pop concert—it was probably jammed. Who can say whether they were there or not?"

"Forget the Bowl," said Mendoza. "Or rather, find out what time the concert ended and go on from there. He said they stopped for a drink, and that might have been around the crucial time. Ask him where."

"So I'm slipping. All right, I see that."

"I was rather hoping somebody might have left a shirt-button or something in the car, but I might have known this joker wouldn't. Almost as careful as our Margaret herself. Yes. Well, let's go and have a quick lunch and then I think I'll have a good look through Margaret's room. They were damn slow getting a warrant. Oh, well, I suppose no harm. Unless, of course—*¡Pues vámonos ya*, let's be on our way!"

# 8

He always liked to do the poking around himself, on a thing like this. The ordinary crude business, the boys would spot anything relevant; but on a thing a little offbeat, maybe what was relevant wouldn't look that way. He took Dwyer along for company, but he'd look himself.

He didn't get the chance, right away. In the entrance-hall of the big house on Franklin Avenue, he was introduced to Kenneth Lord, who was, it seemed, just leaving. Laura clung to his arm; she had been crying. Belated grief? Mrs. Chadwick had not; again she looked through Mendoza.

"There've been all the—arrangements to make, you know," said Lord. "I've been trying to help out best I can."

"We do appreciate it, Kenneth." Mrs. Chadwick thawed with Lord, giving him an almost fond glance.

"You've been wonderful, Kenny," said Laura with a muffled sob. "Just wonderful."

"Well, a time like this—" He was a little embarrassed at her obvious complete adulation. He was indeed good-looking: tall and slim, with one of those perennially boyish faces making him look younger than he was: more fair than dark, with close-cut sandy hair. As if to counterbalance the boyish face, his manner was a little formal; or maybe that was on account of the police. A lot of people didn't like police in the house, and not always because they had guilty consciences.

Mendoza produced his search-warrant, and raised an instant furor. "What on *earth*," asked Mrs. Chadwick coldly, "is the reason for this? I cannot see how prying into our personal possessions can be of any help to you in catching this—this criminal! It's an invasion of privacy—you are obviously incompetent in your duty, to—"

"But I don't understand!" cried Laura, clinging closer to Lord. "Look at Margaret's *things?* But she wouldn't have known the man before! I don't understand—"

Lord said nothing for a moment, but his very blue eyes were suddenly shrewd on Mendoza. "This sounds kind of funny to me," he said then. No, Lord was no fool. "She wouldn't have known one like—like the one it seems killed her. Does this mean, maybe, you're thinking it wasn't just a chance hold-up—that whoever did it meant to?"

"I'm sorry, Mr. Lord, I can't say anything more right now," returned Mendoza smoothly. "If you'd show me Miss Chadwick's room, Mrs. Chadwick?"

"No, I refuse. This is sheer incompetency. We are not—not merely *anyone*, I daresay you are used to dealing with poor ignorant people who know no better, have no influence, but I am a personal friend of—"

"Of His Honor the Mayor?" Under provocation, Mendoza could administer the sharpest of snubs while retaining all his suave courtesy. He smiled at Mrs. Chadwick gently, with pity. "I have here a search-warrant, duly signed by a justice, Mrs. Chadwick. It authorizes me to search these premises or any part thereof. It was applied for and granted in the usual legal manner. I am a police officer—the officer in charge of this case—and whatever I may think requires investigation will be investigated." He was kind, explaining obvious facts to a stupid child. "I have been a police-officer for twenty years, madam, and I have some experience at investigating homicides. I should have thought that you would be only too anxious to give us any help asked in this investigation. I ask you again to direct me to Miss Chadwick's room."

Myra Chadwick's thin mouth tightened, listening; she snapped out one vicious obscenity at him, turned and went into the living-room and slammed the double doors behind her. Laura cried, *"Mother!"* and ran after her.

"Well, well," said Mendoza mildly.

Dwyer cleared his throat. "I'd never 've thought the lady knew such a word."

Unexpectedly Ken Lord chuckled. "Neither would I. You riled her all right, Lieutenant. I didn't think it could be done. But nobody likes being talked at as if he's a backward child. You do that act right nice. *Do* you think so? About Margaret, I mean?"

Mendoza looked at him: looked a little up at him, for Lord topped

Mendoza's five-ten by three inches. "A little early to say, Mr. Lord. We just like to have a look at everything."

"Sure," said Lord. He slapped his soft felt hat against his knee. "Hell of a thing. I never knew Margaret but just so well, you know." He had only a trace of Southern accent. "Confess it, I didn't like her much. Prim and prissy—" he hunched his shoulders— " old-maidish. But— the hell of a thing to happen to her. I guess everybody just naturally took it for granted; a hold-up. Alone in the car as she was. But now, with you sniffing around everywhere—oh, Mrs. Burkhart at my apartment told me there'd been a man around asking—and at the office too." He laughed, and sobered. "I hope you won't do too much asking at the office, is all. Conservative brokerages are—scarey—about publicity. You want to know any more, ask me. You really think somebody had a— private reason for it? Hell, I don't see it. Not *murder*. Margaret—she could be annoying, sure. She didn't like me much, I guess you'll hear that so I'll tell you first. She had a funny idea I'm marrying Laura for her money." The blue eyes told Mendoza nothing at all, and Lord did not go on to deny it, with any earnest protestations of true love. "What the hell, you marry, you get in-laws. But I don't see any reason— Of course, I didn't see much of her. I suppose there could be. It's your business."

"So it is, Mr. Lord," said Mendoza.

"Sure," said Lord. He opened the living-room door and said, "Laura honey, you come here to me." She came, snuffling into a handkerchief. "Now, honey. You stop crying—no use. These gentlemen are just doing their duty, see, what they think ought to be done. No call to get upset about it. Your mother's just a little excited, doesn't know what she's saying."

"Yes, Ken," she said forlornly, sniffing.

"So you show 'em your sister's room and don't bother them with fool questions. I guess they know what they're doing. O.K.?"

"Yes, Ken. Are you—will you—"

"I'll drop by tonight, baby, sure. Maybe take you some nice quiet place for a malt or something, hmm? O.K.?"

"Yes, d-darling."

"All right then." He kissed her lightly, gave her a little push. "Oblige the police, honey. See you."

"See you, Kenny."

He gave Mendoza a careless salute, putting on his hat. "Nice to've met you, sir." She watched him out, said dolefully she'd show them Margaret's room, led them upstairs.

"That Lord seems like a nice guy," said Dwyer when she'd left them in it.

"Um," said Mendoza. Dwyer recognized the symptoms and fell silent. He found an ashtray, sat down on the bed and lit a cigarette. Mendoza prowled, getting the feel of the room. A big room: these old houses had big bedrooms.

She used lavender cologne: expectable, unimaginative. A big wardrobe hanging in a big closet, but the clothes were all—uninspired, conventional. Not much jewelry. (Arden hadn't got her an engagement-ring yet, evidently.) It was a conventional bedroom: modern low-headboard bed, Danish walnut; vanity-table, bureau; a desk under the window, a rather large walnut desk. Everything was very neat, not even a film of powder on the glass top of the dressing-table. She had left this room at seven-thirty on Saturday night, to go to a party, but before she'd left she'd seen that the room was neat. Her mother's daughter.

He opened the bureau-drawers and felt about among piles of lingerie, accessories. A dozen handbags hung on a chain in the closet, from hooks set at intervals. He looked through all of them. Not anywhere near so much of the jumble most handbags held even when not in current use. A few sales-slips, a few books of matches, a forgotten handkerchief. He crossed the room and stared at the desk. "Such a businesslike young lady, by her handbag," he murmured, and sat down in the desk-chair and started to go through the drawers.

Her notepaper was severely plain gray, with name and address printed in dark blue. One drawer was reserved for several manila envelopes, marked tersely *Receipts, Correspondence to be Kept,* and *Tax-Forms.* Everything docketed, labeled, so she could lay a hand on it in a minute. Her father's daughter? Mendoza went through it methodically. Unlike most people, she really had kept receipts only the necessary three years; nothing dated beyond that. And, very businesslike, she had kept receipts only on items which were tax-deductible.

He put them back into the envelope, set it aside, and took up *Correspondence to be Kept.*

Here was a postcard signed *George.* It was from Lake Tahoe, the postmark August of last year. "Dear Margaret, We are having a nice time, not too much of a crowd here, and the weather wonderful. Mike has been taking a lot of pictures, hope they're all good. See you on Monday, Yours, George."

There was, interestingly, a rather incoherent letter from someone who signed herself Janice. It said that of course she understood Margaret hadn't meant any *harm*, dear, it had been just casual talk, but Margaret would understand that John was *difficult*, and it had all been so upsetting, even if he understood in the end that there hadn't been anything *wrong*, about Hunt. And she'd been *so* upset herself, maybe she *had* said some awful things to Margaret, and she hoped Margaret would understand and forgive her. Men *were* difficult, weren't they, and of course it had just been a terrible *misunderstanding*.

Yes. Roberta Silverman had been more forthright. Mendoza set the letter aside; no harm to find out who Janice, John and Hunt were.

There were a couple of letters from the president and secretary of the Good Samaritan Club, dating over a period of several years. They related to "cases" Margaret had visited, and all warmly commended her.

The last item was different. Its envelope was postmarked July fourteenth this year, and that was last Friday. It was a cheap envelope, and the folded letter did not fit it, had been double folded. The page had been torn from a school-notebook, odd-size blue-ruled paper. The writing was in pencil, neat enough but unformed and childish, the large round hand of one not used to writing. It had no salutation.

> Listen Miss Chadwick, you lay off mixing up my wife and telling her all this stuff. Its our own business strictly and we dont want no damn do-good lady charity worker sticking her nose in. You come nosing round any more getting Annie mixed up telling her Im no good, and Ill fix you good Miss Chadwick. You got no right snoop around us and youd better not no more. You better believe I mean this, see.
>
>                                                    Martin O'Hara

"*¿Ya lo decía yo?*" said Mendoza pleasedly. "What did I say? Curiosity killed the cat. Oh, yes, very nice. I think I want a little talk with Mr. Martin O'Hara."

He went on looking, but turned up nothing more interesting than an accumulation of check-stubs and a program for the final performance of *The Drunkard*. "Come on," he said to Dwyer, "we're finished here."

He drove back to headquarters and called Mrs. Rose Larkin. "I wonder if you could tell me anything about the—mmh—cases Miss Chadwick had been seeing lately, this Good Samaritan Club?"

"Oh!" said Mrs. Larkin. "Why, what *in* the world—? I mean, I can't imagine why you'd want— But I mustn't ask questions of the *police!* Of course, if it would help—but I wouldn't know, I'm just another busy little Good Samaritan. I expect Mrs. Ashbrook will know, the vice-president. Yes, of course I can give you the number . . . Janice? That would probably be Janice Headley . . . She lives somewhere in Brentwood . . . Hunt? Well, I couldn't say, I'm sure . . . Oh, not at *all,* Lieutenant."

Mrs. Ashbrook sounded crisp, efficient and distant. Could not conceive why Lieutenant Mendoza should be interested, but of course it was a duty to cooperate, such a dreadful tragedy. Miss Chadwick one of their most enthusiastic members and active workers. If the lieutenant would hold on, she would find her case-book.

Mendoza said to himself, "I'll bet she was. Our Margaret, so good at telling people how to manage their lives. And at finding out the innocent little secrets." Or the ones not so innocent.

"—A family by the name of O'Hara," said Mrs. Ashbrook. "It was one of the children, I believe, needed some dental work and they're not eligible for public relief. We get a number of cases like that. And a hospital case—the General—a Miss Genevieve Walker. A Miss Singer, she's an old lady in a rest-home, Miss Chadwick would just have been visiting her, bringing her little presents, you know . . . We obtain names from several sources. People who are not eligible for public charity, and also—many of them—poor people who are alone, old spinsters, widowers. We try to do what we can, cheer them up, and so on. The little extra treats. Miss Chadwick will be greatly missed—"

"I'll bet," said Mendoza again, as he put the phone down. He got his hat and put the scribbled list of addresses in his pocket. In the anteroom he said to Sergeant Lake, "I'll be back about four, or maybe not at all. Depends. Anything urgent, call me at home."

He wondered, descending in the elevator, how Alison was getting on with the architects. He had a vague idea that architects could be stubborn. But so could a redheaded Scots-Irish girl. His money would go on Alison.

Mr. Martin O'Hara . . .

Alison had begun to cope with the architects. Now, feeling again like Judas, she was approaching Bertha.

"Well, now, that sounds real nice, Mis' Mendoza," said Bertha, beaming. "You know, funny thing, I been thinking lately how nice it'd be, one kinda permanent job. But what you said about *quarters*, I guess I wouldn't want to move—there's Fritz, you see. He wouldn't like it, and it prob'ly would be you wouldn't like Fritz neither. It isn't ever'body understands him. But I'm used to him like, living with him so long."

"Oh," said Alison. Come to think, she didn't know much about Bertha, the perfect servant. Whether she had a husband, a family. Apparently the former anyway. "Well, there'd be no objection—" she said cautiously. Presumably Fritz had a job, would be away all day.

Bertha's ruddy round face broke in two, smiling. "I just guess there *would* be!" she said. "That Fritz, he don't like cats, not nohow. Me, I kinda get a kick out of 'em. Yours, anyways. They're kinda interesting. That Saynyor cat—never know what he'll be up to next. But not Fritz, see. It's a shame, Mis' Mendoza, but there's no changing him. I been thinking though, a real nice change, work just one place alla time." Her tight gray sausage-curls quivered as she nodded violently.

"I—we feel awfully guilty, taking you away from everybody else—"

"Oh, don't you worry, Mis' Mendoza! Wouldn't dream of deserting Mis' Carter and Mis' Bryson and the Elgins, without I put somebody good in instead. They're all nice folk. And there's my niece Mabel—"

"Oh, that's fine!" said Alison, much relieved. "I mean, she's just as— as careful and good as you are? How nice."

"Now she just better be," said Bertha. "I brought her up mostly. And she's married, but she likes to earn. She'd do a real good job here, and I don't hafta say, I'd be real pleased, come to you alla time. Real interesting, work for a real detective like the lieutenant. It's just that Fritz, see, I just couldn't be separated from Fritz, so I couldn't live in. He wouldn't stand for it, Fritz wouldn't. With the cats and all."

"Well, that's all right, I quite understand," said Alison. "It'd be just like a regular job, then."

"Yes, Mis' Mendoza. Acourse I got my own car. It's just that with that Fritz, I couldn't promise no overtime, like when you had a party. He raises such a fuss, you wouldn't believe."

"Oh?" said Alison. Somehow it seemed incredible that the strong-minded competent Bertha should be under the thumb of an autocratic husband. "But if you explained to him—"

Bertha threw back her head and guffawed. "That's a good one, that is! Explain! Just about as much use, I give you my word, as explain to that Saynyor cat! Expects his dinner at six-thirty sharp, see, and I got to be there, give it to him. Won't take it from nobody else. Raises an awful fuss if I'm late. You see how it is. But I'll be real pleased come to you permanent, Mis' Mendoza. I been thinking I ought to take it easier. Only, no denying, Fritz makes it kind of hard. Good thing the landlord don't mind him, I'll say that. On account of he's noisy, sometimes."

"Oh?" said Alison again, having visions of a drunken Fritz throwing things at Bertha, and failing to believe it. Bertha, of all people! To let herself be dictated to—

"*And,*" said Bertha, "having to have his walk, rain or shine, every night. Otherwise he'd get too fat. Though I give him nothing but the *best,* you understand. Ground stew-beef and beef liver. He likes it just seared over. But it's an awful nuisance getting him to take his vitamins. Just like that Saynyor cat with the wheat-germ stuff."

"Oh!" said Alison, dim light dawning. "Oh, I see. What—what kind is he?"

"Fritz," said Bertha, "is a Germing Shepherd, Mis' Mendoza. Awful big even for one of them. I guess it's kind o' silly, person like me keep such a creature, but he's company. He was just the cutest pup you ever saw. Smart, too. I got his papers and everything, he's a real thorough-bred. Only awful big. And he don't like cats no ways at all."

"I suppose not," said Alison.

"He takes out after a cat, and that cat makes tracks, give you *my* word! You can see. I kinda like 'em, but not Fritz. So it's all right with you, Mis' Mendoza, I'd sure like that, one permanent place, and I get my niece Mabel to come in here. Only I better go on living where I do."

"Well, yes," said Alison. On account of the Germing Shepherd. "I expect it'll be about December. Goodness knows when they'll start building." Those architects.

"Oh, sure," said Bertha. "I'll tell Mabel. It'll be nice, sorta looking forward to it."

So, fine about Bertha. But those architects . . .

# 9

"**S**o you're a cop askin' about this letter I wrote Miss Snoopy Chadwick?" said Martin O'Hara. "You might know one like that'd yell for the cops. Well, I done nothing wrong nor I don't mind layin' a complaint against *her*, see? I guess I've got a right, protect my home an' family. Man's home is his castle, they say. Come snoopin' around, tryin' to tell Annie I'm a no-good!"

Mr. O'Hara was about five-feet-three and bulged with muscles. He had flaming red hair, a thick red moustache like a bottle-brush, and dangerous fire in his blue eyes. His wife, a small thin dark woman, fluttered in the background. "Oh, please, Marty. He's a policeman. He'll arrest you if you—"

"Well, I haven't got a warrant on me," said Mendoza. "Suppose you just tell me all about it, Mr. O'Hara."

"You're damn right I'll tell you all about it! Sit down. Have a glass o' beer." Mendoza declined politely. "Suit yourself. *I'll* have a glass o' beer."

"Yes, dear," and his wife scurried to get it.

"Damn rich-bitches come slumming, handing out charity, and think because they got more money 'n me they can tell us how to live! I don't want no charity from nobody, and I said so in the first place!"

"It was Julia's teeth, Marty," said his wife, pouring the beer. She poured it carefully.

"Thanks, Annie. *I* know it was Julia's teeth. But why shouldn't I pay for fixing my own kid's teeth? The clinic lets you pay on time. Just because a bunch of snoopy rich-bitch females like to build themselves up by giving charity where it ain't asked—" He drank, lowered the glass, and fixed Mendoza with a belligerent stare. "I'm an honest working-man, see, I drive a refuse truck for the city. Eighty-five a week take-home pay I get. *And* I support my wife and kids on it. Charity I don't ask nor take, see. But this Annie, she figured, well, it was a break, if they were bound to help pay, and goddam it, she had it fixed up before I ever heard a word about it. I wanted no part of it, and I said so. But would she pay any notice, this Chadwick female? It was fixed, and here she was comin' to drive Julia to the clinic twice a week. Four o'clock, an' I'm off at three, so I'd be home, see. That snotty little snooper." He lifted the glass again.

"I don't s'pose she meant things the way it sounded, Marty. You got to remember she prob'ly lives in a big house an' all, an' just doesn't know how things are for ordinary folk."

"Then let her for God's sake stay in her big house! So I come home," he said to Mendoza, "an' I'm tired. Handlin' that great big truck all day. So I like to sit down an' relax, have a few beers. *I* buy the damn beer, don't I? What the hell right has this Chadwick female to tell Annie I'm a bad husband an' father, guzzling alcohol—that's what she says, a few beers—an' can't pay my kid's dentist! She has the goddam gall to say Annie ought to leave me! Because I like a few beers, an' don't talk English out of a schoolbook, she says I'm a bad influence on the kids! *My* kids!"

"Not very tactful," said Mendoza.

"*My* kids! Annie, I'll have another glass. Let me tell you, mister, I do right by my kids—all six of 'em. I catch 'em actin' dishonest, tellin' lies, they get walloped, an' they know what for. Every Sunday of their lives to church, see? But this Annie. The Chadwick dame gets her all mixed up. You always been satisfied with me before!" he added to the woman.

She poured beer carefully. "Now Marty. It was what she kept saying about the kids. *I* dunno, she's been educated an' knows all those things. I just got to feeling kind of miserable, all she said, an'—"

"Damn right, an' no snotty dame nor nobody else is goin' to come round makin' my wife miserable, see? So she lays a complaint—"

"No," said Mendoza. "She's dead, Mr. O'Hara. Murdered. Last Saturday night."

"Murdered, by Jesus!" said O'Hara. He even forgot the beer. "Well, I'll be damned!" Then he laughed. "An' I bet whoever did it, he had a damn good reason! I bet she damn well deserved it."

"Oh, Marty, you shouldn't! The poor thing! She meant well, I really do believe."

"An' don't the Reverend O'Neill tell us what road it is paved with good intentions," said O'Hara. "Who killed her?"

"Well, we're not quite sure about that, you see," said Mendoza gently. "When I came across your letter, Mr. O'Hara, I wondered if by any chance you killed her."

"*Me?*" said O'Hara blankly.

"Oh, *Marty!* Oh, officer, he *wouldn't!* He talks real sharp sometimes but he's soft as butter really—he *wouldn't*—"

"Me? Well, I *will* be damned," said O'Hara. He didn't sound much alarmed, only interested. "No, I didn't kill her, mister. She was just awful damn annoying, see. But not *that* much. Saturday night? Well, I was at Charlie's bar down at the corner until about nine-thirty, an' then I an' some other fellows got into a little friendly hand of stud, see, I was with them until about two A.M. Annie can say when I come in, account of I woke her up to brag on winning nine bucks. You can ask the fellows—"

Mendoza marveled slightly, getting out pen and notebook, that stud poker should so absorb several grown men for so long: a childish game. Draw was the thing you sat over all night. But people came all sorts. He took down the names and thanked O'Hara.

"*Me* kill somebody," said O'Hara. He was amused—and flattered. "Times I'd liked to've blacked an eye for her, but nothing worse."

"He just *talks*," said his wife desperately. "Why, he'd never lay a hand on a woman, officer—I ought to know—"

"No, not me," and he winked at Mendoza. "Got all those kids by spontaneous combustion like they say—"

"*Marty!* I didn't mean *that!* Please, officer—"

Mendoza, who rather liked Mr. O'Hara, said he didn't think they need worry, and came away. It was four-thirty-five; Mr. O'Hara had been voluble. He didn't think there was any particular point in checking Mr. O'Hara's alibi, but of course it had to be done . . . Our Margaret had certainly meddled, anywhere she found herself . . . He drove back to headquarters and told Sergeant Lake to dispatch men to check: also gave him the names and addresses of Margaret's other current cases and asked that somebody see them, just in case a little something might come out—something she'd said to them, or done.

He decided there was not much more he could usefully do today, and drove home. It was going to be an early, hot summer; the drive through traffic was murder. When he got there, Alison's garage-slot was empty. Still at the architects', he thought: the nesting instinct.

He let himself into the apartment, where air-conditioning met him gratefully. Three of the cats came to welcome him—his own darling Bast and her daughters. he made a little fuss over them. The apartment, where he'd lived so long alone, felt oddly empty without Alison there; unusually, he decided to have a drink, and went out to the kitchen.

El Señor had got the cupboard over the sink open again, and had deposited in the sink, under a dripping faucet, a large package of cereal, a bar of cooking chocolate, and an opened package of rice. He was now sitting on top of the refrigerator, having inherited from his Siamese father a liking for elevated places, and he gazed at Mendoza with a remote, impersonal green stare.

"*¡Señor Malevolencia!*" said Mendoza. "Why can't you behave yourself like your mother and sisters?"

El Señor watched interestedly as he cleared up the mess, and waited until he was in the act of pouring rye to leap lightly down to his shoulder. The glass toppled and smashed. "*¡Fuera—es el colmo!* I'll take you to the pound tomorrow!"

He took El Señor and a new drink back to the living-room, and while El Señor thoughtfully groomed his claws, Mendoza thought about Margaret . . .

As he finished the drink, her key rattled in the lock and Alison came in. "Oh, you're early! I'm so sorry, Luis—I just went out to get cigarettes—"

"Secret of a successful marriage, you can still puzzle me. What are you sorry about?"

Alison laughed, putting down her bag. "Very old-fashioned of me. When a husband comes home, he ought to find his wife with dinner almost ready, complete with apron and appetizing smell. Relic of all my peasant ancestors. I feel guilty if I'm not." She plucked El Señor off his lap and substituted herself.

"Now you've offended him, and he'll think up something diabolical to pay you back. And you do have an appetizing smell—carnation, very nice. Did you see the architects?"

"Don't remind me! All they want to talk about is where the pipes and things have to go, just like plumbers. And explain that that's why they can't use my ideas exactly the way I want. And they kept saying that Spanish design isn't fashionable any more. When it's the only sensible way to build for the climate. Oh, but we *are* going to have Bertha, and I was so relieved, Luis—"

He duly appreciated both Mabel and the Germing Shepherd. "Though I suppose," said Alison thoughtfully, "it might be appropriate for some of them. If they had mange or something . . . Luis, it's going to cost an *awful* lot."

"Well, I've got the money, never mind."

"I know, but—" Alison was silent awhile, snuggling closer, and then she said, "You forgot about the soap again. I put out a new bar . . . I expect there's something in what they say about childhood environment. I don't suppose I'll ever get used to having money. Real money. And neither will you. Silly little miserly economies. You *will* go on hoarding soap until it's just a sliver you can't get hold of."

He laughed. "True. I broke myself of saving half-smoked cigarettes, but not about the soap. My grandmother used to save all the slivers to put together. The six or eight cents wasn't always so easy to come by— and the old man sitting on all that money, if we'd only known—"

"Never mind, darling, she lived to enjoy it quite awhile." He kissed her, and there was a little silence.

"I'll take you out to dinner. Though I shouldn't spoil you. You admit you're at fault, not doing your proper wifely job—"

"*Mi amo,* but I have been! Starting to prepare a home for you—"

"Listen, impudence, don't I know when a woman starts calling me lord and master, that's the time to look out! Go and get dressed for a respectable place."

"You'll have to shave again. And your moustache needs trimming on the left side."

"Leave my moustache alone. *¡Desvergonzada*—shameless! You're a bad wife, trying to order me around. I thought the Cuernavaca. Forty minutes for a shower and so on? I'll phone for a table."

"You'd better feed the cats first, *amado.*"

Mrs. Mary Whipley got off the bus and walked briskly up Montezuma Street. Mrs. Whipley was fifty-nine but she had a lot of energy, and she'd always worked hard so she didn't mind it. She walked up two blocks and turned into Florentina Street. Here she passed several old apartment buildings, not big ones—six-family, most of them—and more old frame California bungalows. Most of the front yards were not very neatly kept up. In the middle of the block, she slowed before one of them, looking up its walk. Hadn't seen little Mrs. Hill for a few days, to ask about her poor sister. Seemed like some people were born under an unlucky star or something—nothing but bad luck. She'd said it was just a question of time. And the sister only twenty-nine; it kind of made you wonder whether the minister was right about God's intentions—didn't seem fair.

Better not stop in now, she'd be busy getting supper. For herself and that cat. Mrs. Whipley was not fond of cats herself. Had to admit he was a handsome creature, but it beat all how Mrs. Hill just doted on him, like he was her baby or something.

She walked on. It made you feel you were maybe luckier than you thought. A lot of trouble and grief—Dan getting killed in that accident, and him only forty-two, and her having to go to work again; and never any kids, so she was all alone. But she was alive, and healthy, and doing all right; barring accident, knock on wood, she felt good for another twenty years, and all her faculties like they said. She could still enjoy the movies, and an occasional dinner out. While some people—little Mrs. Hill and her poor sister—such bad luck, so young. The husband leaving her, it made you wonder, a pretty little thing if a bit softheaded. And T.B., well, it didn't ask ages.

She'd be likely to see Mrs. Hill tomorrow or next day, coming home or going to work. To ask, and sympathize. Meanwhile, she wanted her own supper.

She passed on: watched, unseen, by the great smoke-silver cat.

The cat had no interest in Mrs. Whipley. Mrs. Whipley was not the one he waited for.

Jay Redding figured philosophically it was just one of those things. His usual luck. Well, there were a lot of blondes around, but this one he could have gone for. A real nice girl. You could tell. He'd planned on asking her for a Saturday-night date today. She'd been friendly, he thought she'd say yes.

And here was the foreman saying she'd quit. All of a sudden. The foreman was annoyed, and said things about flighty females, but Redding figured she must have had good reason. What he'd seen, a good steady worker . . . He was sorry. He'd liked her a lot, done a little dreaming about her.

But she was gone, before he'd got around to knowing her better. It was just one of those things.

This was the third night the cat had been alone. He was hungry, and restless, and afraid. In his mind was a great dim longing for all that was so inexplicably not there any more—the soft words, the brushing, the food and milk, the warm lap, the warmth in the house.

He did not understand, and was unhappy and uncomfortable.

It was long past the time she should have come; but he still sat there on the porch, tail coiled lightly around him, waiting.

Sergeant Lake had an important evening coming up—his younger daughter Kathy was to perform in a piano-recital at her music teacher's house—and he was a little excited, pleased and anxious, about it. He carried out Mendoza's orders all right, but he didn't pay much attention to details. It was a little late to send out day-duty men, so he passed it on to the night-duty sergeant, Farrell.

"He wants somebody to see these people. On the Chadwick case. She knew 'em all. They're to be asked if she ever said anything personal about her family and so on."

"O.K.," said Farrell. "I'll see to it." And of course, that was more or less what Mendoza had said, only not quite all he'd said. But Lake was thinking about Kathy.

Farrell sent out a very new ranker, Cheney, to see the people on the list of Margaret's cases. Cheney was a conscientious man, but he had not much imagination. He went and saw these people, luckily finding them all where they were supposed to be, and asked them about their relationships with Margaret Chadwick. He summed up what they told him in his report.

"Walker. Patient Gen. Hosp. Young woman. Says M.C. visited about twice a week, brought candy, fruit. Was pleasant. Never said anything about personal life. Singer. Old lady, rest-home. Strokes. Says M.C. brought her magazines, candy, was nice and pleasant. Never said much about self. Came ab. once a week. Klingman. Midd.-aged woman, out-patient of Gen. Hosp., arthritis. Says M.C. came drive her clinic once a week. Very nice but never said much ab. self. Mrs. K. volunteered didn't like her much, thought she was stuck-up—says talked down at her, if tried to be nice. None knew M.C.'s address or anything ab. family."

It was uninteresting. Cheney got paid to do such uninteresting jobs. He did them conscientiously.

# 10

Today they'd hold an inquest on Margaret, and the verdict would be open: cut and dried. Today also they would bury Margaret, correctly, up at Forest Lawn. Mendoza was uninterested in either proceeding; both were conventions. Hackett would attend the inquest, but that was only a formality.

He sat at his desk and looked at those reports on the cases Margaret had been visiting recently. Very little there, apparently.

"Somebody says he has some information on Chadwick," said Sergeant Lake, looking in. "Will you take the call?"

"Put it through . . . Lieutenant Mendoza speaking."

A cautious male voice said, "Oh. Well, I just thought I ought to call in. After thinking it over. Not that I can really tell you anything, Lieutenant. My name's Hogg. Oscar J. Hogg. I run a private-investigation service. Two-oh-four Alvarado."

"Yes, Mr. Hogg?"

"Well, it's just, you see, this Miss Chadwick. Margaret Chadwick that got killed by the car-hold-up fellow. I saw it in the papers. I don't figure it's anything to *do* with it, Lieutenant, well, how could it be, I mean? But I figured I ought to tell you. You know. We got to cooperate."

"Yes. You knew Miss Chadwick?"

"She called in," said Hogg unhappily. "Saturday afternoon, to ask for an appointment. No, I never met her. I gave her three P.M. Monday . . . No, sir, she never said what about. Just, she had a—a commission for us, and she'd say what, when I could see her . . . No, she didn't ask what it'd cost. She didn't say anything, except ask for an appointment

. . . That was my first free time, yes, sir. That's all I can tell you—just, she called. And I figured—"

Mendoza said it was interesting, thanked him. It *was* interesting. He thought it was time he just sat and ruminated on this for awhile, starting to put pieces together.

"Scarne's got a little something for you, Lieutenant," said Sergeant Lake, and Scarne wandered in and put an envelope on Mendoza's desk.

"I don't know that it's worth much. It's what the vacuum picked up in the Buick. O.K. to release the car? Mrs. Chadwick called in on it."

"Oh, did she? Yes, of course—checking up on material possessions. Yes, all right, thanks." Scarne wandered out, and Mendoza picked up the envelope.

Bits and pieces, all right. The eye half of a black hook and eye. A tiny curved strip of metal, gold-colored, part of a link of something, bracelet, necklace? A flat black leather bow, which might have come off a woman's shoe. A triangular scrap of paper.

He laid them out and looked at them. Picked up the scrap, felt it. It said something to him. Not ordinary paper; it was shiny on one side, dull on the other. A snapshot. This was one corner of a photographic print, almost without doubt an ordinary snapshot, considering its size. It had been torn off raggedly: the shiny paper was evidently superimposed on the other, and more of it had been torn away, but not enough to give any indication of what the picture had been—that part was just light (sky or an inside wall) against the narrow white margin. But he thought the piece had been torn, say one person snatching it from another, and not just dog-eared until it was broken.

And what did it say? Nothing. People in the car looking at snapshots, maybe a group of girls, eagerly reaching, and somebody tearing this by accident. On the other hand, that was tough, thick paper; it wouldn't tear as easily as bond or even typing paper.

He put it down and stared at that tiny curved piece of metal. That was saying something quite fantastic to him. Because most women had jewelry, good jewelry or costume stuff. And a great many pieces of jewelry—bracelets and necklaces—were made up of links, or fastened with a link clasp. Also, these days, small pendants were fashionable, suspended on fine chains, and the pendants had to be fastened to the chains with a ring. This little curved piece might easily have been part of a link, or part of a clasp, the ring which the snap-ring went through.

And it might also have been part of the little ring which fastened a gold charm to a charm-bracelet.

He stared at it for awhile, and then picked up the inside phone and asked if Palliser was around. "O.K., send him in, will you?" When Palliser came, he asked how he was doing on that thing.

"I'm not," said Palliser. "Just nothing to get hold of, until we find out who she was. Nobody's reported her at Missing Persons yet, and I guess it'll take those jewelry firms quite awhile to check through all their back records. Well, you know how a thing like that goes, sir. I've done everything I—"

"Yes. Look at this thing. It could be part of a ring to hold a charm on a bracelet."

Palliser peered at it and agreed that it could. "I'm wool-gathering," said Mendoza, annoyed at himself. "Isn't Margaret enough? Why try to drag in another body? And Art's perfectly right, this is a big town, and two unrelated killers might have had the urge to strangle two unrelated women on the same night. I concede it. All the same—all the same—*was* it coincidence?"

"You think they tie up? But how? I don't see— Of course, we don't know one single thing about the blonde. Yet."

"No. But you might take this to the lab and ask them what it is—gold plate or fourteen-karat. Which will say exactly nothing again. We know the blonde's charm was fourteen-karat. But Margaret had good jewelry, what she had—her friends probably would too. And conversely, the blonde was wearing inexpensive costume jewelry too—and Margaret had some of that, as her friends undoubtedly would. And charm-bracelets—expensive or cheap—are always popular. Anybody at all might have had a bracelet or necklace break in Margaret's car. But no harm to find out about this."

"Yes, sir. Excuse me, sir—" Palliser hesitated. "May I ask you something?"

"Mmh?"

"Well, I was talking with Higgins, and he just happened to mention that—that you'd first met your wife through a case, I mean she was a witness or something. I—"

"Well, yes?"

"Well, I just wondered if it was all right, somebody you meet that way, to—Higgins said it was O.K. I thought there might be some objection. But if—"

Mendoza grinned at him. "Depends on the lady, doesn't it? Who've you been meeting lately? Oh, the Silverman girl. Yes, indeed—unusual type, I agree with you. I don't object if she doesn't. Mmh, yes, Roberta Silverman—"

"You aren't thinking she had anything to do with—?" Palliser sounded uneasily astonished.

"I haven't been, but I could be wrong. It's happened before. I've even been known to draw to an inside straight. She's got a motive. And maybe you'd better hear about that." He told Palliser about Roberta Silverman's motive, and Palliser was indignant over the fiancé of little faith.

"What a heel—why, anybody could see— And that catty Chadwick girl— But, Lieutenant, would it be enough of a motive? After all—" He looked unhappy. He started to say something else, stopped.

"When you've been at this job as long as I have," said Mendoza, "you'll have found out that motives are different things to different people. I've known a man killed over a quarrel about four cents' change —and on the other hand some people will put up with what amounts to slavery or torture and never take any revenge. What motive is enough, that depends on who's got it. How he or she's built. There's not much of a handle on this thing yet, but my first choice for X isn't Miss Silverman. Now."

"Well," said Palliser. "Well, thank you, sir. I'll take this thing up to the lab."

Mendoza lit another cigarette and ruminated some more. He still liked Arden and Darrell—liked them very much, as First and Second Murderers. An obvious motive, if. And he felt ninety percent certain about the if. But here was private-eye Hogg telling him that Margaret had been about to hire him. What for? Most probably, to check up on somebody: somebody she suspected of something, and hoped to get direct evidence on.

Margaret—inquisitive, prying, always expecting the worst, jumping to the worst conclusion— But there was a saying, even fools speak the truth occasionally. People like that were more apt to stumble across some not-so-innocent secret than less perennially suspicious people. A dangerous secret, perhaps, which would thus come out where it mustn't come out. So shut her up before she could tell, or find out more.

But if it had been Arden and Darrell, Margaret's death hadn't been due to her prying, and private-eye Hogg was—extracurricular. Whatever commission Margaret had for him was extraneous. In any case, suppose she had come across something so serious that she intended to hire Hogg to check on it, surely she wouldn't have told the object of suspicion about it—or would she? She didn't seem to have had much finesse—witness Mr. O'Hara. She might have come out with it to X— that particular X—flat and plain: "I think you stole money out of my purse" (one of the maids?) or, "I think you're embezzling from your boss" (husband of a friend?) and added, "And I'm going to set a detective on you." One thing you could say about Margaret's kind, she'd be apt to go all lengths to prove a random malicious suspicion; and she had the money to pay a private eye.

Arden and Darrell. And you could tie them up to that, too. After a fashion. Darrell alone. Maybe he was still working on Arden. Maybe, even after knowing him all this time, he'd never tried to make him as a new boy-friend, had found enough of those elsewhere. And now was. And Margaret somehow found out, or suspected it. And said so to him. That kind was unstable, as he'd said to Art. So Darrell killed her, to shut her up. Or take Arden and Darrell together. Say it was the way he thought—that Arden had been Darrell's little playmate for some time (witness that postcard from Lake Tahoe) and Margaret and the mother, all innocent, had maneuvered Arden into an unwanted engagement. And then Margaret (who would have been, probably, rather innocent about such sordid matters) for some reason began to suspect Darrell for what he was, and said so. Tried to get Arden to drop him, as a bad influence—never suspecting Arden was another one. And when Arden refused, she said she'd hire a private eye to check on Darrell and prove it —not having access to the police-records. And that they couldn't have, because Darrell's record would come out, and Mrs. Arden would hear about it too—remember, she holds the purse strings, and might not be so indulgent to George if she suspected. In any case, Margaret couldn't be allowed to tell Mrs. Arden her suspicions. Get rid of her quick. If it was like that, the private-eye threat just triggered the murder sooner.

He still liked the idea of First and Second Murderers. So much easier to do it the way it had probably been done.

He picked up the inside phone and asked for Higgins. Higgins was the kind of cop Hackett was, if Hackett had a university degree and a higher I.Q.; nobody would ever take him for anything but a cop. He was big, he looked deceptively stolid, and he wore ready-made suits so the shoulder-holster always bulged a little. Mendoza told him to sit down. "Before I send you out again, what did you get on this Janice Headley?"

"I didn't have to ask but a couple of questions," said Higgins. "She just poured it out at me, when I said we had her letter, from Miss Chadwick's things. She's one of those fluffy little blondes, not very bright. Seems about a year ago she let this Hunt, who is one Hunter Caldwell, bond-salesman on Spring Street, buy her a drink once in awhile. At the country club—other places if she ran into him. They sort of went around in the same crowd. He gave her a lift a few times. Nothing more than that—all just casual like. She says. Only Margaret Chadwick thought it wasn't and did a little gossiping here and there—"

"*Chisme averiguada jamás es acabado,*" muttered Mendoza. "No end to gossip. Yes?"

"And eventually her husband John heard it, and was mad. She says it was all just a silly misunderstanding, she made him see there wasn't anything in it, but she practically begged me on her knees not to bring it up again *now*, officer, so I guess John was maybe pretty mad."

"Mmh, sounds like it. O.K. Now I want you to go see two fellows— take Arden first, he has to attend a funeral this afternoon so he'll probably be home. If he isn't, try Darrell's place. Here are the addresses. I want you to be a real old-fashioned tough cop. Act sinister to them—as if we'd just applied for the warrant and are just waiting for it to haul them in and start the third degree. ¿*Comprende?*"

"I get you."

"Ask them both where they stopped for a drink last Saturday night, and about what time. If they give you a name, go there and ask. I'd take a small bet they won't. I think I know where they went, and they'll be chary of admitting it. The more you can scare them, the better. I think Arden might scare easier than Darrell."

"O.K.," said Higgins. He got up, twisting his eyebrows in a sneering frown, and leaned forward belligerently. "Come clean, you bum! Hah, like that? Real nineteen-thirty?"

"You can't overplay it too much, boy," said Mendoza. "I don't think these two know we come any different nowadays."

Higgins laughed and went out.

Mendoza went downstairs for the Ferrari and drove up to Hollywood, to that place on Fairfax. It was called The Victorian Room. A lot of them wore such fancy names. Well, it was a problem, in any big city you got them in crowds—and both sexes too. There were a few places like this for the women. You kept an eye on them, once in awhile raided them just for fun, and sometimes came up with a wanted man.

He parked the car half a block away, walked back and went in. The atmosphere hit him as soon as he was over the threshold: nothing out in the open, just a feel. It was very quiet, and brighter-lit than most bars. Very chichi Victorian décor: red plush, a crystal chandelier, even a dark-red carpet. There were only eight or ten men in the place, at this hour. They sat at tables, all in couples except one party of four. Every eye went to Mendoza as he came in—a stranger. There'd be few strangers ever in here, and most of them would have a hasty password for the bartender—"Joe Smith recommended this place" or something like that.

Mendoza knew if he'd had a woman with him he wouldn't have got three steps inside the door. Somebody would have been there to bar the way, say politely, "I'm sorry, sir, this is a private club."

As it was, they watched him. He went up to the curved mahogany bar, where no one else stood, and said casually to the bartender, "Straight rye."

The bartender was slow to serve him. "You know somebody here, mister? This is a kind of private club."

"That's no news to me," said Mendoza. He wasn't insulted at the implication; as Art said, and contrary to popular fiction, you couldn't tell by the surface. "Sure I do. George Arden and Mike Darrell."

"Oh, yeah," said the bartender. He poured the rye. Mendoza picked up the shot-glass and turned, leaning on the bar, to survey the room. No, you sure as hell couldn't spot them. There was only one man in the place anybody might have suspected, a slight blond youth in blue slacks and shirt, who had delicately-rouged cheeks and lips, painted nails. But that hairy, chesty fellow in levis—the sullen, heavy-jawed man of middle age sitting with a thin, ordinary-looking man no younger—that portly formally-dressed fellow with a corporation, bald and ruddy—the manly collar-ad in well-tailored jodhpurs, showing even white teeth at the ace-reporter-gone-to-seed type—you wouldn't look twice at any of them.

He turned back to the bartender, who was still eyeing him doubtfully. Maybe the bartender, with more experience, had built-in radar that told him, yes or no. Anyway, he wasn't liking Mendoza much, which was just the way Mendoza wanted it; he was eyeing Mendoza's custom-tailored gray Italian silk and Sulka tie with suspicion. He was a big beefy man about fifty, bald and jowled; he looked male as a bull. Only the nose-ring was missing. Oddly enough, the bartenders and/or owners of a place like this were often enough ordinary men. For this reason or that, the fags, the queers, began to monopolize a certain place, and eventually, if the bartender was willing and kept his eyes shut, drove all the other trade away. Some owners figured their money was as good as anybody else's. But whatever they'd been to start with, honest or not, the bartenders sooner or later had to turn a little or a lot crooked, because the ones like this were frequently on the edges of pro crime—and inevitably, too, you got the hysterical open quarrels and knives pulled, that kind of thing.

"Ask you a few questions," he said to the bartender, and pulled out his identification; he didn't lower his voice. "Lieutenant, homicide."

What little noise had been in the place was stilled instantly. Behind him he felt the sudden tension, the alarm.

The bartender laid both hands flat on the bar. "A fuzz," he said. "I mighta known. Is this a raid?"

"What, all by myself? I'm good, friend, but not quite as good as that," said Mendoza. "Even for your customers. And I said homicide, not vice. Just a straight answer. Were George Arden and Mike Darrell in here last Saturday night, and what time, and for how long?"

"Why d'you want to know?"

"I'm the one asking questions. Were they?"

"They say so?"

"You heard me the first time. Were they?"

"Listen, I got my rights, we all got rights, you can't come here an' bully me—I got a right to know what—I don't say nothing about my friends unless I know—"

Mendoza put down his glass, reached across the bar with his left hand and yanked the bartender half over it, toward him, by his narrow string tie. He slapped the bartender once, a ringing slap across the mouth. "You need a hearing-aid, friend," he said gently. "A question I asked you. You answer it, and just maybe I won't ask any more. Such as, have you got a pedigree down at Records? And do you maybe keep a few decks of H. under your bar for special customers? And how much do you baptize the bonded stuff?"

"Goddam you—fly cop come in and— Anybody tell you he scored a fix here, he's a goddam liar—" The bartender struggled like a fish on a line. Mendoza held him hard.

Behind him a little concerted murmur rose, a low ugly hum. This kind, unstable: and he was only one man. He regarded the bartender's reddening face dispassionately and slapped him hard. And he didn't approve at all of this kind of thing, ordinarily; but twenty years' experience with the smalltime pros told him that there was, really, only one thing they understood. You couldn't treat the pros like ordinary people, because they just weren't. And you had to show them that the cops were a whole lot tougher than they liked to think they were themselves, to maintain proper respect. "Brace me, friend," he said. "Speak up like a good boy." If the rest of them rushed him— He let go of the bartender's tie and gave him a little shove; the man staggered back and stood leaning on the shelves behind the bar, licking his lips.

"All right, all right," he said sullenly. "They say they were here, they were. Most Saturday nights they are. Sure. Why the hell all the fuss? Sure they were, I remember."

"What time did they come in?"

"I don't—exactly remember, I was busy—"

"What time did they come in?"

"I don't remember! Whatever time they say, I guess they'd know."

"Come here, friend. Let's see if your memory won't improve."

"No! I don't— Well, I guess it was about—about—"

"Think hard, now."

"N-nine o'clock," said the bartender, and having committed himself regained confidence. "Somewheres about. They were here until we shut. Two A.M. There was a crowd, I— What did they—"

"That's fine," said Mendoza. "You've been a good boy." He laid a dollar-bill on the bar. "You baptize your rye a little too much, but that's not my business. The next time somebody asks you a polite question, answer it a little sooner and easier." He turned and went out. Every man in the place watched him from bar to door, silent and tense.

On his way back to the Ferrari, he thought maybe Art had something, always telling him what a damn fool he was for seldom packing a gun; but he didn't approve of the old-fashioned tough cop, the trigger-happy cop always spoiling for a fight.

And of course, he may have been a fool here other ways. The legality of evidence—it cut both ways.

He drove back to headquarters, and met Hackett going in. The inquest was over: an open verdict, as expected. It was a little past noon;

tacitly they got into the Ferrari and went up to Federico's for lunch. Mendoza brought Hackett up to date.

"Yes, very nice," said Hackett about the bartender. "The D.A. will like that, if it comes to trial. But what if they were there? Later? At the crucial time. Like the boy who cried wolf."

"All right, I know," said Mendoza. "It had to be done."

"Sure. I just have kind of a funny prejudice about railroading people. Even people like Darrell and Arden. So you can't trust what the bartender says, obviously. He'll say anything to oblige his friends—and good customers. Or can you? Maybe they were there all evening, just told everybody about the Bowl as an excuse. Maybe they really did drop in later, and the bartender's just handing them a longer alibi. Point is, if they were there later, and really at the Bowl before, nobody's going to believe it if the bartender changes his story and backs them up, it was from eleven on."

"All right, I've been to kindergarten."

"And you will keep walking into these situations, not so much as a pair of knuckle-dusters on you," added Hackett disapprovingly. "Pack of wild ones like that, never know what they'll do. Nothing to me, of course, but for some reason I kind of like your redheaded wife. You might give a thought to her occasionally."

"Only the virtuous die young," said Mendoza, "didn't you know?"

"And you've got something there." They lit cigarettes over coffee; Hackett looked at his watch. "They're just starting to bury Margaret. One o'clock, at the Church of the Recessional . . . You know what? It'd be a big help to us if we could know what everybody's thinking, sitting in that church listening to the minister tell what a wonderful girl she was."

"And if we did," said Mendoza sardonically, "it'd be inadmissible evidence—self-condemnation. About an hour should see the end of it? I'm going to wander up and meet the mourners presently. I'm using psychology on George—very elementary psychology . . ."

# 11

" 'We brought nothing into this world,' " intoned the rector of St. Anne's, " 'and it is certain we can carry nothing out. The Lord gave, and the Lord hath taken away; blessed be the Name of the Lord.' "

It was a high-church Episcopal service, as prescribed in the Book of Common Prayer. Hot in his robes, even in the biggest church at Forest Lawn, the Reverend Claude Merton let out his trained solemn baritone consciously. He rather prided himself on his reading of Scripture. He paused, and proceeded to Psalm Thirty-Nine. " 'I said, I will take heed to my ways: that I offend not in my tongue—' "

God, thought George Arden, I must be careful what I say. To Them. Coming, asking. As if—as if they *suspect*. We must be careful. Just keep calm, keep our heads. Dear God, we can't all be alike. As if we were freaks or something. But Mike shouldn't, oh, God, have sworn at that cop—shouldn't have said all that— Must be careful. As if it was a crime, to be a little *different*. Mike—put him in jail—put both of them in jail—oh, God, just because—

Margaret. Damn Margaret. Deserved whatever she got. Mother. She didn't understand, nobody understood. Talking at him. Surrounding him. Before he knew, talking about—about— Horrible! Unthinkable! Never, never, never— They didn't understand. Mike said it was just how things were. You had to forget it, forget the cover-up necessary. Most people not mature enough to realize, some of us just *different*. That was true.

But not even Mike had understood how frightened he had been of Margaret—how he had hated and feared her. Somehow, she could make things happen. As if he had been hypnotized, he kept feeling in

spite of everything she'd make *that* happen. And now they were going
to put her in the ground, and it would be an expensive coffin but wood,
he could see, and it would rot, and the worms and the rot would get at
her and make a fearful ugly thing of the body the undertakers had
prepared and painted, the body lying there in masses of flowers, and
inwardly he was shaken with a terrible joy—sheer joy.

He wet his lips and sat still, listening to the rich voice, thinking of
Mike.

" 'For man walketh in a vain shadow; and disquieteth himself in vain:
he heapeth up riches, and cannot tell who shall gather them—' "

Well, that was half a lie anyway, thought Kenneth Lord. Some people
could say. Right now he knew who was going to garner some of the
Chadwick riches . . . He looked down at Laura beside him, gave her
hand an encouraging squeeze. Call it common sense. Laura was a good
girl; not too bad-looking, and down-right game, and blind in love with
him, the only male who'd ever paid her much notice. Only natural. Like
a lot of not-so-goodlooking women, she could be unexpectedly passionate. He really liked Laura, a good girl. They'd settle down all right
together. Especially with the money to cushion it. And, later on, in case
of necessity, she'd be very damn easy to lie to.

She surprised him, Laura did. About certain things. Not the fluffy-
headed nitwit she looked, at times. A real good girl. And everything
plain sailing from now on—parents liking him, trusting him.

You had to look out for yourself, sure as God; nobody else would.

He squeezed her hand again. She looked up at him, pale, with a set
expression, and returned the squeeze. Leaned against him a little closer.

He glanced sideways at Mrs. Chadwick. There was a cold proposition,
all right. Might be at a dog-show or a fashion-exhibit. Women. Well,
she liked him, on account of being such a snob. Good old southern
family . . .

" 'The first man is of the earth, earthy: the second man is the Lord
from Heaven . . .' "

All very proper, thought Myra Chadwick. Really a gratifying amount
of flowers. For such a tiresome girl, the thought slid into her mind
unbidden, and she dismissed it at once, in small panic. She must stop
herself doing that, had she said it aloud? No, of course not. These
strange impulses, lately—to let go the normal hold one kept on oneself,
a lady, and scream out the obscenity, the filth. That day when the
policeman— No, no, no. My dear daughter is dead, I am grieving for

her. Dead in such a way. Police. That policeman, a Mexican, acting as if
he thought he was a gentleman. But real Italian silk; at least two hundred dollars. Corrupt. Corruption. The body there in the casket—already corrupt, three days. She shuddered involuntarily; and her husband
put a hand on her arm. She moved slightly away.

Then they were adjourning to the graveside. It was on an unfortunately steep slope; many people stayed up on level ground, at the road-
side.

" 'Man that is born of a woman hath but a short time to live, and is
full of misery—' "

Misery, thought Charles Chadwick. My daughter there, flesh of my
flesh, and I feel so little. I should feel more. But she kept them away
from me, this pale cold woman. If there had been a son . . . They talk
of a death-wish. Is not a non-life-wish the same? A subtle difference.
Always the tangible—the address, the clothes, the right clubs. No. It
would not matter, if there was a life-wish. A little warmth. She kept
them away from me; they were like her. But did she love Margaret?
What is she feeling now, so still and expressionless there? Is there any
love in her, or is it a carefully dressed shell of a woman, saying the
proper things, doing the proper things? I do not know. Helen could
explain it; Helen is so wise. And warm. This church, now, is cold—so
cold. I am dying for Helen's warmth and I am a fool. For years, a fool.
Nine years. I was forty-two: still a reasonably young man. I could have,
we could have. *Money*. It should not come back to money, but it does.
Inevitably. Helen, my darling . . . My daughter there, young, violently
dead, I should be feeling— But how should I? I did not really know her;
I did not really like her. That was a shocking thought. Terrible. But it
was not a human law. That because one performed a more or less
instinctive act upon the body of a woman (a woman tensed, awkward,
disliking the entire business) one must necessarily feel love for the result
of the act.

As he stood, he clung desperately to the thought of Helen, warm
good Helen who would give him comfort when he could get to her.

" 'The sting of death is sin, and the strength of sin is the law. But
thanks be to God, which giveth us the victory through our Lord Jesus
Christ. Therefore, my brethren, be ye steadfast, immovable—' "

All through that long time, Laura Chadwick thought only, I hated
her, and she is dead, thank God. That's wicked, but I can't help it. She
hated Ken, my darling. She was jealous. I hated her, and she is dead,

thank God. She moved closer to Ken: felt his solid warmth, his warm hand. Thank God she is dead, I should feel wicked but I can't, I hated her.

" 'Thou knowest, O Lord, the secrets of our hearts; shut not thy merciful ears to our prayer; but spare us, Lord—' "

Rose Larkin felt conventional feelings, which she would forget within several hours. Roberta Silverman, who had attended the funeral somewhat to her own surprise, felt oddly guilty because she found her mind wandering to that police-sergeant, who had so apologetically called to ask her out to dinner on Saturday night. She was also surprised at herself for accepting . . . That Lieutenant Mendoza. He would find out. Alison Mendoza—funny combination—he'd be a tricky one to get on with, day to day. Maybe a little too intelligent. Uncomfortable. Sergeant John Palliser . . .

Janice Headley thought righteously conventional thoughts; and wondered if the new navy cloche was quite as becoming as the clerk had assured her. Mrs. Sylvia Ashbrook was one of the few people present who earnestly prayed, along with the rector.

There were reporters, photographers hovering. A scattering of curious strangers.

" 'The grace of our Lord Jesus Christ, and the love of God, and the fellowship of the Holy Ghost, be with us all evermore.' Amen," said the Reverend Merton, and shut the prayerbook.

Those at the graveside turned and began to straggle back up the slope toward the road and their cars. Flashbulbs flared. Someone—Roberta thought it was Laura Chadwick's fiancé—protested in an angry voice. She found she was plodding upward beside Rose Larkin, a silly woman she'd never much liked. She said something conventional. And there was Margaret's boy-friend, George Arden—sufficiently goodlooking, conventionally neat and sober-faced, in a dark suit and tie.

"Everything just as dear Margaret would have liked it," said Rose Larkin in a hushed voice.

Roberta thought irreverently, Oh, yeah? She stepped over the flat bronze name-plates set into the earth. Came to the top of the slope, the lines of parked cars.

There was a new car sitting in the middle of the narrow road. A long, sleek, black, shining strange car that said blandly, Money; that said, Power. And he stood casually leaning on the driver's door, as if waiting. He looked, Roberta thought, rather like an old-fashioned screen villain.

The narrow line of moustache, the casual sophisticated confidence. Only too discreet; not swaggering enough. The very good clothes, the poised cigarette. You couldn't exactly call him handsome, but—nuances —the authoritative male. Oh, very much so. In a discreet way.

He waited, and at exactly the right moment, as George Arden came by, giving him a nervous side-glance, he dropped his cigarette, stepped on it, and said, "Oh, Mr. Arden. Excuse me. I hoped to catch you here."

Roberta passed by, toward her own car; stopped and looked back.

"Oh—er—yes?" said Arden nervously. He stopped.

"I'm so sorry to keep troubling you," said Mendoza, "at such a time." The Chadwicks, Kenneth Lord, were just behind Arden, coming up the road. "Very—er—tactless. And painful. But I'm afraid we work twenty-four hours a day, Mr. Arden. What time did you and Mr. Darrell arrive at the Victorian Room on Saturday night, Mr. Arden?"

Arden went muddy white. "The—I don't know what you mean, I never heard— What the *hell?*—damn fly cop persecuting— I don't have to tell you one *thing*—Mike said—none of your business! I—"

"The bartender," said Mendoza very gently, "says you both came in about nine o'clock. Now obviously somebody's lying, Mr. Arden. You said you were at the Hollywood Bowl, and stopped for your drink about eleven. Which was it, Mr. Arden?"

Most of those within earshot had stopped dead, listening.

"I—I—you goddam *cop*," said Arden. "I—what the hell does it m—I told you the truth! *We* told you! I can't help what damn fool silly lie Al tells you—I'm not sure exactly what time—what right've you got—"

"Not even a little guess at the time, Mr. Arden?" purred Mendoza. "Ten-forty-five, eleven, eleven-fifteen?"

"Goddam you to hell!" screamed Arden suddenly, and ran. He ran, stumbling, up to the shabby gray Chevvy, threw himself in, started the engine, gunned the motor.

Mendoza made not one move after him. He leaned on the long low black car, and he got out a new cigarette and lit it with a flick of a silver lighter. He looked after the Chevvy as if mildly interested.

Reporters swarmed around him. "What's the line, Lieutenant?" "Was it a personal kill?" "Did the boy-friend do it?" "Give us something for the night editions, Lieutenant!"

Mendoza said nothing. He leaned on the car and smoked. And Charles Chadwick pushed through the knot of reporters to face him.

"I would have expected common courtesy," said Chadwick coldly.
"That you would have the decency to allow us to— Not turn a religious
service into a three-ring circus, create such a scene!"

Mendoza expelled twin streams of smoke from his nostrils. Oh, a
showman, thought Roberta. "Mr. Chadwick," and his voice was soft,
"we have to get our work done how we can, and where, and when. On a
homicide case, we have to look in a lot of places, and sometimes—
sometimes, Mr. Chadwick—we find skeletons in closets. If you know
what I mean."

Chadwick took a step back, away from him.

"We may not like it," said Mendoza, "and people resent it, Mr.
Chadwick. Understandably. But we have to look into private lives. And
things show up. Some of them irrelevant things. We just have to separate the wheat from the chaff. And once in awhile we have to act a little
tough. That's all."

"I—" said Chadwick. And then he turned quickly and shepherded
his wife past, toward their car. Laura and Ken Lord followed.

The old Chevvy with George Arden was long down the hill. Roberta
paused beside her middle-aged Studebaker and looked back again. The
Chadwicks were getting into the new Pontiac. Ken Lord was helping
Laura into his six-year-old hardtop Oldsmobile. Other people getting
into anonymous cars parked along both sides of this narrow winding
road.

The man from homicide still leaned there on his great low black car,
smoking. Not looking at anything in particular.

Roberta got into her car. He seemed to be quite a fellow, Luis Mendoza, that you could say; but she didn't know that she'd like to be
married to him.

But he'd probably find out.

# 12

Higgins had said that Arden had been scared. Not Darrell, or not as much. "But he's cop-shy. Naturally." Mendoza agreed.

"Arden's the one to keep working on. If he gets scared enough, if we can bluff him into thinking we know more than we do, he may do something silly or let out something. I'd take a small bet it was the pair of them, but there's damn all in evidence. I'm going out to scare him again, after the funeral. Now I want some good men to stay on their tails close. Very close. Very obvious. Who's available?"

Higgins told him. Dwyer was due for some night-tours; he put Scarne on Arden now— "He can pick him up at the Forest Lawn gates—" to be relieved by Dwyer. And Bailey on Darrell, to be relieved by Glasser.

It went a little wrong from the start, because they couldn't find Darrell. He'd been at home when Higgins saw him, still in a dressing-gown, unshaven. Now he had vanished. Bailey, who ought to have known better, did a little chasing around—to Arden's, to the Victorian Room—before he called the studios Darrell had worked for. Darrell, it appeared, had gone off with a crew to the desert near Palm Springs, where they were shooting part of a T.V. Western. Yes, it had been a sudden decision; Mr. Darrell had been notified only at eleven o'clock, around there. He would probably be back tomorrow night. Bailey called in to ask should he go to Palm Springs? He sounded resigned; he didn't like the desert, especially in July. It was hot enough here.

"No," said Mendoza. "We'll concentrate on Arden."

Arden gave Scarne less trouble. Scarne picked up the gray Chevvy as it left Forest Lawn at two-fifteen. Arden made a beeline for Detroit Avenue in Hollywood, driving erratically and too fast. He didn't apparently realize he was being followed; when he glanced at Scarne, pulling

up behind him at the curb, as he started for the apartment, his face was
blank misery only. Scarne waited. About ten minutes later Arden came
out, slower than he had gone in; he stood at the curb, looking uncertain,
looking desperately anxious. Mendoza had figured that Arden wouldn't
have heard of Darrell's sudden departure; evidently he hadn't. Scarne
watched the man steadily. Finally Arden moved, looked up and saw him
sitting there. For some reason, momentarily, observation seemed to
steady him; he walked down to the Chevvy and started the engine.
Scarne promptly turned his own ignition-key. Make it obvious, the lieutenant had said; let him know he's got a tail. He followed the Chevvy
very close, too close, and it wasn't long before Arden realized it. The
Chevvy speeded up in panic, slowed down, began to turn corners.

Scarne called in at five-thirty. "We've got him good and rattled, Lieutenant. He spent quite awhile trying to shake me. Then he tried Darrell's apartment again. Drove around some more corners, finally went
into an Owl and tried the public phones—hunting Darrell, I figure.
Then he comes back to this Victorian Room . . . What you mean, am
I in it? Would I be let in? I'm in the drugstore three stores away. I don't
think he'll pull out before Bert gets here, he just went in five minutes
ago."

Arden was still there when Dwyer relieved Scarne.

It was the time again, the time for her to be coming, and the cat sat
waiting. She would come at last, as she should; she would do something
about the nagging little pain in his side where the foxtail was eating in,
and there would be food and milk in his own dishes, and the knots
combed out of his coat, and the soft words.

He sat patiently, long after the time had passed.

It would come again; and he would wait again.

El Señor demanded instant notice, someone telling him what a handsome cat he was, someone smoothing his sleek fur coat which fitted him
so well. This was a rare occasion, and both the humans who lived with
El Señor responded satisfactorily. Alison said, "What a beautiful cat!
¡Un gato muy hermoso, mi gato elegante!" Mendoza handed her the
very minute object they had been looking at and picked up El Señor,
reassuring him that he was a king among cats, none so handsome,
clever, or bold a he-cat as El Señor the magnificent. Which, as Alison

pointed out, was rather silly because after all, strictly speaking, he wasn't a—

"Be quiet, he'll hear you," said Mendoza. "If he ever finds out—!" El Señor turned around a few times and coiled himself on Mendoza's lap, satisfied that he had received his just due.

"I should think," said Alison, reverting to the former subject, "that it must be the smallest clue anyone ever had."

"It's not a clue at all, damn it," said Mendoza. "How could they tie up? So the lab says it's fourteen-karat. It's not a clue until we know that nobody Margaret knew in the ordinary way ever had a piece of jewelry break when they were in her car. You'd remember a thing like that—especially when it was a piece of good jewelry."

"You'd remember anyway, because it would be so annoying," said Alison. "And, Luis—I should think it can't have been too long ago. Because she was a little like you."

"Translation, *por favor.*"

"You're not only orderly by nature, but you automatically take care of things. Unlike most men, you don't really need a wife at all, for things like sending suits to the cleaners and being sure there are clean shirts. And you have that—that Italian hot-rod washed every week, and in between if it's got rained on or something. And at those places, they clean the inside pretty thoroughly too, you know. I think Margaret probably had her car washed fairly often, the same way. And a little thing like this, just on the floor—unless it had got pushed down a seat-crack—"

"Mmh. Yes. I don't think, if it had, our vacuum would have pulled it out—too small. Yes, that's a point. But it doesn't say anything, damn it. We don't know the blonde. Until we do, we can't say whether there was a tie-up. And, damn it, why would there have been, how could there have been, if it was Arden?"

"You think it was."

"I think so. It's so neat, then. Arden and Darrell. Only Margaret—" Mendoza stabbed out his cigarette. "Only I also think our Margaret was —what's the word, not innocent, but blind—blind about sex. Because she was generally uninterested herself. It would have had to be something overt she saw or heard, to tell her about Darrell. Because I think it must have been Darrell she found out about, not Arden. If she had found out about Arden—and come to think, it's rather odd she didn't, because he'd have probably betrayed himself at once if she showed she

expected him to kiss her, anything like that—only, not being interested
except in the surface appearances, she didn't— If she had found out
about Arden, I don't think she'd have done anything but drop him,
after telling Mrs. Arden. Because it would have reflected on her, made
some gossip about Margaret for a change, that she'd taken up with one
like that, couldn't tell the difference . . . What I can't see, considering the kind of people she knew otherwise, is her stumbling over something else so serious among them that it was—worth a murder. Of
course, motive—as I said to Palliser . . . *Not* the tie, Señor Diablo!"

"*Amado*, come home from the office," said Alison. "I want to show
you my ideas for the house. After all, you're going to live there too. The
architects don't like the way I draw plans because I don't put in all the
plumbing-connections, but this is more or less the way it's going to be—
excuse me, Señor— This is the living-room, nice and big, and the dining-room here—and your den—"

"Why do I want a den? I am not a tiger."

"You are—a big black jaguar, *mi incomodidad de un marido*—pay
attention! In this other wing, see, the bedrooms—"

"Too many of them. What the hell are you plotting? This I'd better
look into. Women. You respectable ones all the same, look at a man as a
mere private stud—"

"Well, as far as that goes," said Alison, "I will say—"

The phone rang in the bedroom. She went to answer it. "—Signed
testimonial," she said over her shoulder, "any day. Hello? Yes, just a
minute." She reappeared, looking resigned. "Your office."

Mendoza handed her El Señor, getting up. El Señor, annoyed at
being moved, left her and went and sat on top of his mother on the
couch. Bast woke up and cuffed him.

"—Don't you think, Lieutenant? I mean; it sounded a little funny,"
said Sergeant Farrell. "About ten minutes ago. Bert called in, and said
he was in the Ardens' place, see. Said Arden was acting damn wild and
talking sort of crazy, reason he'd gone in, and he figured he'd better
bring him in for his own good, way he was talking about suiciding. And
then the line went dead, bang, like that. Well, you get failures, all of a
sudden—but it sounded funny. So I called the phone company and
they're checking, but I thought—"

"O.K., yes. No chances. Just in case. You shoot a patrol car out there
—no siren. I'm on my way." Mendoza put the phone down, opened the

top drawer of his bureau and took out the .38 police special, reached for his hat.

"Luis—" she said in the doorway. Her eyes were on the gun. "You never, unless it's something—"

"Women," he said. "Jumping to conclusions. Don't fuss, *chica*. I said to Art, only the virtuous die young, but it occurs to me I've been acting damn virtuous lately." He kissed her, deliberate and slow. "Brood over your house-plans. I'll be home when you see me."

"Yes," she said. Her hazel-green eyes darkened on him. "Silly to say, be careful."

"I have been. For twenty years last month. I'll be home." He kissed her again and went out.

Alison looked at the pages of her house-plans, scattered on the couch. Every time he leaves, she thought. And paying the salary, all of it, into the police pension fund, because he doesn't need— Angel said it too. All the time he was away. Because you never knew. Never, when somebody would come, awkward, nervous, kind, to say, Sorry, but you've got to hear—

So people, ordinary people, could feel safe, and be safe.

She picked up the papers and mechanically straightened them into a neat little stack.

He'd told her, smiling, about Sergeant Palliser and Roberta Silverman. Alison had a sudden impulse to call Roberta and say, Don't. Don't get involved with one of them. Shortening your life, whenever they go out with the gun in the holster.

It would be nothing. He'd come home, put the gun away still loaded, and tell her about it. They would build the house on Great Thunderbolt Avenue, and live in it forty years and have four kids—she'd decided on four—and turn into baby-sitters for grandchildren.

The gun was just insurance.

He got to the house on McCadden Place just as the black-and-white patrol car pulled up. He was out of the Ferrari and up with the two anonymous navy-blue uniforms in three seconds. "Easy and quiet, boys," he said, "we don't know what we've got here." He identified himself. "Let's take a look before we start in." Arden was still here; the Chevvy sat in the driveway, and he spotted Dwyer's car in front of the house next door.

They went up to the house silently, across the lawn. As they went, they heard a voice talking; warm summer night, windows open. It was a typical California bungalow, a narrow porch across the front, roofed and shadowed more by a vine on a trellis at each end. The porch-light was not on; they would be in deep shadow there. They went up three cement steps to the porch.

*"Persecution!"* said the voice. It was high and hysterical. "Mike said —I can't stand it any more, I just can't—! You *followed* me—as if I was a criminal or something—I won't stand it any more! I—I—I—You stand still! Don't come near me, don't try—"

The windows, each side of the front door, consisted of one wide stationary pane, and two side casements opening inward. Mendoza shoved the two big patrolmen gently aside, slid up to the nearest open screened casement and looked in, obliquely. From here he couldn't see Arden; this was the casement nearest the front door, and the window obscured that end of the room. What he could see was Mrs. Arden sitting in an armchair opposite him—and Dwyer. Mrs. Arden's cane was propped beside her. A gentle, stupid woman, gray-haired, ordinary-looking and plumpish, about sixty. She wore a frozen, incredulous expression. At the end of the room to the right, across the narrow wall, was a brick hearth. Against that stood Sergeant Dwyer, tense and alert. There was a spreading red stain across Sergeant Dwyer's light-gray, rumpled summer suit, across the shoulder, and his right arm hung limp. But his eyes were watchful; he was all there, though he leaned on the mantel.

Mendoza stepped back, slid quietly down to the other casement. This one opened the other way, and he could look down the length of the room. There was an archway, that would be between living-and-dining rooms. Just inside the archway, a little into this room, stood George Arden. He was white, sweating, trembling. He held a gun, pointed but wavering.

"—Gone!" said Arden. "He's gone, run away and left me—to face it. Looked for him, oh, God, I—after that, after that cop said— But he's gone, he knew what they'd— Left me to take it all alone, and I— Oh, Mike! I can't—I can't— You stand still! There're still bullets—"

"George," said Mrs. Arden. "George, I don't understand. Who is this man? Why did you— That's your grandfather's old pistol, I didn't know there were any bullets for it anywhere. George, do be careful— I don't understand—"

The gun, Mendoza saw, was one of those old Colts. A .45 six-shooter.

He also saw that it was loaded; that open revolving cylinder, you could see at a glance, cartridges or no. There was one, anyway. Maybe four more. Apparently one slug in Bert. And the neighbors putting it down as a backfire, of course.

A very awkward spot. These damned bungalows, with no entrance-hall. The front door, even if it was probably unlocked, opened direct into that room, about six feet from George Arden. Just nice time and space for him to turn and fire square at anyone coming in, even fast. The dining-room windows, behind Arden, would be impossible: same narrow width as these, not wide enough to admit a man. And Mrs. Arden was more or less in the cross-fire position.

These damned unstable, neurotic queers, thought Mendoza. He moved back, touched the man on his left. They went silently down to the lawn again. "Try the back. If you can get in without making any noise, O.K."

The man vanished. Mendoza went back to the porch. Very probably the sooner Dwyer got to a doctor, the better. Bert had run into more than his share of this kind of thing, this last year.

"—Just gone and left me, run away! Not worth it—dodging around corners—sneaking— What the goddam hell, just because we're *different!*" Arden was almost sobbing; incongruously, tears poured down his white face. "And you—with that *Margaret!*" He swung on his mother. "You never understood— Oh, *damn* Margaret, that's finished now, but— Like we're freaks, I won't stand any more of it— And Mike gone, I can't find Mike, he'd tell me what to— Kill myself before I— Kill all of you, *all* of you, and *then* myself— I just can't stand any more persecution, I'll— Don't you move! You don't believe me! You think I wouldn't have the nerve, but I would—I will! *What's that?*" He flung around; and Dwyer went for his gun, awkward with his left hand.

He'd never make it, Mendoza saw; he was too slow. Arden's glance shot back, and he fired at Dwyer. But he fired too fast, without aim, and the bullet shattered a china ornament on the mantel. And would that bring neighbors? Mendoza did not want neighbors; damn fools getting in the line of fire. He was extremely annoyed at this neurotic, worthless bastard Arden. He got out his own gun.

"George, dear, I don't— George, all this violence—" Mrs. Arden was struggling to get up out of her chair.

"You! All the time, how nice for me, have a dear girl like Margaret! Never knew how I hated her—hated, hated, hated her—Christ damn

Margaret! But Mike's run away— Kill you all, and might as well kill myself—"

Apparently there was no getting in the back without making a noise; or the patrolman was incompetent. Regrettable, but necessary. Mendoza moved the second man aside, remembering Hackett's jeers on the last range-test; he'd never claimed to do more than stay up to minimum requirements, at target practice. He did not enjoy gunfights. He took careful aim and shot the old Colt out of George Arden's hand. Inevitably, he hit the hand too.

Arden screamed. The first patrolman appeared suddenly behind him, in the dining-room. Mendoza lunged for the front door, found it open, and got in, the other patrolman behind him. Arden, still screaming, turned and ran. The three of them got in each other's way, after him; and the rest of the house was dark. He banged a door—they were in a narrow hall—they heard a key snick in the lock. It was too narrow to get much of a run at the door. They shouldered the door, hearing beyond it Arden weeping hysterically, incoherent. "Get back!" panted the biggest patrolman. "I can do it, these old doors—" He took a sideways run at it; it shuddered. The third time it gave. They broke it in the rest of the way by their combined weight.

"All right, go call an ambulance." Arden had not been competent even at suicide. He had tried a razor, but the slash on his wrist was slight. The mangled hand was a more serious wound; it was bleeding freely.

Mendoza was annoyed at incompetence. He went back to the living-room, to see to Dwyer. "He jumped me," said Dwyer, sitting down on the couch. "Cut the phone-cord, and shoved that canister at me. Well, one like that, trigger-happy, I'm not so crazy as to ask for it. The once I thought I had him off-guard, he— I don't think it's bad, but—"

"But!" said Mendoza. "All right, not your fault. But I should have used more imagination. One like that, it doesn't take much to send him off. I think I've been stupid here." He was annoyed at himself.

"I guess my arm's broken," said Dwyer resignedly. "This is the third time this year I've run into a bullet, you realize that, Lieutenant? Why can't they pick on somebody else for a change?"

# 13

They cleaned things up as well as they could. Arden, who was probably not very bad off, was carted to the General along with Dwyer. Dwyer had said he'd heard Arden start shouting in here, about ten o'clock, and as he was shouting about killing himself, he'd been debating about going in when Arden spotted him on the porch and began raving at him and about police persecution. So he'd gone in, and on the point of taking Arden in for his own protection, had faced the gun. Arden, he said, had stayed at the Victorian Room until around nine, and when he came out he was a little high, by the way he drove. Maybe the alcohol, relaxing inhibitions, had set him brooding on how he was being persecuted. But no, it didn't take much to trigger the ones like Arden; that, Mendoza should have remembered.

He couldn't get through to the old lady at all. He tried to explain the situation to her, as gently as possible, but she refused to listen, to understand. "There's some mistake, officer," she kept repeating, shaking her head. "Not my son, oh, no, this is all some horrible mistake—George is a nice boy, well-brought-up, officer. He was upset, no wonder—I must go to the hospital with him—all that blood—you're all great bullies, shooting an innocent boy for no reason—it's all a mistake—"

In the end, Mendoza sent for a policewoman to spend the night with her. Maybe a policewoman would have better luck explaining to her. Or maybe she'd always go on thinking it was just a mistake. In self-defense; because they said, didn't they, it usually went back to some mistakes on the part of the mother? And about that, he didn't know yes or no either.

He drove down to headquarters and called the General. Dwyer had a simple fracture and had lost a little blood; they'd keep him overnight. Arden's condition was more serious but he was in no danger.

Mendoza sent out men. One to the General, to sit beside Arden. "Take down anything he says. He's under arrest—material witness to start with. You can tell him that when he wakes up." One to Palm Springs. "I want Darrell brought in *pronto*. Material witness. I want a warrant to go through his apartment. Also the Arden house. I am now going home. If Arden wakes up and confesses to the murder, call me. Otherwise, not—I've had a full day."

He got home about one o'clock, and found Alison sitting up in bed leafing through a magazine. "You needn't have waited up, *querida*," he said, taking off his jacket.

"Occasionally you astonish me," said Alison. "Did you really think I'd go to bed and to sleep when you'd gone out packing a gun?"

"It's never any use worrying. What happens, happens. And what happened was damned annoying." He told her about it as he undressed. "These over-emotional neurotics. The whole thing so unnecessary. Running around shooting up my men—and it would be Bert, of course . . . Well, it doesn't prove anything. But Arden just might break down and give us a nice confession, after this. We'll see."

Arden did not. Waking up in the hospital, uncomfortable, to find himself under arrest and a police-officer at his bedside, Arden turned sullen and refused to say anything except that they were persecuting him.

Darrell had been lodged in the County Jail at seven-thirty A.M., after a tiresome night-drive to Palm Springs and back. He was, the arresting officer retorted, acting very tough and cocky, and yelling for a lawyer. Mendoza, who had been regaling Hackett with the night's events, said let him yell. He could have a lawyer after he'd been questioned. "Which I'm going to do at once."

But as he stood up from his desk, Sergeant Lake came in, shut the door behind him, and said, "Mr. Chadwick wants to see you, Lieutenant."

"Well, well, does he indeed? On second thought—Art, you run over to the jail and start the softening-up process. I'll come along later. All right, I'll see Chadwick, Jimmy." He sat down again and lit a cigarette.

Chadwick looked indefinably older and grayer. He came in, said good morning, sat down in the chair across the desk from Mendoza. "I suppose, very likely, you can guess what I came in to say, Lieutenant."

"Can I?" Mendoza offered him a cigarette, lit it politely.

"What you said to me yesterday, at the—funeral. About skeletons in closets. I don't pretend to know why, but apparently you think that my —that Margaret was—killed deliberately. By—someone she knew? The way you seem to be—prying into her private relationships, into her family and friends. A search warrant for her— I don't understand it, why you should think that."

"There were several little things, Mr. Chadwick. No need to go into detail."

"So, I suppose," said Chadwick bitterly, "you're probing into private lives. I suppose you've found out about Mrs. Ross."

"I'm aware that you called on a Mrs. Ross on Sunday night," said Mendoza noncommittally.

"And last night," said Chadwick. "I don't know what you think it could have to do with Margaret. But I'll be quite frank with you, Lieutenant—does this kind of thing have to come out? It's—irrelevant. You said that, that you find out a lot of irrelevant things. I—my wife—if this should come out, she—"

"We aren't exactly gossipmongers here, Mr. Chadwick. Anything that's irrelevant, we forget it. But if you'll excuse me, you haven't had much experience at—mmh—intrigue, have you? Why come in here and hand me this, gratis? For all I might have known, Mrs. Ross is a family friend or a cousin, and you went to see her to break the news about your daughter." His eyes were amused.

Chadwick leaned forward. "You didn't really think that, did you?"

"No, Mr. Chadwick," said Mendoza equably. He did not add, after meeting your wife, but perhaps it was in his voice.

"What *did* you think?" said Chadwick in sudden anger. "Shall I tell you? I know! You thought, they don't get along, but he sticks to her for the money she's got—didn't you? Didn't you?" His face reddened; a muscle in his neck twitched violently.

"Did I?" said Mendoza. "It's one reading, of course." So helpful when people lost their tempers; things tended to slip out.

"Goddam it!" said Chadwick. "We've never been—compatible. Long word for it. But how could I, when the girls were still kids, and not enough money for two households— But I asked her. I did. When—I met Helen. And she said if I tried to divorce her she'd sue for as high alimony as she could get. In the kind of—circles she moves in, divorce is still disgraceful. Particularly when it'd be someone wanting to be rid of her, not the other way round. It was before she inherited—that money. Margaret was still a minor. I didn't dare—I didn't dare. Helen was only thirty-one, there might have been other children. And after she had that money, it wasn't much different. She said that, that the courts—you never know what a judge will do. There was a case in the papers, about then—the woman had a good private income, and the man just a salaried job, but the judge set alimony-and-support at five hundred a month. And when Myra would be the injured party—you see. I couldn't—I didn't dare. Now I think I was a fool. I know I was. I should have taken the chance."

"It's not too late, Mr. Chadwick," said Mendoza.

"Isn't it?" Chadwick sounded tired. He put out his cigarette. "I don't know. But I'm telling you this frankly, Lieutenant, so that you can see it's—one of your irrelevances. I don't know what—happened to Margaret. I'm afraid I don't know either of my daughters very well. A long time ago she—had monopolized them, perhaps they were more like her—if there'd been a boy—I—in a sense, I had—given up on it. Long ago. They—Margaret—seemed to have little feeling for me, it was all—the surface, conventional thing. Maybe if I'd made an effort to get closer—to be closer—" He passed a hand across his eyes.

"No, I don't think so," said Mendoza. He was sorry for Chadwick—the man in a trap—but he did not think, There but for the grace of God. Chadwick had been muddleheaded, paying some lip-service to convention himself. A stronger man would have got out, damn the consequences. But— "I don't think so," he repeated. "You knew something about her, Mr. Chadwick. How she—liked gossip. And repeated it."

Chadwick's expression tightened. He sat back in the chair. "I knew that," he said quietly, "yes. She was—very like her mother. In many ways. Are you trying to tell me that—it was some motive arising out of that? That she—"

"It could be. You'll be interested to hear that we have Mr. George Arden under arrest."

An expression of utter incredulity came over Chadwick's face; he half-rose. *"Arden?"* he exclaimed. "That—incompetent young fool? But why—he'd have no reason to—"

"Oh, yes, he had," said Mendoza, and told Chadwick about Arden and Darrell. Chadwick listened, still incredulous.

"My God," he said, "I never suspected—no one would suspect. Just on—surface manners. It's incredible. None of us— I'm sure Margaret herself—"

"Well, she might have—at the last, you see. That might have been the motive. We don't know. We'll find out." I hope, Mendoza added to himself.

"My God, what a thing. It—I can hardly believe it. I know these things happen, but— Of course, that's your business, finding out." Chadwick's voice was dull again. "What I came in to say—about us— this is all in the papers. If not in sensational headlines. It's not exactly enjoyable for any of us. And when my—friendship with Mrs. Ross is so utterly irrelevant, I hope you won't—"

"We don't," said Mendoza, "persecute innocent people, Mr. Chadwick. But as long as you've come in and—mmh—volunteered so much, perhaps you'd answer a few questions. You said you've asked your wife for a divorce. I assume that the relationship between you is—shall we say, one of surface courtesy and no more? Then why are you anxious that your wife shouldn't learn of your—friendship with Mrs. Ross? Hasn't she, very likely, assumed something of the sort?"

"I—" said Chadwick wretchedly. He looked down to his clasped hands. "It's—not very pleasant for me to say all this. She—Myra—can be, well, needlessly vindictive. Can you understand me if I say that— that she doesn't want me herself, but—in a sense, by law I am bound to her, her property. She wouldn't care, personally, about—that. But it's quite probable that she would feel vindictive toward Mrs. Ross. Would —try to harm her in some way. And the firm Mrs. Ross works for is old and conservative. If it came to their knowledge that—that—"

"I see," said Mendoza. Very much her mother's daughter, Margaret. And at the moment he was more than half-way convinced that he had Margaret's killers, if not much useful evidence on them; but at random, ideas connecting, he asked, "Tell me, Mr. Chadwick, do you think that Margaret had any suspicion of your relationship with Mrs. Ross?"

Unexpectedly, almost shockingly, Chadwick went white. For an instant he looked as if he might faint. "I—no, of course not," he said chokingly. He stood up hastily. "Of course not. How could she? That's all I wanted to say, Lieutenant. You're—very understanding. I mean, when it's quite irrelevant. Yes, well, thanks very much—good morning."

Mendoza looked at the closing door and said to himself, *"Esto me da que pensar*—this gives me something to think about. I do wonder. Considering our Margaret. Yes." But Arden and Darrell were much more immediate. He thought it was time he joined Hackett at the County Jail, and got his hat, and went out to the anteroom.

Here he was delayed further by Palliser, asking if he could see him for a minute. Mendoza took him back into his office. "What is it?"

Palliser looked miserable. His long, dark, normally good-humored face, with its heavy bars of dark brows and wide mouth, was almost drawn. "It's nothing, sir," he said wretchedly. "*I know it's nothing at all —but I've got to tell you. It's—it's about Miss Silverman.*"

"Yes?"

"I—you see, I went out there. To where she lives, in South Pasadena. On Monday evening. I thought—well, you know, it'd be better than phoning. I'd only met her once, I thought she might not exactly remember my name and so on, if I just phoned. Anyway, I went. It was about seven, I'd just come off duty, and she wasn't home yet. I hung around waiting awhile, you know, and after about twenty minutes she came home and I— But the point is, while I was waiting the woman in the next apartment came home. A Mrs. Davenport. She asked if I was waiting for Miss Silverman and so on—she was talkative, you know— and something was said, she brought it up, about Miss Silverman having been at the party Margaret Chadwick was at too, the one who'd been murdered. I don't know, maybe Miss Silverman had mentioned it to her." Palliser stopped, looking more miserable.

"Well?"

"Well, sir, Mrs. Davenport said—she was being chatty, you know— that it must have been a nice party, because Miss Silverman didn't come home until quite late. She heard her come in—she was still up, couldn't sleep and was sitting up reading. She sounded pretty positive. She said it was five minutes to two that morning."

"*No me diga,*" said Mendoza. "You don't say."

"But it doesn't mean anything, does it?" said Palliser. "She—dropped into a newsreel theatre. Or went to see some other friends. Or something. It was Saturday night, maybe she didn't feel like going home at eleven o'clock. You know. And a woman couldn't have—"

A tall, fairly strong young woman. But when there were Arden and Darrell, so nice and obvious— "I don't know," said Mendoza abstractedly. "I see." He looked up at Palliser and smiled. "I don't really think so, John," he said, deliberately using Palliser's given name for the first time. "I thought she was a nice girl myself—though nice people commit murder too. You sat on this for twenty-four hours."

"Yes, sir," said Palliser expressionlessly.

"Next time, don't. But it's O.K. Trust your uncle Luis not to misread evidence." He stood up. He came round his desk and touched Palliser's arm lightly. "Most fellows who take the oath as rookies really mean it. Almost have to, committing themselves for that salary. On this force, we find out the ones who don't very quick. This could be a little black mark against you, John, but I'm human too. It's O.K., forget it. I don't think it means anything either."

"Thanks very much, sir."

"Forget it. Go and work on your anonymous blonde."

"Yes, *sir*," said Palliser, and went out.

"I want a lawyer," said Michael Darrell.

"You can have a lawyer any time," said Mendoza. He leaned against the cell-door, hands in pockets, regarding Darrell detachedly. Hackett had got nothing out of Darrell at all. "It's no charge. Yet. Material witness, Mr. Darrell. All I want from you is a statement about where you and Mr. Arden were last Saturday night. With, if possible, names of witnesses who can testify to it."

"You go to hell! Damn smart cop, trying to frame—"

"It would be a help," said Mendoza, "to you as well as us." Darrell was a Samson, as Hackett had said. About six-three, leonine blond, muscled. A square primitive-looking face, wide-nostriled, square-jawed; small agate-colored eyes; a smooth hairless chin, and a blond rinse on the naturally curly hair. He wore gray slacks and a blue-and-white printed sports shirt.

"You've got no right—just persecuting—"

"You're monotonous," said Mendoza dispassionately. "That's Mr. Arden's favorite word too. Answer the question, please."

"You've got a hope! I want my lawyer—"

"Mr. Darrell, please," said Mendoza gently. "Listen to me. I'm investigating a homicide. Margaret Chadwick. I think it was a personal motive, against Margaret. Obviously—once I knew the background—Mr. Arden has a motive. So, in a way, have you. You are both under grave suspicion of this murder. Now will you calm down and give me information, please. About where you were when. Forget your notions about frame-ups and corrupt cops, and tell me. If you have any kind of alibi that will stand up, tell me. Even if, as is very possible, it ties you into something else. Because I don't have to tell you that there's a good deal of difference between a vice-rap, or a dope-rap, and a homicide charge."

Darrell stared at him. A lock of his curly blond hair had fallen across his forehead; he swept it back. *"Murder!"* he said blankly. "Nobody said —I thought it was on a—Margaret Chadwick? You think Georgie and I did—*that?* You're nuts! We—what the hell, I thought that was some hopped-up pro."

And he sounded remarkably surprised, confounded. He said, "You damn fool! Anybody trust Georgie, in a *homicide?* Go to pieces if anybody looked at him crooked!"

As, of course, he had. Yes.

"Just give me a straight answer," said Mendoza. "It's to your own advantage, if you can prove you were elsewhere."

"Where the hell's elsewhere?" countered Darrell. But he was thinking. He sat on the narrow jail cot, thinking; his small shrewd eyes blinked up at Mendoza. "Homicide!" he said. "I never—what the hell? Georgie lost his head, 's all. That sergeant told me how Georgie got to acting last night—figured I'd be rattled. Poor damn fool George—that gun. Made him feel big to have a loaded canister on him. You know? It didn't mean anything. He got scared. I suppose you arranged to scare him. With the idea he'd come out with something." He laughed.

"Maybe he did, Mr. Darrell."

"So try to scare me!" said Darrell contemptuously. "Cops! You haven't got a thing on either of us. To make up any charge."

"Don't be too sure. Mr. Arden came out with some significant remarks last night. About how he'd hated Margaret—and how Mike would tell him what to do—as, presumably, he had before."

A spasm of alarm crossed Darrell's face. "Don't you try to pin this on me! What the hell, a murder— All right. All right. O.K., we've got the alibi. So Georgie didn't part, but I will. If I've got to. Not that it's anything, see? Homicide, that's just funny, Lieutenant, neither of us 'd do a thing like that. An alibi, sure. I'll tell you. You can check. You bastards, put Georgie in the hospital, just on account he got a little nervous! I'll tell you. All that about the Bowl, it was strictly for Mrs. Arden. We were at the Victorian Room from about nine to eleven, eleven-fifteen. Look, Georgie, he can't take much liquor, see? You know some guys are like that? Three drinks, you'd think they'd had ten. He was—under the weather. And his mother—well, he couldn't be let go home like that. I mean, you know, she gives him an allowance, all nice and easy, and if he— Well, she wouldn't like it, if she got the idea he was running with a wild bunch. You see what I mean. A couple of us took him up to my place, sobered him up so he was O.K. to go home. I guess it'd 've been about one A.M., around there. That's all."

"Names and addresses, please," said Mendoza.

"Warrington," said Darrell sullenly, "Joe. Somewhere in Hollywood —Rowena Street, I think. Allen Foster. One-oh-four Mansfield. Keller, Hans Keller, five-forty-two Hobart. They can tell you. They stayed on awhile after Georgie left. Now, if you're holding me, I want a lawyer."

"By all means," said Mendoza. "Thanks very much." For what? For the names of three habitués of the Victorian Room who would, naturally, back up Darrell's story. Where did it get him? Unfortunately, the passionless law made no differentiation between credible witnesses and otherwise, on such evidence as past records and association. Juries, of course, did. Having some sense, if not always as much as one might wish. But—

It didn't say anything the D.A.'s office would like.

Mendoza was annoyed. Because it was so nice and neat, Arden and Darrell, the motive and everything else. But no legal evidence. No proof, that Margaret knew about Darrell—about Arden. Had made any threats. If she'd been a closer confidante of her mother, her sister, anybody—come out with some hints. But she hadn't.

Of course, these witnesses— He thought of Al the bartender, and sighed. It could be on the cards that they'd come out glibly with the same story Darrell told, because Darrell and Arden had thoughtfully arranged the alibi with them, say some time Sunday. And of course in that case, they might not know it was an alibi for a homicide. Something there. But—

So, hope that Arden would come out with something. Something definitely incriminating. But if he didn't—

# 14

"All right, Arden," said Hackett. "Say it. 'Miss Chadwick.' "

"You can't make me," said Arden sullenly. "I don't have to."

"Look," said Hackett patiently, "you say it wasn't you that called Miss Chadwick. O.K., then your voice won't be recognized. Say it."

"Miss Chadwick," said Arden unwillingly. He looked up warily from the pillows; he was unshaven, ill and white.

Hackett looked at Angel. Who shook her head helplessly. "It was so short, and I wasn't really thinking about it. You know."

"Well," said Hackett. They went out to the corridor.

"The other one was a little more like it, I think, Art. Darrell's voice. But I couldn't swear one way or the other."

"Couldn't expect it," said Hackett, sighing. "All right." They got into the elevator. "You be careful on the way home. Stay off the freeway."

"I'm not going home. Now I'm here I'm going up to the May Company to shop, and then I'm going to lunch with Alison because she wants to show me the lots they've bought."

"Oh. I don't like your gadding around so much. The doctor said—"

"The doctor said I'm fine. Really, you'd think I was made of china or something. Men. Don't be silly, Art. Is there any chance that you'll be home for dinner? Or say by at least seven-thirty? Because I came across a new recipe for tournedos of beef and I don't want to waste it, and it won't keep servable indefinitely, like a casserole—"

Hackett said wistfully that her guess was good as his. "I'll try to let you know, anyway." He hoped he could; he thought of the tournedos of beef and, sighing, also thought of Dr. Towner telling him he ought to take off ten pounds. It was easy to say. But with a wife like Angel, who was earnestly enthusiastic about cooking, what could you do? More exercise, Hackett thought vaguely: I won't get that power mower, use the old-fashioned kind. And try to get in a walk every day. He knew he probably wouldn't. Maybe if they got a dog, a big dog that had to be walked?

"Like a Great Dane," he said aloud as they got out of the elevator.

"Well, really, Art!" said Angel. "I know I'm not looking my best, who *could*, only two months to go, but you needn't remind me of it!"

"What? Oh, I didn't mean you, darling, I was just—it doesn't matter. Of course I didn't mean— Now you be careful driving."

"I will, I will. Don't dither at me. And try to come home on time." She stood on tiptoe to kiss him, got into her car. He watched her off, and got his own car and started back to headquarters to tell Luis that she hadn't recognized the voice. They hadn't really thought she would, but had to check.

It was a situation that came up once in awhile. You thought you knew, but couldn't get one damn thing to prove it legally.

They now had Darrell charged with unlawful possession of narcotics; they'd found a hundred made-up reefers in his apartment. They couldn't charge Arden with anything but assaulting an officer and attempted suicide.

Those three witnesses had backed Darrell, up to the hilt. Warrington, clerk in a men's clothing store, about forty, no record. Foster, also a studio extra, about twenty-five, no record. Keller, a door-to-door salesman, thirty-five, one vice-rap (a year) and two arrests, not charged. Mendoza had seen them himself, and they'd all told the same story and sworn to the same times. They were informed that this might be a first-degree homicide charge, and perjury was a serious offense: did they want to think again? No. They came out with various remarks about the cops framing innocent guys just because they liked to persecute people, but they stuck to the story.

Which, of course, said not one damn thing.

The phone-call. It was difficult at best to trace a dial call—impossible in this case. Arden said he didn't have any idea where Margaret was going that night, but admitted that the last time he'd seen her had been that Saturday morning; she had brought his mother some flowers and stayed about half an hour. She could very well have mentioned it before him, saying Angel's full name, mentioning that it was Highland Park— or told his mother, who could have told George afterward.

So they asked Mrs. Arden, who said no, Margaret hadn't said anything about where she was going that evening. But Mrs. Arden might
say that anyway, because she had by now grasped what this was all
about, and was steadfastly maintaining that George was a hundred per
cent innocent (in all ways) and hadn't known what kind Darrell was, it
was a mistake, George wasn't like that, he was a good boy.

There was no evidence for a homicide charge at all. There probably
never would be.

"And the worst of that is," said Mendoza in exasperation, "there's
nothing to clear them definitely, either. If we had something one way or
the other! But now we waste time and men—very probably—looking
elsewhere."

"How sure do you feel about Arden and Darrell?" asked Hackett.

Mendoza fiddled with the ashtray, pushing it round in circles. "Fifty-
fifty," he said at last. "Or maybe sixty-forty, yes. And it'd be Darrell
masterminded it, obviously. It's natural, in a way, there shouldn't be any
tangible evidence. It wasn't a very intricate plot."

"No, but do you think Darrell is smart enough to dream it up and not
make any mistakes?"

"He did make mistakes," Mendoza reminded him. "He wiped off the
handbag. He left the cigarette case. He underestimated our I.Q.'s,
which is a thing cop-haters are always doing."

"That's so. Still, I— Well, so we go on looking in a different direction?"

"Damn it," said Mendoza, "if we only had something definite!"

Fate obliged him within the hour.

It so happened that Sergeant (third grade) Henry Glasser had a young
cousin, Fred Victor. Some eighteen months ago young Victor, having
done his military service, had asked Glasser about the police force: he
kind of thought of joining, how did Glasser like it and what was base
pay and so on. The upshot was that Victor had joined the force, and
after his rookie-training (where instructors had smiled on him for his
army-acquired sharpshooting and excellent coordination) he was as-
signed to the Hollywood (Wilcox Street) precinct office. Right now he
was riding patrol-cars.

It further happened that, as a rather rare coincidence, both Glasser
and young Victor were currently working night-tours; so they were both
able to be present at the family picnic in Griffith Park to celebrate

Glasser's mother's fifty-seventh birthday. They were, in fact, the only two males present, as Mrs. Glasser had been a widow for two years and all the other immediate male relatives were respectably at nine-to-five jobs. In these circumstances, it was not surprising that, glutted with the inevitable potato salad, baked beans, rolls and jam and pickles and olives and celery and iced coffee, with a cocoanut cake afterward, the two men sat torpidly a little apart from the women and talked desultory shop.

It was Glasser who did most of the talking to start with, as the experienced senior and attached to Headquarters, Homicide. As, moreover, a man working under Lieutenant Luis Rodolfo Vicente Mendoza, with something of a reputation on this force. Glasser mentioned a few cases, talked about Mendoza. Quite a guy, he said. Funny, some ways. One thing, if *he* had all that money like Mendoza, catch him working round the clock! Like Mendoza did it for a hobby, you could say. He'd even heard rumors Mendoza didn't collect the salary, but paid it all into the pension-fund. Crazy, that was. But it'd be like him. It just went to show, among other things, you couldn't generalize. "Like this one time," said Glasser, "a fellow who had a pet-shop got killed. By a hopped-up punk after what was in the register. That Mendoza. He got the kid all right, but he was so damn worried about those puppies and kittens and birds all alone, he spent all his spare time in the place for a week, looking after 'em, until the guy's niece showed up to take over. Of course, he's married now. Not that I guess that'd bother him, if he figured something had to be done. He was the hell of a chaser, I've heard tell, before. I can believe it. What they call charm, you know? But he's got a damn goodlooking wife, I'll say that—she's come in to meet him a couple of times. Redhead she is, and really something . . . Well, what we're on now, it's kind of up in the air. He's all hot and bothered about it, but it doesn't look like anything to me. This girl who got killed in her car—strangled, and dumped."

"Oh, that," said Victor. "I saw it in the papers. Looks like somebody jumped her for what cash she had. A nut of some kind, maybe, killing her."

"I guess he thinks different," said Glasser. "It's bothering him. I heard something from Higgins. He—the lieutenant I mean—thinks maybe it was her boy-friend. Because it seems he wasn't. It turns out he's a fag, and for a hundred percent sure, leery of being jockeyed into wedding-bells with a female."

"She didn't suspect? Must have been a real hot number," said Victor with a grin. "That's a funny one. I've been seeing something of that kind lately. One of their hangouts is on our route—place called the Victorian Room, on Fairfax. They make you feel—I don't know," he moved his shoulders uneasily, "well, queer."

"Is that so?" said Glasser. "Higgins said that was the hangout this Arden used, him and his boy-friend."

"Oh?" said Victor. "Well, let's hope there aren't more than half a dozen joints like that around. We get a little business there three-four nights a week. Picked up a pair last night, matter of fact, pretty high and having a fight on the sidewalk in front of the place."

"Guess you would," said Glasser. "Anything last Saturday night? This pair were supposed to be there then. They say."

"Oh, there's almost always something, Saturday nights," said Victor. "Sure, but we didn't take anybody in. There was another fight, and later on there were the drunks. That one guy was really stinking. And another one, great big blond guy, he was pretty high too." He laughed. "He kept saying, Poor Georgie, poor Georgie, about the other one. You'd never have picked him for that kind, either. Big hefty guy he was."

Glasser came wholly awake suddenly. "Georgie?" he said. "You sure?"

"Sure, why? It was just this one guy really high, and the rest of 'em said they'd see he got home O.K., so we didn't take him in. What time? Hell, I couldn't say to the minute, it'll be on our time-sheet, but it was around eleven-thirty. Why?"

"Because," said Glasser, "going by what Higgins told me, it could be you've got some evidence for the lieutenant on this thing. By coincidence. We're going down to headquarters right now so you can tell your story to Mendoza."

So there at last was the definite alibi for Arden and Darrell. A better one you couldn't ask for, sworn to by two police-officers. Fred Victor and his partner identified Darrell, Arden and Keller absolutely, Warrington and Foster less surely, as the men they had talked to, just outside the Victorian Room, at eleven-thirty-eight on Saturday night. They had stopped because they'd seen a man being sick into the gutter (Arden). Had taken a look at him, in case he was a drunk-and-incapable to take into the tank overnight. The four men with him had been high, but not incompetent, and had said they'd see Georgie was O.K. So the patrol-car had gone on, satisfied.

And obviously, if Darrell and a drunk Arden had been along there on Fairfax at eleven-thirty-eight, they hadn't had anything to do with murdering Margaret some time between then and midnight, somewhere fairly near the S.P. freight yards.

"¡Caramba y Válgame Dios y Santa María y diez millón demonios desde infierno!" said Mendoza.

"A nice little ride on the merry-go-round," said Hackett. "Now will you try a second round for double the money, Lieutenant?"

"¡Venga más! Sure, sure. Tell me I'm a fool. The hunches don't always come out. Damn it, it looked so likely, Arden and Darrell."

"Oh, I know, I know," sighed Hackett. "Seems it's a little more complicated. Or maybe a little less, Luis. Maybe, after all, just the random hold-up boy jumping a car?"

"No," said Mendoza. "That it isn't. And there's Hogg. Yes, so we're back to that. She stumbled across something—" He fell abruptly silent, staring at the desk-lighter.

"¿Y qué esto?"

"A couple of things I'm thinking of now—again," said Mendoza slowly. "That Silverman girl. A nice girl. But—for one thing—not a type who's obviously goodlooking, attractive. Very possibly a girl—no-nonsense, intelligent, and secretly very passionate—who doesn't annex men very easy. She tells a good plausible tale that she's got over it, resented the gossip but reacted very sensibly, if that's the word. I'm wondering. Whether she didn't brood darkly over what Margaret did to her. It's only a couple of months ago, after all. Depriving her of the man she'd managed to catch. Maybe he broke the engagement. Yes. She left your place just after Margaret, but she didn't get home until five minutes to two. Palliser—" He told Hackett about that.

"But a woman—" began Hackett doubtfully.

"Oh, it could be. She's a big strong girl. I'll say one thing," said Mendoza, "it clears up a major point. Margaret would have stopped for a woman. Especially a woman she knew. ¿Como no? This leaves the telephone-call out, that was irrelevant. I can see this the way it might have gone. Roberta Silverman says she followed Margaret's Buick down Figueroa to York. Just suppose that somewhere along there—mmh, yes—she first passed Margaret and then stopped, and when Margaret came by honked at her, called out the window and asked for help. Said she had engine-trouble, said she suddenly felt faint. Anything. And our Margaret always so ready to take responsibility! Can't you see it? See her

neatly parking the Buick, coming over to Roberta all very helpful . . .
She could have."

"I know you've got an imagination. Build it from there."

"Say it was as far down Figueroa toward York as possible," said Mendoza. "Roberta got her in the car and killed her at once. Drove into the
nearest side-street and hoisted the body over the seat down to the floor
in the back, out of sight. That's going against the doctor, but he wasn't
positively definite on the time—there's leeway. All right . . . How
would I do it? Damn, it's the hell of a long trip . . . I'd have done it in
relays, I think. Drive the Buick down Figueroa to, say, Avenue 61. Park
it. Walk back six blocks, drive the Study down to around Avenue 54.
Walk back, pick up the Buick with the body. Drive it down to Pasadena
Avenue. Walk back for the Study, take it down to Avenue 42 . . . Like
that. Short hops. She wouldn't be afraid to leave the body in the car, out
of sight, with the doors locked. Who'd look, a car parked for a short
while? She'd have been able, that way, to dump the body by one-thirty
or so, and get back to South Pasadena at five minutes to two."

"It's very damn complicated," said Hackett. "I don't like it, Luis.
Even not having met the girl. I mean, look at it from her view. She
wants it to be taken as a car-hold-up. O.K. That can happen anywhere.
She knows people can say she left the party at almost the same time as
Margaret, and her natural way home is down Figueroa, same as Margaret. So she stages it as looking as if it happened just after she would have
turned off, onto York. Wouldn't she? So much easier. She puts it around
Avenue 60—after she's presumably lost sight of the Buick, going in the
opposite direction." He was looking at the map. "Look, right here convenient is the Highland Park Playground, recreation center deserted at
night. What better place to leave the body? Why go to all that trouble
to take it down to the yards? And she's only got about six blocks to walk
back to her car."

"Maybe that's why. It would leap to the eye," said Mendoza. "She
had to leave right after Margaret, to catch her. People would remember.
There are plenty of people to testify to the motive. So she made it
subtle. Just in case we didn't fall for the random killer, spotted it for a
private kill."

"You," said Hackett, "have a tortuous mind, is all. It's possible, but I
don't put it any higher than that. Relays! My God, a good six miles
she'd have to do her relays, at six or eight blocks at a time! It's too
complicated. Nobody would."

"All right," said Mendoza amiably, "how do you like Chadwick and Mrs. Ross? Or Mrs. Ross alone?"

"For God's sake!" said Hackett.

"Not so fantastic. He reacted very visibly when I suggested that Margaret had known about Mrs. Ross. She may very well have known. Have taken the trouble to find out. We know she liked to pry into things. The psychologists tell us, Arturo, that men around Chadwick's age are liable to sudden violent emotions—especially in love-affairs. He says very frankly that he was afraid, if his wife found out about Mrs. Ross, she'd do her harm with her employers—and also, of course, with her friends—by gossip, scandal. It looks like a very mild motive for murder, but what motive is enough depends on who has it—as I said to Palliser. Yes. Chadwick says to me, he wasn't at all close with either of his daughters. Just suppose Margaret did know—had pried, and found out. And threatened, all righteous and prim, to tell Mother?"

"For God's sake," said Hackett, "*no*. His own daughter."

"So, Mrs. Ross alone? It is, I'd lay you any money, a truly romantic affair. Chadwick's not paying her rent, not paying for anything. Not a—mmh—love-nest. Neither of them is young or especially—" he shrugged — "sexually attractive. Look at it—we know human people, Art. This will be Helen Ross's last grasp at Romance, at true love. It's on the cards she *is* in love with him, passionately. And he with her. She'd go all lengths to keep him, protect their romance. So suppose Margaret goes to her, says righteously, you break with Daddy or I'll tell Mother—and suppose Helen knows, one, that Mrs. Chadwick will be vindictive and spread scandal about her, and/or two, that Chadwick depends on her for money—"

"No," said Hackett. "Not that. He's not like that. Soft, sentimental, but not weak. The money doesn't mean a damn to him."

"All right, I don't think so either. That's wrong. Why, then? Of course—don't you see it? With Margaret's threat over them, knowing the consequences, Chadwick would play Sir Galahad and voluntarily walk out of Helen's life to save her reputation. Just the thing he'd do, whether she protested or not. And that, she'd know. So, seeing Chadwick being taken away from her—"

"How did she know where Margaret was?"

"Damn it, it could be she knew," said Mendoza. "It could be the two of them, you know. Neither of the girls close. And a late, violent love-affair, it could outweigh—any little paternal feelings. From what we know of Margaret, I think it'd be difficult for anybody to love her very much. With her threatening—"

"I don't like it," said Hackett, shaking his head. "No, Luis. Not Chadwick. He's—a basically nice guy in a trap. Not wanting trouble, is all. And conventional."

"All that," agreed Mendoza. "But when it comes to sex—" He looked at his cigarette. "And that age. For him too, the last romance. Call it that. Don't they say, the strongest life-urge?"

"I guess it is, sure," said Hackett.

"There are those don't worry about it," said Mendoza. "Don't nag themselves about it, in connection with their ages or anything else. It's just there to stay." And Hackett thought, having known Luis Mendoza a long time, that's you, boy. That so often went with the high I.Q., whether it was expressed or sublimated. And this kind of thing Luis Mendoza understood without a blueprint, so maybe he was right about Chadwick. "But most people— You take Chadwick. He's feeling damn guilty about something. And it could be it's just the affair. Conventional, yes. Maybe it just worries him, being underhand. The affair, not a clean divorce and remarriage. But also—"

"Shouldn't he?" asked Hackett involuntarily.

He got an amused glance. "My Arturo! Depends on the people involved, doesn't it? Myra Chadwick—he was caught, the poor innocent boy, at nineteen. And she's the one responsible for the affair, not him."

"I just don't like Chadwick in it. Just possibly Mrs. Ross, as you sketched it. Only how did she know where Margaret would be?"

Mendoza considered. "Chadwick may have known, of course. But equally of course, it's not exactly the kind of thing to come out in casual conversation between those two, is it? Another thing. Even if Chadwick knew, even if for some reason he mentioned it to her, how would he most likely put it? Margaret's going to a shower for an old school-friend, a Mrs. Hackett. Or, Angel Hackett. He wouldn't add, at 5126 Springvale Street in Highland Park. And from just the name, how would she get the address? Even if he said, Mrs. Arthur Hackett, which isn't likely, you're probably not the only one in five phone-directories. How would she get the address? I'll tell you how I see it. If it was Helen Ross, it was Chadwick too."

"I don't like it," said Hackett obstinately. "You're grasping at straws."

"Hardly," said Mendoza. "Just going on to the next set of clues."

# 15

It was not yet the time for her to be coming, and the cat was not on the porch. Increasing hunger had sent him ranging as far from home as he dared. He had found, a long block away, an empty lot where a house had burned, and in the tall underbrush grown up there, a few field-mice. These were easier to catch than birds, but there was less meat on them; and there were not many families of field-mice. Still, he was hunting in the lot, until he had caught them all or the remnants took fright and moved out.

He had caught four that morning, and was now hunting again. He caught another before his time-sense began to tell him it was almost the time when she might be coming.

Obedient to life-long habit, the cat started for home. He slid cautiously through back yards, under or over fences. He was much thinner now, but his long coat concealed that. The foxtail was festering in his side, starting a small abcess. He came to his house, came around it to the front, and sat on the porch, half-hidden by one of the porch-pillars, waiting.

He was still sitting there half an hour later when Mrs. Whipley came by. Again she glanced at the house but did not turn up the walk; she was tired. She thought maybe she'd come back to see Mrs. Hill after supper. She did not see the cat.

A long while later the cat rose, walked stiffly around the house, and used his own little shutter-like door to enter the kitchen. The kitchen smelled of long-eaten food; there was none there now. His water-bowl was long empty. There were things here, familiar things, but not edible. The cat went over and sniffed at the white plastic handbag on the floor, under the table. Things had spilled out of it—a handkerchief, a lipstick, keys, a coin purse. Among the other things lay one round gold-and-white earring. All the things smelled of her, but the scent was fading. There was an empty bowl on the table, quite clean, and an empty clean saucepan.

The cat stalked unhappily from room to room, in this place where content and well-being had been and were not. Finally he leaped up to her bed, where he had always slept, and curled himself to a tight, unhappy ball of matted fur.

A long while after that, he heard the doorbell sound. It was dark by then. He only lifted his head a little, dropped it again. That was not her. The bell rang twice, an interval between, and then stopped.

Mrs. Whipley said to herself, turning away, "Out. It'd be real nice if she found herself some good kind young man. Well, I'll probably see her around tomorrow or next day." Meanwhile, there was that new picture at the Roxy . . .

So they were starting all over again, and Mendoza had a little new idea to work on. "Let's try to find out," he said, "who was Margaret's current target among her acquaintances. Who she'd been gossiping about lately. It might be a lead."

"To a deliberate homicide? Because she was telling everybody Marion shops at Graysons' instead of Magnin's—or was going to tell Henry that his best girl Gloria dyes her hair?"

"Now don't belittle, Art. She could have come across something serious. And it's a delicate little job, get those women to talk. I want you and Scarne on it, I think. I'll do some of it too, but tonight I'm going to call on Mrs. Helen Ross." He had called her at her office at four o'clock, asked if it would be convenient. Her answering voice had been warm contralto, level and oddly unsurprised.

"Of course, Lieutenant. I'd rather been expecting you to call. Eight o'clock, that's quite convenient, yes."

A level-headed woman, he said to himself. An intelligent woman. A woman who wouldn't fly off the handle.

Now he went home, and found Alison sitting on the couch grimly engaged in altering the hem of a new dress. The cats sat in a row watching her with round astonished eyes, and she was muttering a number of words no lady should have used, in either of two languages. "Don't speak to me," she said, and stabbed her finger again and uttered a little shriek. "*How* I loathe sewing! All the damned generalizations, any really feminine woman— Oh, *damn!* Oh, this blasted nylon thread! Now I'll have to thread it again—"

Mendoza removed needle and thread from her, neatly threaded the needle at the first attempt, and handed it back. "In all good shops," he said, "there are alteration departments. For a small nominal charge the thing is done for you. And you accuse me of practicing silly automatic economies."

"I know, I know! It's a form of penance—my puritanical Scots streak coming out. I'll bring myself to it gradually, like other things I never could afford. Oh, *damnation!*"

"If you used a thimble," said Mendoza, "you wouldn't stab yourself so often."

"I can't sew with a thimble any more than I can drive in gloves. For goodness' *sake* go away and don't stand there *watching* me!"

Mendoza picked up Bast, who patted his moustache fondly with a soft paw. "This is the warm welcome of the loving, fond wife eager to make a happy and comfortable home for her lord and master. When, worn with the day's labors, he arrives home—*Cuidado*, look out, you'll hit Bast!" He dodged the sofa-cushion, put Bast down on it where it fell, and escaped to the kitchen.

Here he devoted some unaccustomed time—for he was not a devotee of mixed drinks, or indeed, much liquor at all—to preparing a shaker of very cold, very strong Margueritas. He set a wet glass inside the refrigerator. Measured a careful six ounces of tequila into the shaker. Added two ounces of Triple Sec and four of chilled limejuice. Broke out six ice-cubes and put them into the electric ice-shaver. Tore off a paper towel and poured onto it, in a neat circle, a generous supply of salt. Put the ice into the shaker and mixed all the ingredients thoroughly. He listened, and heard silence in the living-room.

"Well, of *all* the jobs!" she said thirty seconds later.

Mendoza retrieved the frosted glass from the refrigerator, set it rim down on the salt, upended it, filled it and took it in to her. She was licking a wounded finger, the finished dress folded beside her.

"*¡Amante!*" she said. "For an amateur at the job, you make a very fine husband. Just what I wanted . . . Are you trying to get me drunk?—these are awfully strong. Don't you want one?"

"Not that stuff. Not anything much, but I'll join you for company." He got himself a small drink of rye. "This thing has come all to pieces again," and he told her about the alibi.

"Oh, poor Luis. How provoking for you."

"I can think of other words. I'm going out after dinner to start all over again."

"I've got some frozen haddock fillets," said Alison helpfully, sipping her drink. "They say it's brain-food, don't they? . . . Well, I shouldn't have another, but I will. That's enough. You'll have to help finish it, darling, you shouldn't have made so much."

And he didn't especially like tequila, but he filled another glass with the bonus left and took it to the desk with him while she attended to the fillets. He got out a pack of cards and shuffled them absently, as if telling his own fortune—laid them out at random. He had had a date tonight, at his Hollywood club, for some poker. He picked up the cards and shuffled them again, reflecting that the prosperous used-car dealer who'd been one of his intended table-mates hadn't sounded just so regretful to hear that Mendoza wouldn't be sitting in. Some day he'd have to give up poker. Some day when he couldn't find anybody any more to sit in a hand of draw with Mendoza the Menace. Be reduced to solitaire.

He laid out the cards for solitaire and stared at them. This damned thing. No handle to get hold of at all. He wished Margaret Chadwick had never been born, to plague him like this with her death.

And God knew she'd been small loss. But—the jigsaw puzzle—he had to fit the pieces together. Way he was built.

He started to lay out cards, red on black, black on red.

Around the Silver Lake Reservoir were a number of very good, very expensive houses: very high-priced rental units; and, around the lower end of the reservoir, middle-priced, fairly new units. There were few apartment-houses: the rental units were in little pleasant courts, one-storey in front, two-storey at the rear, painted bright cheerful colors.

The court where Helen Ross lived was painted apple-green, and she had the lower apartment of the rear building, 6707½. She answered the chimes promptly. "Lieutenant Mendoza? Do come in."

It was a pleasant living-room. Neat, but lived in. There were books in a tall bookcase, magazines in a rack; the room was beige, with a beige carpet and green and orange accents deftly added in cushions, curtains, lamps, ornaments. There were only two pictures, both reproductions. His education in art had been improved lately; he recognized both. The larger was a good copy of El Greco's *Portrait of a Man;* the other was an

equally good copy of Moroni's *The Bergamask Captain*. Unusual, interesting, and seldom-reproduced portraits. Apparently, like himself, Helen
Ross did not particularly care for art minus life. The landscape, the still
life, said nothing to him; portraits he liked.

"Sit down," she said politely, "won't you?" Helen Ross was a tall
woman with a fine figure, if an unfashionable one. She did not look her
forty years. Her face was roundish, with a perfect skin, unlined; regular
features, a generous mouth, brown quiet eyes under slim brows, and
dark brown hair untouched with gray. She wore gray, quietly; and her
slender hands were beautiful. Not, thought Mendoza, very big hands,
for her height. Smallish, well-cared-for.

"Thank you," he said. "I expect you can guess why I wanted to see
you." This was an intelligent woman. But he had half expected to find
Chadwick here.

The brown eyes were steady on him. "Charles was worried," she said.
"For no reason, really, but he was. He said you were no fool, Lieutenant
—and that you seemed to think she was murdered for a—a personal
reason, however it may look. That you were—prying."

"As Margaret did," said Mendoza. He offered her a cigarette. She
took it, bent to his lighter.

"Yes, she did, didn't she? Poor girl. I only met her once, but I was
sorry for her, a little." Helen Ross smoked reflectively. "Having to—find
an outlet—in that kind of thing . . . But are you sure, Lieutenant?
Really? That it wasn't just some man holding her up for what she had in
her purse?"

"I'm sorry, I can hardly discuss evidence—"

"No, no," and she gestured impatiently, "I'm only asking because
this seems to me to be—casting rather far afield. Are you really thinking
that *I* might have murdered her? Or Charles and I in collusion? His own
daughter? Of course, I suppose you ordinarily meet the kind of people
who might do such things—"

"People are people, Mrs. Ross. One of the coldest-blooded killers I
ever met was an upper-class lady with quite a little money, who among
other things tried to frame her own daughter for a murder."

"Well—" she said. "Of course, Charles isn't—close—to either of his
daughters. Which isn't his fault. He said he told you that. I didn't tell
him that you'd called, by the way. I think he's a little afraid of you,
Lieutenant Mendoza."

"Has he reason to be, Mrs. Ross?"

She moved sharply. "No, of course not. The whole thing's absurd. I see we've—we've got to be frank, here. In the circumstances. I—it's difficult for me, I'm not used to—parading my emotions. He told me he had—rather come out with a confession to you, when he was angry. But you said—about irrelevances, that you don't—" She put out her cigarette. There were ashtrays here. Which was perhaps a basic reason, thought Mendoza: comfort and convenience. "Lieutenant," she said abruptly, "I read the papers. I'm aware that we have a very good police-force here, when it comes to honesty and efficiency. That you don't—make blunders often. And I've come across your name a few times too, I gather that you have a little reputation at your job. I said to Charles, we should be frank, anything you want to know, that you wouldn't jump to conclusions. I mean, it seems incredible that you could think— But he was nervous about it, because of the possible publicity. He's so afraid of scandal about me. A lot of men don't realize how tough women are."

For the first time Mendoza gave her his sudden charming smile. "Much tougher than we are as a rule," he agreed.

Helen Ross eyed him thoughtfully. "Aren't we, though. I'll trust you to judge people accurately. I expect you already know a good deal about Margaret, poor thing. What she was like. As I say, I only met her once, but I grasped what she was like. It showed very clearly. And the answer to what you're wondering about is Yes. You don't think anyone as—delightedly—suspicious as Margaret wouldn't have got to speculating, when Charles said he had work at the office four nights a week?"

Mendoza liked that *delightedly*. The very word. "I wondered," he said, "yes. So I did."

"You needn't. If you want to know, I think Myra Chadwick never questioned it because she's not that interested in him, and she's out a good deal herself, at her club-meetings and so on. But Margaret—took the trouble to check up. Not that it was much trouble, actually. She followed him one night. He came straight here, and my name is in the slot over the mailbox."

"And what," asked Mendoza, "did she do about it?"

"Exactly what you might expect. She had to meddle—had to manage. She came to see me one Saturday afternoon. She told me she couldn't 'approve' of our 'sordid relationship,' and that she thought her mother should be informed. I tried to keep my temper—I saw what kind she was, and Charles had told me a few things. I said that it was scarcely any of her business, that she had no right to meddle in her father's private life, or mine. Oh, you can guess how it went, what we both said. Such a tiresome girl—very spinsterish, if you know what I mean. I'm afraid at the last I said some rude things, but she never lost her temper, just went on looking righteous and—and repeating all the conventional things. As if—" she made a little grimace of distaste— "she'd found him paying a chorus-girl's rent. Like that."

"Yes. And of course you told Mr. Chadwick about it."

"No," said Helen Ross calmly. "Because I knew how he'd react. He knew his wife, that while she wouldn't—excuse me—give a personal damn, she'd be pleased to spread scandal about me. Perhaps lose me my job. Yes, you're thinking that Margaret was her mother's daughter. So she was. I didn't tell him—because I hoped to God the girl would tell."

"Ah," said Mendoza. "Did you? I see."

"Do you? So it'd be—in the open, then. It's not that he's *weak*," she said almost desperately. "He's not. But he's—so damned *chivalrous*." She laughed nervously at that. "He wouldn't take the chance, on account of me. On account of the scandal. Of—quite possibly—having to get along on very little money. I wanted him to take the chance. I've argued with him— *Do* you see? Can you understand? I wanted her to tell! It wouldn't matter about the scandal, to me. Not if we could—have it open, make a clean break. It's not as if Charles' business would have been affected. There wouldn't have been headlines about it. And these days, people don't— She'd never divorce him, but it might have been the one thing to stir Charles up to divorce her, once the consequences had already arrived, if you see what I mean."

"Yes, I see that."

She quieted. "I didn't care, really."

"When was this, Mrs. Ross? Which Saturday did she come to see you?"

Helen Ross was lighting another cigarette. "Last week. The Saturday before—before she—"

"I see," said Mendoza noncommittally. "Did she give you any ultimatum?"

"I—don't know what you—"

"Did she say, you break with Daddy within a week, or I'll tell? Or a month? Or tomorrow?"

"I—no, of course not. No. What are you thinking? That I— that we— It's ridiculous," she said scornfully. "Not even—alarming. Neither of us would— And I didn't tell him, because as I say I hoped she would tell. And that it would stir him up to divorce— He should have left her, divorced her, years ago."

"And maybe I agree with you," said Mendoza. "All the same, Mrs. Ross, I'll ask you where you were last Saturday night."

She looked at him incredulously. "I? I was— You can't think that! All right, I know you have to ask. I'm sorry. Charles—they keep up a kind of social pretense—he was to go out with his wife, to a dinner. I was just here. I came home about six-thirty, got myself dinner, and read all evening. I—if it means anything, which it doesn't, the new Lockridges' detective novel. I went to bed about eleven-thirty. But—no witnesses, are there? You can't think—Lieutenant, how would I know where she was? Know where to—contact her?"

And now Mendoza was remembering that Chadwick had an alibi. Did he? They'd got home about twelve-thirty, they said. Yes, but the doctor could be wrong. A little leeway there, quite a little, in fact. Also, Helen Ross—like the Silverman girl—a strong, active woman. It just could be that—

Hell, it was still very wide open. In all directions.

He thanked Mrs. Ross, said a noncommittal goodnight and went out to the car. He had the feeling that she was startled at his abrupt cessation of questioning; but he was, for the moment, finished with her. He wanted to think about something new.

All of a sudden, just now, he had seen the case upside-down, as it were; and that, of course, was the only way in which Chadwick could have been involved in it.

Because Chadwick *had* known that Margaret knew about Helen Ross. He was not a good liar; he had betrayed that in Mendoza's office this morning. So perhaps Helen Ross had told him—or suppose that Margaret had also gone to him breathing righteousness.

And suppose Margaret had come straight home from the party and been in her room when the Chadwicks came in. It was a hundred to one that Myra Chadwick had a separate room. Suppose Charles Chadwick, being clever, providing himself with an implied alibi (just in case the police didn't buy the random killer) had gone to her room and—what? She'd have been undressed by then, very likely. Would he have known what she'd been wearing when she went out? They had probably left at about the same time. What fancy story would he tell her, how would he persuade her to put on the same dress? He wouldn't try, of course. He'd kill her there and then. Strangling, if you were strong enough, was a very smart way to kill, because it left no mess—no chance of inconvenient blood-stains. He had heard Laura come in, say, before he moved. Not long before, because you couldn't go much over the doctor's ruling. The doctor said, eleven-thirty to midnight, nearer midnight. The Chadwicks would have got home about twelve-thirty. Yes, and Laura and Mrs. Chadwick still awake, within earshot, when he killed her. All right, he waited, then, until they were asleep. He redressed the body in the light-blue dress, and waited in the dark until, perhaps, two o'clock. Dead of night. He carried the body down through the house— And all this was something of an athletic feat, wasn't it, for a sedentary fellow of fifty-one? Well, for a strong incentive: and he was a big man, in good condition. He could have— Carried the body down, no servants sleeping in, and left it inside the hedge around the lawn, hidden. He had her car keys, and he wore gloves. He got her Buick, drove it to the house, got the body and put it in the car. Only a short distance from hedge to curb, and at such an hour—

He had arranged with Helen Ross to meet him in her car, at the freight-yards or thereabouts. He abandoned the body, left the Buick on Amador Drive, being tailed by Helen Ross, who then picked him up and drove him home. And drove home herself.

How about that?

Well, it might sound fine in a detective-story, thought Mendoza. He turned the ignition key and started home himself.

# 16

Evidence, *por Dios,* he thought, sitting at his desk next morning. Usually there was something to give them a lead. Here, it was all nuances. Now that the obvious lead on Arden had blown up in their faces. And Hackett was riding his favorite hobby horse.

"You want to make it complicated because you've got a tortuous mind. That's all. I still say it could be just the random thing."

"No. Another little point says no, there. The car. The car was worth something. That kind of smalltime pro would have kept the car, dropped it off at some car-fence's lot, for what it would fetch. But this boy wasn't interested—he left it at the first convenient spot, to be rid of it. Mr. Sanchez says that he first noticed the car there at about five-thirty on Sunday morning when he left the house to attend early mass."

"Y-e-s," said Hackett. "I take that. All right. But there's nothing to get *hold* of, damn it!"

"Are you telling me! And why I say 'he' I don't know. I'm feeling right now as if it's likelier it was 'she.' Yes, well, let's get busy and see if we can't find something. Here we have a list of the women Margaret would have been seeing most frequently. Rose Larkin, Betty-Lou Cole, Esther MacRae, Linda Warren, Sue Porter, Sandra Norman. We'll see all of them, and ask politely what gossip Margaret had been retailing lately. You take Larkin and Cole, give Scarne Porter and Norman, and I'll take MacRae and Warren. O.K.?"

"O.K.," said Hackett with a sigh, "but—gossip. So, Linda's dyeing her hair. Sue's husband is cheating on her. And murder done over it?"

"*¡Animo, manos a la obra*—let's get to work! You're so optimistic."

But before he went out to visit Miss MacRae and Mrs. Warren, he sat at his desk and looked back, deliberately, at every scrap of factual evidence they had gathered on this thing.

The fingerprints left in the car had belonged to Margaret, to Laura, to Mrs. Klingman whom Margaret had driven to the clinic. No prints on the wheel, gear-selector, or driver's side of the dashboard, which argued that somebody else had driven the car after Margaret had.

If that nice detective-story plot about Chadwick and Helen Ross was so, his alibi up to midnight didn't matter. But the Porters backed him up on it, as to the time. For what it was worth.

Mr. Martin O'Hara's incomprehensible alibi involving several hours of stud poker was also backed up by his fellow players. For what that was worth.

The waiter and the cashier at the Club Afrique remembered Laura Chadwick and Kenneth Lord quite well; they frequently came there. They had come in about nine-forty (after the leisurely dinner at Frascati's) and had left somewhere between ten to eleven and eleven. Lord had supplied the name of the second place they'd gone to—Giuseppi's, Sunset Boulevard, where a currently popular pianist was playing and had an eleven-thirty session. They were remembered there as fairly frequent patrons too, by the waiter; they had come in just in time for the show, about eleven-thirty; the pianist was late and the show didn't go on until eleven-thirty-five.

Laura had said she had known Margaret was going to a shower for a girl she'd known in school, but not the name or where it was. Mrs. Chadwick ditto. Chadwick hadn't even known what kind of party it was. There were twenty-four people listed in her address-book who had not attended the shower; all of them disclaimed any knowledge of it. Helen Ross said she'd had no idea where Margaret was going that night, why should she have?

Roberta Silverman, thought Mendoza. Well, yes. And, by a natural association of ideas, Palliser's blonde. How wild could you get? Margaret was enough to cope with.

And Oscar Hogg. He had been asked to come in and make a statement; he had done so. As near as he recalled, said Mr. Hogg, Margaret had called his office about three on Saturday afternoon, and asked for an appointment. He had given her one at three on Monday afternoon, and asked—"We like to have some idea—" what sort of job it was she had for them. She had said something like, "Oh, just something—" or "some facts"—"I want checked into." And that was all.

And there was, of course, the phone-call. When you thought about it, it was, call it seventy percent, sure that that tied in. Because nobody (as Alison said) would make an unimportant phone-call to a guest in someone else's house. But questions had to be asked, of people who might have wanted to talk to her about something quite irrelevant to the murder. (Mrs. Ashbrook?) People knowing where she was, other friends not invited to the shower but knowing about it. How? Well, rather easy to imagine. Margaret talking about it, a shower for Angel Hackett—talking to Mrs. Ashbrook, other friends—adding, "Rather a tiresome drive, out to Highland Park." So, if a little something came up—say on one of her "cases"—the phone number could be found; there was probably not more than one Hackett in Highland Park.

Or was there? Mendoza got out the relevant phone-book and checked. There were three. Arthur J., John P., and Randolph.

Well, all right, even on a casual thing, not much trouble to dial three numbers, knowing one of them had to be right. He wondered if John P. and Randolph had had any wrong-number calls on Saturday night.

So the phone-call could be irrelevant. Ask around.

And then there was Helen Ross . . . Go on building the stories about it, looking for the one that fitted best . . . He liked Helen Ross, but some killers were likable. He thought she was very deeply in love with Charles Chadwick, and she was an extremely competent woman. He liked the idea of Helen Ross alone one hell of a lot better than the detective-story plot about Chadwick and Helen together; but how could she have—

He was a fool. Of course she didn't need to have known where Margaret had been. On a Saturday night, she could expect that Margaret would be out somewhere. She'd be taking a chance that Margaret would be out with Arden, who'd bring her home. But Chadwick had probably said a little something about that affair (which had been all Margaret's and Mrs. Arden's pushing, so Arden would have showed as lukewarm), and she could surmise that there was a good chance Margaret would come home alone. Fairly late. And along there on Franklin—a darkish street, few pedestrians at any time—it would be safe. It was a chance—would have been—and who was to say she hadn't tried, and missed, before? It was a way a single person could have done it.

She'd pick the spot—the S.P. yards, dark and deserted late at night. But it might have been any other place like that; it just happened to be the yards. She'd drive down there, say, around nine-thirty. Park the car inconspicuously, lock it, and walk up to Sunset to get a Hollywood bus. Get up to the house on Franklin by around ten-thirty, and wait there inside the hedge. When Margaret came home, step out and accost her, say she'd been thinking things over, wanted to tell Margaret her side of the story, if Margaret would just listen—couldn't they sit in her car a few minutes and talk? The chances were, Margaret (welcoming the opportunity to air her righteous views again) would fall for it. Yes, she wouldn't be afraid of another woman. And in the Buick, Helen killed her. Smallish hands, yes. But a very determined woman. And rather brief pressure in just the right spot brought unconsciousness very soon. Then, how easy. Drive down to the area where she'd left her own car, dump the body, abandon the Buick. Pick up her car and drive home. And—public transportation, even the few passengers at that hour— nobody would be able to swear to her. She would have put a scarf over her head, maybe wore reading glasses and put those on.

He liked that—liked it a lot better than mixing Chadwick into it.

But there was also the Silverman girl. With what might be a good motive too. And damn it, in a way Art was right, saying his idea of getting down there with two cars in relays was too complicated—unnecessarily complicated. But she could have done it other ways. People were constantly underestimating the police. She (or somebody else) could have assumed that the police would take it on the surface for what it looked like, the random car-hopper after cash, and wouldn't look further . . . And another little point here, too, that just occurred to him. Art pointing out that there were other, nearer places to abandon a body— deserted places. So there were. But someone like Roberta Silverman or Helen Ross—people with no knowledge of professional crime—would want to connect the body to what they'd think of vaguely as "the slums." And in L.A., to most people like that, that said, Main Street— down around the railroad yards. If it had actually been a small-time pro, it might have been anywhere . . . So, all right, Roberta Silverman. Keep it simple, how could she have done it?

She knew Margaret would be at the shower. Rose Larkin might very well have mentioned the names of others who'd be there. So she had come prepared. She had annexed Margaret, after the party, as he'd outlined to Art, saying engine-trouble, saying sudden illness. Help, please. And killed her in the car—Roberta's car. Parked the car on a side-street. Brought Margaret's Buick around, and transferred the body to it. Drove down to the yards, left the body. Abandoned the Buick.

Walked up to Main or Sunset, and picked up or called a cab (no buses running then). There too, the head-scarf, an assumed accent, some kind of crude disguise (just as cover, because she wouldn't really think the cops would be looking for an inside motive)—and, probably, take the cab only up to some corner on Figueroa within walking distance of where she'd left her own car. And so home.

He liked that too . . . Long experience at unraveling homicides (and a lot of them, of course, didn't take much unraveling) had taught him that the two basic motives, recurring over and over again, were sex and money. You could say that they were the two basic *motifs* of human life. Here were two women hypothetically frustrated about sex. In a way, Margaret had taken a man away from Roberta and maybe was just about to from Helen. There was some evidence to back that up. Either of them could have done the murder. And the only evidence that might be obtainable to say Yes would depend on a bus-driver, a cab-driver.

Inquiries would be sent out, on the chance.

Alibis—

Well. Mendoza, about to stab out the latest cigarette and reach for his hat, suddenly stopped and looked again at the topmost page of reports before him. Vague memory nudged him . . . He'd been a cop in this town for a long time. He'd stood on corners regulating traffic, he'd ridden patrol-cars—awhile back. And in that time the town had changed—changed, and gotten the hell of a lot bigger . . . He had taken the oath as a rookie in the June after Pearl Harbor, of the year he turned twenty-one. They hadn't known about all the money then, and he'd had to borrow to buy his uniforms. The old lady had been so proud —a good honest respectable job, with a pension promised, instead of that gambling-den. Well, he'd picked up some change at The Blue Cat; people—a human instinct, gambling—*croupier* at the roulette table, a silly game. Later, spotting the pro sharps for Sammy; because he knew all the tricks, could spot a deck of readers at twenty feet. Couldn't remember back to the first time he held a deck of cards. And he'd been helping pay the grocery-bill, at seventeen, by running a Spanish Monte bank. But not a job that meant anything, somehow. That challenged you . . . Joined the force, and ridden patrol-cars—and then the old man dying, and all the money—the hoarded, miser's money—and that was very nice; but he'd passed the sergeants' exam by then and, well, the job got hold of you—the money was an extra, but the job . . . What was his mind doing, what the hell, casting back all those years?

The town had changed. Under a million people then, to over six million now, take in the county. Second largest city in the nation. Biggest in the world in area—four hundred and fifty-seven square miles. Something about that, his mind was saying. He knew it—he had to know it, the city—like the palm of his hand. The color divisions, the economic divisions.

He stared at the report. It was Dwyer's. Dwyer's laconic report about Laura Chadwick and Ken Lord, where they'd been and what they'd done on Saturday night. The Club Afrique, and Giuseppi's.

"¡Ca!" he said softly to himself. He'd ridden a patrol-car around there, awhile. The city had changed drastically; but some few parts and places in it had not. He wondered if this had. He pulled the phone-book toward him.

No. The Club Afrique was listed as in the seventy-nine hundred block of Sunset. Not quite up to the Strip. And Giuseppi's was listed in the seventy-seven hundred block.

"Qué interesante," he said, and got up and reached for his hat.

"Oh, well," said Linda Warren, "people do talk about—er—people they know. I mean, it's only human."

Mendoza agreed. He had spent a good twenty minutes listening to pretty, fluffy-headed, incoherent Mrs. Warren, agreeing that Margaret's death had been just terrible, that it was hard to imagine what these awful men were *like*, and—latterly—being vague about how it could *possibly* help him to know—well, what he was asking. Because of course, just some awful hold-up man— "What she'd *talked* about, the last few times I saw her? But I don't understand—I mean—"

At last he'd got her down to it. He hoped. "Well," she said deprecatingly, "I guess we do—gossip. Some. Human nature, isn't it?"

Mendoza agreed that it was natural. "You said you'd seen her last Wednesday. Let's take that. What was she—"

"Oh, I just can't bear to think—we were all so happy, so casual—never dreaming—"

"Yes. Maybe just the casual gossiping?" He was putting out all his charm; she arched her brows at him, girlish, automatically responding.

"Oh, *well—!* You know. I suppose so. And I just can't imagine why you should want to know, but there's no secret about it, I guess. Anyway, Rose or Esther could say too. We talked about—well, I guess it was mostly Eileen. I mean, such a surprising thing. Because, well, Eileen and Jim—she's always acted as if she was just crazy about him, and they've only been married six months. You know."

"But I don't," and he gave his most winning smile, all his male force of personality. "Fill me in, please. What and why?"

"I just can't *imagine* why you're— Well, Eileen Thomas. Jim Thomas, it's Thomas and Walters, his father I mean, and he's in with the firm too. Some of us, well, I mean Roberta and Margaret and Rose and I, were at college with Jim and his sister, that's where we met him. And so naturally we got to know his wife. I think he met her when he was in the army. Up north somewhere. And I like Eileen," said Linda Warren, "really. We all do. She's nice—we all thought. But it did seem —odd, what Margaret said. About maybe another man. Well, I mean, we just talked about it a little. The way you would."

"What did Miss Chadwick say?"

"Oh, well, I don't suppose it was anything really," said Linda Warren, wriggling uncomfortably. "I mean, sometimes Margaret sort of—built things up, you know? But she said once when she was there Eileen had a phone-call, and acted upset—saying, I can't talk now, I'll call you back —like that. And later on Margaret happened to see her in a car—on Hollywood Boulevard—with a man. She said, a very distinguished-looking man, and he had his arm around her. And then they went into a hotel together, Margaret said she saw them. It did look sort of odd, as if Eileen— Well, we just talked about it, but I don't really think— Because you can tell, Eileen's just crazy about Jim. And she wouldn't—"

Linda Warren was uneasy, apologetic, feeling guilty now about the artless gossip. Yes, thought Mendoza, Margaret's opening gambit. As time went on, they would have wondered more about it, and *it looked sort of odd* would turn into, *My dear, have you heard.* Gossip. Females. Not that Alison—well, of course not Alison. They came all sorts, like the opposite sex, naturally.

He didn't get much more out of Linda Warren. He thanked her, and came away. Put somebody on this Eileen Thomas and her husband. Find out—if there was anything to find out. But—murder, just over the casual extra-marital affair? With people, you never knew.

It was eleven o'clock.

He sat behind the Ferrari's wheel. Alison. Like to go home now to Alison, his darling. Well, yes, the mind that marched with his own, but in addition— Indeed, in addition . . . He had a job to do, damn it. See Roberta Silverman, and ask her questions. Alison. Damn it, she'd be at the architects' office, or— And you could say, disgraceful. A man of his age. She might not be at the architects'. She might be home.

This damned case. No handle.

Alison.

He said to himself, *"¡Qué tipo—pero!* Get on with the job, boy." She would be there when he got home. When he got home, early.

He started for South Pasadena.

And then he stopped, pulled over to the curb, and used the phone he'd had installed in the Ferrari to call his office. "Have somebody go and see this Eileen Thomas, Jimmy." He'd got the address from Linda Warren, a Bel-Air address.

"O.K.," said Sergeant Lake. "Pallister all right? He's right here, at loose ends. What's he supposed to ask her?"

And that was a good question. Mendoza hesitated and then said suddenly, "Cards on the table. Ask her if she knew Margaret was telling tales out of school, about Eileen—who's a bride, by the way—meeting a man on the side. And if she did know, had she said anything to Margaret about it. Just for the reactions."

"Right," said Sergeant Lake.

And, reflected Mendoza, proceeding on his way, he'd take a bet that the second and third times Margaret had "happened to see" Eileen and her extracurricular boy-friend hadn't been happenstance at all. Meddling Margaret. Inquisitive Margaret. She'd seen Eileen with a strange man in a car, so she made it her business to check up, even to trailing her. Some time at the first of last week, by what the Warren girl said.

Well, it was probably nothing, or nothing to do with this; but they'd look.

# 17

Roberta Silverman looked at him with incredulity and amusement. And then with something like alarm. "You don't think I—! How on earth did you find out what time I got home that night?"

Mendoza explained about Sergeant Palliser and Mrs. Davenport in the next apartment. "For heaven's sake," said Roberta. She was silent, and then said, "The unforeseen witness. That's always what trips up so many murderers, isn't it? Or so detective-fiction tells us. Sergeant Palliser— But I see, I suppose he had to tell."

"As an honest officer with a good record," agreed Mendoza. "Just where were you, Miss Silverman, between ten-forty-five and five minutes of two?"

She looked at him steadily. "The answer is still no, Lieutenant. Not out murdering Margaret. How could I have? You said before, you didn't think I could have."

"Well, I've thought of a way you could," said Mendoza. "Rather a— mmh—neat way."

"I'll bet you have. I'll bet you're pretty good at that kind of thing. But I'd have thought you were better at—reading people. As to whether they would or wouldn't, according to their characters. Well, I'll tell you —and I do see you have to ask, of course—but you won't like it. And I'm afraid I can't prove it. You see, that—that was the first time I'd seen Margaret since—the row. When I accused her of slander and all the rest of it. I don't think, if I'd known she was going to be there, I'd have gone. But I went, and there she was. Well, it wasn't too diff·ult to avoid her, in that crowd, without making it look pointed. But I don't deny it —well, upset me a little. Brought it all back. You know." She shrugged. "I got away as soon as I could, politely—but I was thinking about it all over again. Not brooding, Lieutenant—not thinking dark vengeful thoughts about Margaret, I assure you. But I knew I wouldn't sleep if I went home, I didn't especially want to go home. It's an old habit of mine, which you wouldn't know, when I'm thinking something out, or worried, I just like to drive around at random. Maybe that sounds funny, but anyone could tell you, I do. I suppose we all have a few odd little personal habits. Anyway, that's what I was doing. Just driving." She looked at her cigarette, and then she added, "If you want to know, I wasn't thinking much about Margaret. I was trying to figure out why I'd ever—got involved—with a man like Lee Stephens. Why I hadn't— spotted him as a rather weak, spoiled man, before. I like to think I know something more than that about people."

"And what conclusion did you come to?"

She inhaled deeply, blew smoke. "If it's any of your business, I decided it was because of my job. Cooped up with a lot of other women and the kids most of the time. Not meeting many new people. I think maybe I was in the state of mind where unconsciously I thought I'd better take what was available. And that's all I was thinking about, Lieutenant."

"I see. Can you give me any idea where you went driving?"

"Oh, yes—not that it'll be much use to you, I'm afraid. I started home, as I said. Down Figueroa to York and left on York. But about then I realized I wouldn't sleep, and wanted to—think this out. So I went down York to the Pasadena Freeway and followed that down to the exchange, downtown where they all come together. There was a little traffic there—Saturday night, you know—and I didn't want to stay on a freeway, when I'm driving around like that I don't like to drive too fast. So I got off, somewhere around North Broadway, and went down to Venice Boulevard and straight down to the beach. There wasn't much traffic there, and it was a nice night, it had cooled off by then."

"How far down Venice?"

"All the way to Ocean Park. I wasn't noticing the time, I didn't care. I suppose it'd have been around, oh, twelve-fifteen or twelve-twenty when I got to the beach."

"Did you stop anywhere?"

"Not to meet any witnesses," said Roberta ruefully. "I stopped at an all-night gas-station along Washington Boulevard, but just for the ladies' room, the attendant probably wouldn't remember. I can tell you the time then, it was a quarter to one. I was starting back. I came back

Washington to the Harbor Freeway, up to the exchange, and then on the Pasadena Freeway. There was hardly any traffic. I got off the freeway at York and came on home. That's all."

"You're quite right," said Mendoza. "I don't like it. Could you remember which gas-station? You could. Well, we'll see if the attendant does remember. All right, thanks very much."

No handle at all. No way to check for definite facts. This whole damned business was like a handful of quicksilver, you couldn't pin it down.

Well, of course there was also the Club Afrique and Giuseppi's, with a block and a half between them.

He looked at his watch; it was twelve-five. He might catch Kenneth Lord on his lunch-hour. He took the Pasadena Freeway downtown, left the car in a lot on Spring Street, walked back to the tall office-building which, partially, housed Bridger, Fallon and Golding, Brokers, Member New York Stock Exchange. Went in and inquired for Mr. Lord. Mr. Lord had just left on his lunch-break. But, added the snub-nosed receptionist helpfully, he nearly always went just down the street to the Paris Grill, maybe Mendoza would find him there.

He did. Lord was sitting on the end bar stool nearest the door, over a drink. Evidently he was alone; he was not talking with the man beside him. Mendoza came up behind him. "Hello, Mr. Lord. I hoped to find you here."

Lord turned so quickly, cat-startled, that he nearly fell off the stool. "What the hell— Oh, it's you. Hello. That a trick of the trade, try to scare a year's growth out of a suspect?" But he sounded amused. "Sorry, can't ask you to sit down, as you see."

"Quite all right, it's just one little question . . . Rye, straight," he said to the bartender. They were private, at this curved end-section of the bar here. He waited until his drink came, tasted it. "Those last two places you and Miss Chadwick went on Saturday night. The Club Afrique and Giuseppi's. They're only a block and a half apart—about five minutes door to door, including parking and walking in. Yet by the evidence we've got, it took you between thirty and forty minutes. Why?"

Lord drank all but a mouthful of his Manhattan. "Why, Lieutenant, I figured you might know about the birds and bees—enough not to have to ask about that. But if you want it in plain English, Laura and I are engaged, after all—we were just doing a little parking. Seemed a kind of

convenient time and place. The parking lot there, there's no attendant
—not a really classy place like out on the Strip, you know, if they do
have a cover-charge." He finished his drink.

And of course that was just what Mendoza had expected him to say.
"Where? Which place?"

"Matter of fact, neither lot's got an attendant. But we drove down to
Giuseppi's and parked there. That all you want to know?"

Mendoza shrugged. It was, he supposed. Like so much else in this
damned thing, there was no way to check it. And he could use his
imagination and build up motives for Laura and Lord, though not as
strong motives as for a couple of others; but how to prove anything? It
had taken longer than half an hour to do that kill and set up the picture
of the car-hopping killer.

He thanked Lord and drove up North Broadway to Federico's for
lunch, where he found Hackett poring over the menu. He sat down
beside Hackett and said, "Try the Special Protein Plate for dieters."

"You go to hell," said Hackett uneasily. "A little more exercise is all
I— . . . None of your business how much. Well, two-eighteen, but
after all I'm six-three-and-a-half. I—"

"You'd better have the Special, you'll never pass your next physical.
What interesting gossip did you get?"

The waiter came up; Hackett ordered roast beef and, defiantly, a
baked potato with sour cream. "Only it's not like Angel's, she puts
something else into it, I don't know what—and she always pours wine
over a roast—"

"Very fattening," said Mendoza severely. "Bring me a small steak,
Alfred. That's all. Coffee now."

"Yes, sir. Medium-well. Something to drink, Lieutenant?"

"No, thanks. Take your mind off your stomach, Arturo, and tell me
whether you too heard some juicy gossip about Mrs. Eileen Thomas of
Bel-Air."

"Oh, that. Sure. It seems to have been her latest piece of scandal.
Though she'd just finished doing some gossiping about Rose Larkin.
This I got from Betty-Lou Cole, of course. It seems that—just like I
said, didn't I?—our Margaret had dark suspicions that Rose Larkin is
touching up her hair. Now I ask you, Luis. I just ask you. And don't tell
me motives vary with who has them."

"All right. We have to check. I know, I don't like this thing any better than you do. I've got Palliser on Mrs. Thomas. We'll see what he turns up, if anything."

The woman lying restlessly in the hospital-bed said, "It's Thursday. I know it is."

"No, my dear," said the pretty Negro nurse quietly. "You've skipped a couple of days. It's only Tuesday. Really it is."

"No. It's Thursday. Visitors, Sundays and Wednesdays. And she didn't come. Something's wrong, I know it is. Jenny *would.*"

"Now, my dear. You remember she told you she couldn't come on Sunday, because—"

"I know, I know. But she wouldn't miss Wednesday too. Not when— She wouldn't! Something—"

Ada Brent, the pretty nurse, tightened her lips. She didn't think kindly of Jennifer Hill. She didn't know much about her, because on visiting afternoons the nurses tried to keep away from the wards as much as possible, let the patients have their time alone with family and friends. But she surely looked, the Hill girl, like an empty-headed blonde, all her mind on clothes and men probably. She must have been told how near the end was. But she couldn't bother to come and spend an hour with a dying woman.

She went on trying to soothe her, trying to convince her it was visitors' day tomorrow. Perhaps cruel? But then, she might not be here tomorrow. Nobody could say for sure. It might be tomorrow, it might be next Sunday, it might be a week.

"You just rest now, my dear," she said. And she had to go on to other patients.

What Palliser had got didn't turn up until about three-forty-five. Mendoza had devoted some time to looking over the other cases Homicide had on its hands right now, to some last red-tape on the Benson thing. And informed Sergeant Lake he was going home early.

(Alison . . . to be hoped, at home.)

He took the elevator down; and just inside the main entrance met Palliser arriving.

"Oh, Lieutenant—can I have a minute?"

"What'd you turn up?"

"Well, I don't know if I did it right, sir, but I figured—I mean, on this, almost anything might be important. I'll tell you what happened. I

went to see this Thomas woman, and—it was queer right from the start
—I nearly gave her a heart-attack. When I told her my name and who I
was, I thought she was going to pass out—she turned green. And then
she got almost hysterical—she was scared out of her wits, it was obvious."

"You don't say! What about?"

"You can search me, sir. It's a big new house, real class, the taxes
must be something. I'd looked up the firm before I started, it's a brokerage. Established 1872—like that. Real money. And conservative, as
you'd expect. She's a pretty little thing—if you like 'em that way—
about twenty-four, dark, big brown eyes, oh-please-don't-hurt-me type,
you know. And she was scared to death," said Palliser, "of a cop. Any
cop."

"*¿Para qué es esto?*" said Mendoza. "Now what's this?"

"Your guess is as good as mine," said Palliser, "sir. Except that it
seems she is playing around on the side. Because— And another funny
thing, she didn't seem to care that Margaret or anyone else had been
gossiping about her and another man. She—sort of brushed that off.
Kept asking *why* had I come? And looking as if she thought I'd come to
march her off to the gas-chamber then and there. Well, I didn't know
what you might want me to do, but I figured if I could find out any
more—and if it was something to do with a man she'd been seeing
secretly, she just might rush off to see him instead of phoning. I don't
know whether I did right, but I waited around the corner to see if she'd
come out."

"That's my bright boy," said Mendoza. "I would have myself. And
did she?"

"She did," said Palliser. "About—"

"Let's go back up to the office, we may want to do something about
this." They started for the elevators. "Go on."

"About ten minutes after I'd left, she came out in a hurry, backed out
the drive in a new Pontiac hardtop, and started for Hollywood like a bat
out of hell. With me on her tail."

"Yes. Where'd she go?"

A third man came up to where they waited for the elevator, sneezed,
and said, "How's it go, Luis?"

"Hello, Saul. Lieutenant Goldberg—Sergeant Palliser."

"How do you do, sir," said Palliser correctly. Goldberg nodded, fish-
ing for Kleenex.

"Where'd she end up?"

"At a fourth-rate hotel called The Banner way out on Vermont. She had to hunt for a parking-space. So did I. She—"

Mendoza jabbed the elevator-button again. Goldberg blew his nose.

"—Went in, and by the time I got there she'd gone upstairs. There's not much of a lobby to hide in, but I waited —behind a newspaper, you know—and about half an hour later she came down with a man. He's a very handsome fellow, about forty-five, curly silver-gray hair, nice profile, and dressed to the nines." The elevator landed and they all got in. Mendoza jabbed the button for Goldberg's floor—Burglary and Theft was just under Homicide. "They went out, and I figured I had time— they had to walk up to her car—anyway, I went up to the desk, showed the clerk my I. D. and asked who the man was who'd just gone out."

"All according to Hoyle. Who is he?"

Goldberg sneezed again and said, "Damn allergies."

"He's registered as Derrek Dominick, of Chicago," said Palliser. "He's been there about two weeks—"

"Excuse me," said Goldberg, "that wouldn't be, maybe, Derrek Dominick with two R's? Five-eleven, a hundred and eighty, forty-nine last birthday, three-inch scar left forearm? Late of Ossining, N.Y.?"

"Now don't tell me," said Mendoza, swinging around. "A pro? You know him? Talk about luck! Maybe mine's changing in this case!"

The elevator landed. Goldberg stowed Kleenex away and said mildly, "Don't you glamour-boys upstairs ever read the papers? Much less the Wanted posters? He's wanted, but good. Since last January when he broke parole. You want to look at his official pretty picture?" Dumbly, they got out and followed Goldberg down to his office.

"Who and what is he, Saul?"

"Kind of distinguished, in his own way," said Goldberg. "Sit down. Ben, these gentlemen from Homicide are slumming, they'd like to look at a picture of a burglar for a change. Domenici, Joseph, alias Joe Domino, alias Derrek Domino, alias Derreck Dominick. I forget his New York jail-number . . . And funnily enough, a very nice guy, you know. Moral as hell, outside working hours. Never known to take a drink. Never misses a Sunday mass. Never looked at another woman, while his wife was alive. And a very skilled man at the job. He specializes in jewelry. Knows quite a lot about it. He goes for the big collections, very wealthy people who've maybe got a quarter of a million in jewelry—real good stuff. He's slick, smart, and lucky. He's only served two terms. One in San Quentin—I was in on that arrest, nearly twenty years ago, how I know him. I guess I could say," said Goldberg, "he's the only pro I ever really liked. A nice guy. He took it all very philosophical—just the breaks—and we never did get back the stuff, of course, he'd already fenced it, so he could afford to be philosophical. He had a damn pretty wife, Bianca her name was, and a little girl. Lived in Culver City, quiet as you please—neighbors thought he worked swing-shift somewhere . . . Thanks, Ben. That him?"

Palliser looked at the official photographs and said it was, sure. And he'd be damned.

"He got off light, first offense—one to ten. He was a model prisoner, only served six. When he came out, after his parole time was up, he took his wife and the kid and headed east. I was kind of interested," said Goldberg, "to hear news of him again, when this was circulated. You can see he didn't get caught again—though I always figured he was behind that Collier job in Chicago in '49— God knows how many jobs he's been behind—until New York dropped on him in '55. He got another one to ten, and was paroled last January. And promptly broke parole—which isn't like him, and I wonder why. But I'm very happy to know where he is. We'll stake this hotel and oblige New York by picking him up. But I guess you boys are slipping all right, Luis, not glancing over the Wanted posters at least."

"We're kept busy—but you're right," said Mendoza ruefully. "And how the hell does a gentleman burglar fit into this damned thing? Just tell me how!"

"Well—excuse me, Lieutenant," said Palliser diffidently, "but—I mean, I just thought—er—you said a wife and child, Lieutenant Goldberg?"

"He had. Wife died in '53. I don't know about the kid."

"A little girl. How old was she when you—"

"Oh, roundabout four or five, near as I—"

"*Damelo, yo caigo en ello*—so, call me a fool," said Mendoza. "Crook's daughter makes good, marrying into a conservative old broker-age and money. But, just like in all the romances, remains loyal to Papa, whatever he's done."

"Well, I just thought—" said Palliser.

"Like the bright boy you are, yes. Saul, when you pick him up I've got some questions to ask him. We haven't heard where he and fond daughter went."

"They went to a kind of tea-room on Vermont," said Palliser. "And, if you'll believe it, had tea. Waitresses with organdy aprons—that kind of place. I left them there—I mean, I hadn't any reason to question him."

"Well," said Goldberg, "I'd better get some men on that hotel. Thanks very much for the handout, boys."

"I wish it meant as much to me," said Mendoza. "I am now going home. At last. Anything important comes up, Palliser can handle it— Palliser the brain. I'm getting senile."

"Oh, well, it was just luck really," said Palliser.

Mendoza went home—early—and Alison was there.

"Luis," she said.

"Mmh? Cigarette, *querida?*"

"Not right now." They'd been talking desultorily; he'd brought her up to date on this thing. "Luis, it's—too much like a detective-novel. Too many motives. Aren't there? Not natural. There's Roberta— though I'll never believe she would have. And Helen Ross and/or Chadwick—though I can't see him either. And even if you know they didn't do it, George Arden and Darrell. And just maybe her sister, though I don't see why. And now this—fantastic thing about the Thomas girl. It's not natural."

Mendoza turned and looked at her. "Motives," he said meditatively. "I said to Palliser, what motive's enough depends on who has it. But there's the opposite side of the coin too. It's a fact that—nine out of ten people, somebody's got a motive for wanting them out of the way. A lot of the time, several somebodies."

"Oh, don't be melodramatic."

"I'm not—it's a fact. Now take me. You've got a wonderful motive for murdering me. A nice legal will leaving everything to you."

"For heaven's sake!" said Alison.

"All right. So I know you—mmh—seem to think enough of me alive not to be tempted to put arsenic in my coffee—"

"There's British understatement for you."

"*¡La dama perfeccionar!* Who are you calling Anglophile?"

"I am not either a perfect lady. At least—"

"I'm lecturing. Pay attention. Take Angel Hackett. She inherited a little money. More than Art has. Art has a motive for wanting her dead."

"This is absurd."

"I'm talking about facts. How they look, on the surface. Take George Arden. Without doubt, he'll inherit what his fond mama has. I don't for one minute suppose George wants her out of the way—he's far too attached to Mama, who waits on him and takes care of him. The point is, in hard fact it *is* a motive. If. What it comes down to is, you and I and anybody who knows them are aware that Art is far too much in love with his nice domestic little Angel to contemplate murdering her—"

"You're unfair. She's a nice girl, Luis."

"If you like nice domestic little things. And I suppose a few people who know us fairly well are aware that you prefer your indulgent husband quick to dead—"

"You want to watch that understatement, it'll get to be a habit. But I do see what you mean. To anyone who didn't know us— We're neither of us what you'd call—demonstrative people," said Alison thoughtfully. "Are we?"

"Well, considering—"

"Idiot, you know I meant in public. And not terribly social, so there wouldn't be scads of people who know us well, to say. It'd be what showed on the surface."

"Exactly. And especially in a thing like this, that's seventy percent of the job, sizing people up. Would he, would she have done it, because of that? I don't suppose," said Mendoza, "there's one soul in this city who could honestly say, there's nobody with a reason to want me dead. And in a great many cases, more than one. No, this set-up isn't unnatural."

"That's—frightening," said Alison, moving closer.

"The way things are. The great majority of people never do anything about it, of course. Oh, the random thought—when Uncle Charlie's dead I'll get that money, and I'll take a trip to Hawaii—but they don't put arsenic in Uncle Charlie's soup to get to Hawaii any sooner. Only we have to check to see if they did, if Uncle Charlie gets to be a morgue-case . . . This damned thing. Nowhere to check."

"But you still think it was a personal motive."

"I'm damn sure of it. Besides his leaving the car, and the handbag, and the cigarette-case and so on, there was also her wrist-watch. Only good piece of jewelry she was wearing—her earrings were obviously costume stuff, and she hadn't any rings on—"

"No, because she had on colored nail-polish— I remember she said—" She told him about that.

"I grant you, she had on a jacket and the watch was hidden. But a pro would have looked . . . Oh, what the hell. Why are we talking about murders? *Poco importa—dolemos la hoja,* let's change the subject, *chica.*"

"*Me dejo convencer—* I allow you to convince me . . . Quite disgraceful, not six o'clock . . . *¡Bueno, bastante—yo renunciar!* Yes, I do . . . But, Luis, dinner . . . All right, we'll go out to dinner later . . ."

# 18

**M**endoza called Palliser at home at seven o'clock. "I have a congenial little job for you. Somehow felt you wouldn't mind putting in some overtime on it. How'd you like to call Miss Silverman and ask her to ride down to the beach tonight to try to check her alibi?"

"Yes, *sir!*" said Palliser.

"Might give you the chance to explain why you had to pass on her guilty secret in the first place. And better take her car, the attendant might recognize that if he doesn't remember her."

"Yes, sir, that's so. I'll call her right away, Lieutenant." Palliser, Mendoza felt, just refrained from adding thanks. He put down the phone, picked El Señor off his clean shirt and put it on. Alison was just applying lipstick.

The cats had been fed. They left a light on against return after dark and went out, to the Cuernavaca.

Ada Brent wasn't supposed to be doing anything like this, but there came a time, she thought, when a person had to do something. She'd like to give Jennifer Hill a good piece of her mind, but of course she wouldn't. She'd say politely that Miss Walker was very worried because Mrs. Hill hadn't been in yesterday, and hoped she would come on Sunday. And if she had the nerve, she'd like to add that of course Mrs. Hill realized that by Sunday, well, Miss Walker might not be here to visit.

You'd think anybody with ordinary decent human feelings would be willing to go to a little trouble, give up a few hours—and a sister, too. Empty-headed little blonde.

She was doing this on her own, and she didn't suppose the floor-

supervisor would approve. But that poor young thing, lying there worrying— And, of course, there was an outside chance that there had been
an accident. Only you'd think—

She had got the number from May in the office. Now she stood at the
pay-phone in the corridor of the nurses' dormitory, and listened to the
bell ringing at the other end.

(In the house, the cat lifted his head and listened too. When it
stopped, he put his head down on his folded forepaws again.)

She let it ring seven times. Her lips tightened. That girl. Out dancing
somewhere, probably. She replaced the receiver, and came out of the
box to face Carlota Del Valle just coming up the stairs. A good many of
the nurses (and doctors or internes on the staff) at the General were
Negro, and Mexican, and so on, because it was a place they could get
hired. Carlota was on the same floor as Ada, and knew Miss Walker.
Ada found herself telling her about it, as they walked down the hall
together.

"It breaks your heart, hear her worrying about it. She's a good person,
Miss Walker, too generous and loving for her own good. Over the kind
of sister won't come near her when she's dying. I just thought, if I could
get Mrs. Hill on the phone, I could at least tell Miss Walker she's all
right—"

"Oh, but she's not like that, Ada, not at all," said Carlota. "You
wouldn't know, I suppose, Miss Walker's only been in Ward D the last
three weeks. Before, when she was in A, I got to know Mrs. Hill a bit
because there was that Mrs. Gorman in the next bed, I had to come in
to her pretty often even in visiting hours, you know. Mrs. Hill's nice, as
nice as her sister. Well, not many brains, I guess, but—nice. And she's
awfully fond of Miss Walker. Really, I mean, not just putting it on with
a lot of sweet words. You can tell. She hasn't come the whole *week*?
Not Sunday either?"

"Well, Miss Walker said she'd explained she couldn't come Sunday,
and was sorry. They wanted her to work a Sunday shift, extra, and
because they're nice where she worked about letting her off Wednesday
afternoons, she said, she thought she ought to. But Miss Walker expected her on Wednesday, and she didn't come. It's a shame—and
she—"

"But she would have come, if she could," said Carlota. "She never
missed a visitors' day, all the time I had Miss Walker. And if something
came up so she couldn't, she'd call and explain. I know she would, Ada.

She's nice. And thoughtful. You know, she always thanked me for taking good care of Miss Walker, and as if she really meant it too. Which most people don't."

"No," agreed Ada. "But—then why didn't she?"

Carlota's large brown eyes got larger. "Maybe she *was* in an accident or something. It happens. She might even have been killed. And no papers or anything to say who was her nearest relative, so—"

"It'd have been in the newspapers," objected Ada. "She'd have had things with her own address on her, and I suppose there are things with Miss Walker's name—and where she is—letters and so on, in the apartment."

"House," corrected Carlota. "They had a little house their aunt left them. Well, maybe so—but—things happen. Maybe it only happened yesterday, on a lonely road somewhere so the car hasn't been found yet —something like that. I tell you, Ada, Mrs. Hill wouldn't just not come and not phone or anything. I know, just like Miss Walker knows. She's not very brainy, no, but she's the kindest little thing. Suppose something's happened to her?"

"It'd have been in the papers," repeated Ada.

"Maybe not—they've got a lot of news to print these days. Or on a back page somewhere. We ought to find out."

"Well, how?"

"There's the police. They'd know about accidents."

"Oh, but, Carlota—just not much reason at all, bother them for—"

"That's what they're there for." But Carlota wasn't sure either what they should do. "We ought to do *something*. Try to find out," she said.

They looked at each other doubtfully.

"Well, gentlemen," said Joseph Domenici mildly, "it's the first time I've ever been suspected of murder, and I must say I hope it's the last. Of course I haven't killed anyone. This—Chadwick woman. I never saw or heard of her. And if you're thinking that Eileen— Why, that's quite absurd, gentlemen. My little girl just wouldn't be capable."

Mr. Domenici looked very mild and meek, certainly. He blinked gently at Mendoza and Goldberg. "It's not like you, no," said Goldberg.

"Of course not. I never raised a hand in anger to any person in my life." He looked it. You might have taken him for a successful small businessman, or perhaps a technician of some kind; he was a goodlooking man, and nothing in his speech or manner suggested the pro crook.

They had picked him up when he came back to the hotel at ten
o'clock, and he had surrendered quietly, saying only that Eileen would
be upset and he hoped very much their relationship could be kept quiet.
He'd said that only after he knew they knew. He'd been more upset at
learning that than to be arrested.

He leaned back in his chair, there in Goldberg's office, and said, "My
poor little girl. She was christened Luisa, for my mother, but she felt it
gave away her—er—racial parentage. I hope you won't feel vindictive,
gentlemen, because she dislikes police-officers. I'm afraid that was my
wife's influence, all through her formative years. Actually, I've nearly
always found them to be very nice fellows. Especially of late years, when
standards have improved so much. I do hope you needn't bring her into
this." There was anxiety in his fine dark eyes. "It might ruin her marriage. I know that technically she's guilty of harboring a wanted man,
but— When she's done so well for herself, and been so happy—it
would kill her, I do believe, if her husband and his family should find
out about me. I can't ask anything for myself, but, please, gentlemen—"

Goldberg said, "Well, we're human too, Domenici. I guess I can
promise you that."

Domenici relaxed, got out a handkerchief and wiped away genuine
tears. "Thank you, thank you, Lieutenant. That's real Christian charity," he said earnestly; and Mendoza enjoyed the rare spectacle of Saul
Israel Goldberg looking disconcerted. "I can't tell you how I appreciate
this. I hadn't seen my daughter—well, for obvious reasons—since she
was eighteen, but we've always been very close. I did my best for her,
you know, she's had every advantage—private schools—"

"I can guess," said Goldberg. "On the proceeds of how many fat
hauls?"

Domenici ignored that. "She always wrote to me faithfully. You
mustn't think she was ashamed of her parentage, because she changed
her name and called herself Eileen Webster—she felt very deeply the
prejudice some foolish people have against minority groups, you know.
And I was delighted to hear of her engagement. That, of course, was
why I broke my parole—I felt I must be present to see my dear daughter married. She told me there had been some difficulty over a Catholic
ceremony—her in-laws were—er—rather distant about the son marrying into another faith—but she's a good devout girl, she held out. She
tells me they have thawed and she feels really attached to them. And I

have seen the young man at a distance, and she's told me— He seems to be a fine upstanding young man. I've been so pleased and thankful about it, you know. My little Luisa, so well settled in life."

"I can imagine," said Goldberg. "You wanted to attend the wedding, that was all?"

"It was a beautiful service," said Domenici. "I managed to slip in easily, as it was a large wedding. A High Mass, of course. Beautiful."

"And you've been here ever since?"

"Well," Domenici had shut his eyes over the beautiful wedding and did not open them, "the spring is so nasty in New York. I like California. I was—er—quite well provided for."

"Picked up some loot stashed away from beforehand," translated Goldberg.

"In a modest way. Of course I haven't called attention to myself. I have moved about from hotel to hotel, but I've been thinking of taking a small flat. And of course I could see L—Eileen when she could slip away. We've spent many happy afternoons together. Such a dear good girl, and settling down so happily. I can't thank you enough, Lieutenant, for promising to keep her out of this."

"Yes, well, about this homicide," said Mendoza. Mr. Domenici opened his eyes.

"Oh, no," he said mildly.

"Your daughter never said anything to you about Margaret Chadwick? How Margaret had seen you together, jumped to the conclusion that you were having an affair, and was going to tell young Jim Thomas?"

"Disgraceful! Certainly not. If this Chadwick woman *had* seen us, L—Eileen certainly did not know it. She would have been—alarmed, and she wasn't, until, of course, that police-officer came to see her today."

"Where were you last Saturday night, between eleven and one A.M.?"

"Dear me, let me see. I dropped into a movie-theater—the latest Disney, very good—I'd have been back at the hotel, I think, by eleven, and I went directly to bed."

"With no witnesses," said Mendoza resignedly.

"Most certainly not, I'm a moral man, what do you take me for, sir?"

"For an irrelevant nuisance—I think," said Mendoza. "I begin to feel that *I'm* in a movie-theater, watching the same film over and over. This is where I came in."

"I'm sorry I can't help you," said Domenici mildly.

"Oh, take him away, Saul," said Mendoza. "Send him back to the New York boys. Just another ride on the merry-go-round. This is not a case I'm enjoying. Good-night to you both."

Sergeant Palliser and Roberta Silverman drove down to Ocean Park together. On the way, Palliser tried to explain about his job, about how —in a sort of way—his oath as an officer compelled him to give up all information to his superiors, even if—well, even if he didn't think it meant anything, or was misleading. Miss Silverman understood what he meant.

Miss Silverman said she did, and the way she said it, he thought she meant it, and really did. He approved of her driving; some women (and some men, of course) had poor judgment, poor coordination, and it set your teeth on edge to ride with them; but she was a good driver. Easy and natural. He told her so, and she smiled and said she guessed that was a compliment from an authority. Palliser said he guessed so; they had to take a special course in it. In the technique (for one thing) of pursuing at high speeds. He said that course was really something, and she said she believed him, and asked about it. So he told her.

They got on quite nicely, and Palliser began to have the pleasant feeling that she wouldn't mind a detective-sergeant (third grade) pestering her at all. The lieutenant couldn't be seriously thinking— All the same, he wouldn't let her know he knew the ins and outs of her— hypothetical motive—just yet. Might turn her a little shy, knowing he knew. Let it ride awhile.

They didn't have much luck at the gas-station where she'd stopped. Same attendant who'd been on duty, but he couldn't positively identify either her or the Study. "A lot of people stop," he said. "Maybe yes, maybe no. I couldn't say, when it wasn't a sale."

Well, it couldn't be expected, maybe . . . He drove back, and they stopped at a nice place on Sunset and she let him buy her a drink, a Gibson she liked, and he dared to wonder if maybe they'd remember it as the first place they'd been together. A damned attractive girl. A damned nice girl. The kind you liked as well as—all the rest.

The evening wasn't wasted for Palliser.

The call got relayed up from Traffic at nine-thirty-seven. The night-duty sergeant, White, took down meager particulars, asked questions. It was a little unusual, of course, because generally it was relatives who re-

ported. And this didn't have to be anything for them at all. Even relatives (my God, you'd think people were all blind sometimes) couldn't
always give you very definite details—exact height, weight, eye-color
and so on—and this one had only a vague general description. But he
took it down, and the name and address. Florentina Avenue, somewhere
in Alhambra that would be. He took down the informant's name and
address, and the particulars, which were a little—unusual.

Of course, there wasn't much to be done about this tonight. This
late. In this particular department, unlike some, most of the spadework
had to be done by daylight.

He set up a tentative file on it, and left the report on the lieutenant's
desk.

The majority of people who called in to report missing persons did so
before six P.M., so the report on Jennifer Hill was the only overnight
thing to meet the eye of Lieutenant Carey when he came in on Friday
morning at eight-thirty. He read it twice; and then he got out another
report and read it over. He then went up to Homicide and asked for
Lieutenant Mendoza.

"Here's a funny one," he said. "Nurse at the General called last night
to say that the sister of a patient—patient in dying condition—missed
the last visitors' day, Wednesday. She says, the sister's the kind who
always came in, wouldn't miss, or if she had to would have phoned. And
have we a record of an accident to her or something? She got Traffic
first, and they haven't anything on her, so they relayed it up to us. Nurse
says as far as she knows there aren't any other relatives. The thing is, by
the description it just could be that she's that blonde you found the
other day. A very long chance, but I thought you'd like to know."

"You're so right," said Mendoza. "Wait a minute," and he summoned Palliser.

"The nurse says the woman's name is Mrs. Jennifer Hill, listed as
only relative of the patient, and she's about twenty-five, medium height,
blonde with blue eyes, pretty, hasn't much money so she'd be dressed
inexpensively. Separated from her husband. Of course, it's a thousand to
one she's just gone off with a boy-friend somewhere, or had to work
extra, and figured one visitors' day wouldn't matter—in spite of what
the nurse says. But of course we'll check her."

"Yes. What's the patient's name?" asked Mendoza idly.

"Oh, a Miss Genevieve Walker. Dying of T.B. And I—"

"*¿Cuanto, como dice?* Walker—what the *hell*— Wait a minute. Wait a minute," said Mendoza. "Walker. And our Margaret was— Have you got an address, Carey?"

"Sure, 2620 Florentina in Alhambra. It was just an idea, I thought—"

"*Bien.* Let's go. Now," said Mendoza. "All of us. I have the feeling— is it bad luck to say?—this may be the break!"

It was a shabby middle-class neighborhood. A good many small rental-units, low rent, in need of paint. Some single houses, and also houses with smaller houses in their rear yards. The average vintage of the single houses was forty years, old frame bungalows with ill-kept front yards. Toys were scattered everywhere and tricycles were left on the cracked sidewalk. The address they wanted was a house sandwiched between a four-family apartment house and a court; it was a dingy white-painted California bungalow. It had cement pillars holding up the porch roof; a yellow pot with a dying ivy-geranium in it sat beside the left pillar. There was the usual driveway, two strips of cement with devil-grass generously scattered in the grass between, and a ramshackle single garage. The house looked, somehow, empty, though through one big stationary window they could see a lamp with a green shade.

They got out of the Ferrari and went up the cracked-cement front walk. The grass here hadn't been watered for a week, and was almost all brown.

"It's just a long chance," said Carey. "I don't get why you think— It's nothing, really. She might just have gone off with a boy-friend—"

Mendoza stopped. He said in an odd tone, "No. Oh, no. This is the place."

They looked where he was looking. Beside the right pillar, on the porch, crouched a cat. The cat had long smoky-silver hair, much tangled and matted—a coat that stared as a sick cat's does. Near the throat old, dark blood had matted the hair. The cat's green eyes were dull slits. Burrs and foxtails were caught in the long coat. The cat crouched there, tail coiled around legs, with dignity still, but a cat ill, hungry, in pain, unhappy. A cat uncared-for.

"Yes, this is the place. For whatever reason," said Mendoza. He took out his car-keys and handed them to Palliser. "Stop where you are, both of you." He took off his suit-jacket. They looked at him in surprise, with curiosity. "Poor boy—poor boy. No one came. They left you all alone, and you're not used to that, are you? No, poor boy—such a beautiful cat. You know I don't mean to hurt you, boy—" He was advancing on the cat sure and steady, his voice soothing. "It's all right, boy, don't be afraid—"

The cat got to his feet and turned away; turned back. The cat, like most cats, did not like strangers, and he was more used to women than men. But in the cat's short life, most humans had been kind and friendly; he was disposed to be friendly (if in cat fashion) to humans. He was only cautious. The pain from the foxtail in his side, festering, made him fretful; and he was very hungry and thirsty. He had started for the drainage-pipe, but the weakness of hunger had halted him. He had somehow dragged himself back here to his own place. Now these new humans came, and instinctive caution impelled him away from them. It was a kind voice, speaking soft words—the words she had said, Beautiful Cat, and the word which was his name, Boy—but it was necessary to use caution.

"Poor beautiful boy. Don't be afraid, now. Come here. Come here to me. It's all right. You're hurt—that was a wandering tom, way he's raked your neck—and a job it'll be, get all those matts of hair untangled —poor boy, it's all right, you know I won't hurt you—don't be afraid, boy, come here." He came up on the cat slowly, talking, soothing.

The cat hurriedly skipped over to the edge of the porch. A strange human—

"My poor beautiful boy. I won't hurt you, you know that . . . Stand still, for God's sake, both of you!" Carey and Palliser stood still. "It's all right, my beautiful cat—I only want to help you. Poor boy, left all alone . . . It's all right now."

The cat stayed still, pressed up against the house-wall. Mendoza bent and picked him up, draping his suit-jacket over the cat, wrapping him in it lightly. He stroked the cat's head. After a moment the cat produced a small rusty purr. "Poor boy. Beautiful cat. It's all right now." He turned to Palliser. "Probably not used to cars, most Persians don't take to it. You'll drive. I'll tell you where. All right, boy, don't fight me, beautiful cat, we'll take care of you now. Come on."

"Drive—your car, sir? But why—I mean, we came to—I mean, where?"

Mendoza stared at him in utter astonishment. "Why, to the vet's, of course, John. To see that this boy is taken care of first. I'll direct you— Dr. Stocking, on Los Feliz. You look over the house, Carey, I'll send reinforcements and be right back too. There, boy, it's all right. You'll soon be comfortable again—soon better. The Valley freeway, John— hurry."

"But I've never—this car—"

"Make it snappy, come on, nothing difficult. All right, pretty boy, don't struggle now. Soon have you happy again. Poor boy, she didn't come, I know, but you'll be all right . . ."

They left Lieutenant Carey standing on the curb staring after the Ferrari in bewilderment.

# 19

**P**alliser waited awhile in the paneled anteroom of the small-animal hospital, while Mendoza presumably conferred with the doctor. Palliser was still a little shaken from his first experience of handling a Ferrari, moreover somebody else's Ferrari, and was just as happy to sit quiet awhile.

When Mendoza came out, he had his jacket on again. "Well, at least he's had a good meal and some water. I don't envy whoever works on his coat—hell of a job. Shorthairs are so much easier to keep."

"I don't get this about the cat, sir," said Palliser. "Why it seems to tell you so much. I mean—"

Mendoza looked at him as they got into the car. "You don't know about cats, I see. Or cat people. Well, in words of one syllable, it's a fallacy that cats can take care of themselves. Especially in a city. Nothing to hunt, except birds, and even a very good hunter would have to keep at it eighteen hours a day to get enough. That cat is a purebred longhair—Persian—and not much of a hunter by nature. Kind of cat somebody pampers, takes excellent care of. I'd say he has been, up to the time he was—left. There was that gold charm— Somebody thought a lot of that cat. For one thing, he cost somebody around fifty dollars as a three-month kitten."

"Fifty *bucks?*" said Palliser. "For a *cat?*"

"A purebred smoke Persian," said Mendoza, lighting a cigarette. "They come a little lower in price than some other more exotic cats. I paid a hundred and a quarter for Bast, but then Abyssinians were just coming into fashion then." Palliser stared at him. "Whoever bought and cared for that cat wouldn't just walk away and leave the cat. Would know the cat couldn't take care of himself. I don't know whether this

Jennifer Hill is your anonymous blonde, or what happened to her—but something unexpected happened to her, because—not of her own choice—she went away and left her cat uncared for. And I think the odds are good that she is the blonde—because Margaret Chadwick knew her sister, Genevieve Walker, who was one of her cases. And the blonde was strangled on Saturday night."

"But what's the connection?"

"I haven't the vaguest idea," said Mendoza. "We'll have to find out, that's all." He had had Palliser use the car-phone to call in and have some men sent out to the house in Alhambra. It suddenly struck Palliser now that this was a sin of the deadliest kind. That Alhambra was an incorporated city, one of many within Los Angeles proper, and not under the jurisdiction of headquarters. Hesitantly he pointed this out to Mendoza.

Mendoza shook his head, threading the Ferrari through traffic. "That's O.K. That street's just outside the line, technically in City Terrace."

"Oh," said Palliser, wondering how anybody could possibly memorize the technicalities of a Los Angeles County map—where no fewer than one hundred and fourteen separate communities made up the city of L.A. itself and no fewer than sixty-one separate incorporated towns (with their own police and fire departments) also existed, cheek by jowl. He said so, not asking if Mendoza was sure, and got an amused glance.

"You boys get promotion too fast these days. I rode patrol-cars long enough to memorize a few elementary facts." And then Mendoza lapsed into silence, and Palliser, out of deference to his mental labors, did the same, the rest of the way across town back to the empty house.

It was no longer empty. Hackett's Ford sedan stood in front, and as they slid up to the curb, Higgins came out and started down the drive to the garage.

Mendoza sighed deeply, making no immediate move to get out of the car. *"Es difícil,"* he said. "What the hell am I going to do about it?"

"Oh, you'll unravel it sooner or later, sir," said Palliser, daring to encourage him. "It looks pretty complicated, but something may show up—"

"Oh, the *case!*" said Mendoza. "Oh, sure, of course. It's that cat. We can't take him—El Señor would never stand for it. And naturally, Stocking can't take him, with that jealous boy of his own. What am I going to do with him? A nice cat."

"But it belongs to this Hill woman—"

"Who, I'll lay you a hundred to one, is dead. Who is, at the same odds, your blonde. And her only known relative is dying in the General. Damn. Everybody I know," said Mendoza, "who likes cats, has got cats. Very awkward. Well, let's get to work." He got out and went in. Palliser followed him.

Hackett was in the living room, watching Scarne dust for prints. "There's a pretty picture," he said, and led them into the front bedroom, pointed at a framed studio portrait on the double dresser. It was signed across one corner, *For Ginny with love, Jenny.* It was a photograph of a pretty blonde girl—chocolate-box pretty, with wide-apart eyes and a Cupid's bow mouth, smiling.

"It could be," said Palliser.

"This is one of your wild ones," said Hackett to Mendoza.

"Not at all. Her sister was one of Margaret's cases. That's the connection. Tenuous, I grant you. But I don't think, shall we say, tenuous enough to be pure coincidence, Art. Not when they were both strangled on Saturday night."

"I see what you mean," admitted Hackett. "What d'you want, the works? I figured."

"Yes, print everything." Mendoza, hands in pockets, began to wander and look.

It was a shabby old house, the furniture old and not in especially good taste. Palliser thought suddenly that it didn't look like a house where two young women had lived, but like the house of a much older pair of people—a settled middle-aged couple, say. He could almost see them, middle-class retired farm-couple, conventional, strait-laced. The heavy furniture from Sears, Roebuck, the too-colorful lithograph (a seascape) in a cheap frame over the mantel, the American-Oriental pattern rug, the ruffled lampshades. He decided that the two young women had inherited the house from parents, or an aunt and uncle, and changed very little in it—probably because they couldn't afford to.

There was a living-room and dining-room combined, as in most of these California bungalows, one long room across the front with the front door in the middle. Kitchen off the dining-room end. Out of the kitchen, a dark hall, too narrow, with another door into the living-room and on the opposite side doors into two bedrooms and a bathroom between. There was a dripping faucet in the bathtub. The white porclain had been kept clean.

Out of curiosity, Palliser was trailing Mendoza.

Mendoza looked into the medicine-cabinet, which held ordinary things and was neater than most medicine-cabinets. He wandered into the rear bedroom. There was a double bed, old-fashioned high head-board, a bureau, a vanity table, a lamp-table beside the bed. A walk-in closet full of women's clothes. It was a room very neat, old-fashioned but comfortable. A rug, much worn, was too small for it. The bedspread was royal blue chenille.

The other bedroom was slightly larger. Twin beds here, newer, maple. A big double dresser. A vanity table. A walk-in closet, more sparingly filled. The rug was brown, the bedspreads tan chenille, and the sole blanket, folded neatly at the foot of one of the beds, matched the rug in color.

Mendoza wandered on into the kitchen. "Look at this," said Hackett.

"Oh, yes, I see." A white plastic handbag had fallen from the table, spilling its contents. "John."

"Yes, sir?"

"Look." He pointed. "Is that the mate to the earring that was on the blonde?"

Palliser looked and said, by God, it was. "So that settles that," said Mendoza. "Very nice." He contemplated the table, which was an ordinary square plastic-and-chromium table, its top yellow. He opened the refrigerator and looked inside. Opened cupboard doors, carefully using his pen hooked through handles to avoid disturbing prints. The shelves were neat, protected by gay shelf-paper. He wandered out to the old-fashioned large service-porch, where there was an old automatic washer, a tub. He looked at the back door. Into the lower panel of the door was set a curious-looking affair rather like an enlarged version of a butterfly camera-shutter. Mendoza reached down and felt something attached to one side of it.

"Oh, yes, I see."

"Observe the master detective at work," said Hackett. "What happened here, when?"

"Let's see, we're on Daylight Saving," said Mendoza. "Dark about seven-forty-five, isn't it? O.K., whatever happened, it was before that time Saturday night."

"I'll bite, Sherlock. Why?"

"The cat's door wasn't locked." Mendoza nodded at the shutter arrangement. "That's a patented pet-door. Cat or dog pushes at it, it opens out—or in, of course. But it can be locked from inside. Nobody who thinks anything of cats—or dogs, of course—lets them wander at night. We've got one too, of course Bast won't use it, but anyway it gets locked after dark. Mrs. Hill was prevented from locking this one— sometime before about seven-forty-five on Saturday evening." He came back to the kitchen and looked at the table again. "She was just starting to cook something. Methodical. Got out saucepan and bowl—the bowl to mix something, eggs maybe?—but before she got out the ingredients, she was interrupted. Yes. She came in—straight to the kitchen, because she laid her bag down there. Probably talking to the cat. She got out the bowl and pan. She was going to cook something either for the cat or herself—"

"Cook for a cat?" said Palliser involuntarily.

"Some cats," said Mendoza. He said again, Palliser didn't know about cats. Palliser admitted he didn't. "It's unconstitutional," said Mendoza. "Organized slavery. They demand attention . . . And just then she was interrupted. By the doorbell? By a knock on the back door? Some-body came in. Presently there was a little struggle, and the handbag was knocked off the table. And she lost one earring. That charm . . ." He went on staring at the table, as if it told him things. "And that was before, too. Why tucked down in her bra? Instead of in her handbag? Answer, either it happened when she didn't have her handbag with her, or— No. No, that was it. It must have happened when she was at work, the charm's ring breaking, and she tied it in her handkerchief and tucked it inside her bra. And later, didn't bother to transfer it because it was safe where it was. That little piece of gold—part of the ring—yes, it could have stayed loosely hooked through the charm until the last min-ute, and maybe got tucked down there too, caught up in the handker-chief—but loosely enough to fall out later on. If. I wonder." He went back to the service-porch and out the back door to the garage.

"Well," said Hackett after a pause, "he sees things. He's right a lot of the time. But what the hell's the connection?"

Palliser said he'd be damned if he knew.

Mendoza came back again and said, "The screen door squeaks. Two women. Helpless. Just a little oil in the hinges . . . Art?"

"Well?"

"Does your Angel like cats?"

Hackett looked very much taken aback. "Well—she does, yes. There

are some people down the street, their cat's expecting kittens, and she
said maybe we'd take one—"

Mendoza beamed at him. "That's just fine, boy. Tell her not to. She's
got a cat—a beautiful cat. A purebred longhair—we ought to come
across the papers somewhere here—and I'll pay the vet's bill. I don't
think he's over two or three, and a nice cat. I'll tell her how to feed him,
and you'll have to keep him in awhile, be sure he knows where he
belongs and so on. But he'll settle down, with good treatment. This
relieves my mind."

Palliser felt, uneasily and wonderingly, that Mendoza might have had
most of his mind on the cat all the while.

Hackett laughed and said he'd tell Angel. "A very nice cat," said
Mendoza. "Never offered to scratch or bite me. Of course, Persians—
In the same circumstances El Señor would have objected strenuously.
On the other hand, of course, he'd probably have been much more—
mmh—efficient at taking care of himself. Well, Angel will like him, he's
a good cat." He wandered into the rear bedroom.

Scarne was finished here. He had taken the drawers out of the bureau
and laid them on the bed. Mendoza looked at them. At their contents.
He said, "Cheap. Rudimentary taste. Grayson's—Lerner's." He picked
up a black lace brassiere and dangled it, illustrating. "On sale, two for
one-sixty-nine plus tax."

"You're just the boy to know," said Hackett.

"¿Y despues, de insulto, you think I pay female charge-accounts at
such places? Sure, I know. Can read kindergarten signs." He added,
"Somebody, I think, has been all through here before us. She kept
things much neater than this in the kitchen, the bathroom. Well,
maybe natural." He went back to the living-room. Scarne had passed on
to the front bedroom. Mendoza looked at the desk. It was a gimcrack
ladies' desk, vaguely French in design: two small drawers, a narrow
center drawer. Mendoza pulled that open. A thorough search hadn't
been started, until the printing was done. He looked down at a couple of
ballpoint pens, dime-store variety; a pack of dime-store envelopes; a
cheap brass letter-knife; a pair of scissors. He opened the left-hand
drawer. A tablet of cheap stationery. A new bottle of ink, Sheaffer's
Skrip, Washable Blue. That was lying on its side, and the tablet had
been thrust back upside down. A little pile of old letters, neatly tied up
with ribbon. He lifted that out, cocked his head at it. "Oh, very nice—
very suggestive. The ribbon's been untied and retied very recently. Look

at it—the color's faded, except where it was protected by being knotted. You can see quite plainly where the old knot was, here. Something was removed from this little package of nostalgia—if that's what it is—and somebody was careless not to notice that ribbon."

"I still don't see the connection," complained Hackett.

"*Tengo paciencia,* it will emerge . . . Maybe Miss Walker will know about how he was fed—what and when. You'll want to be careful, not change his diet for awhile, to upset his digestion. If it wasn't quite right —his diet, I mean—change over gradually. Beef mostly—lean beef, but liver three times a week. I'll give Angel a list." He opened the right-hand drawer. "He's a nice cat, she'll like him."

A cheap table-lighter. Probably not working, thrust away in a drawer. Can of lighter-fluid. A package of catnip. A ping-pong ball. "For the cat," said Mendoza. "They like them to play with." An address book. That was all. "She didn't do much writing."

The drawer, like all the other drawers they had seen, was neatly lined with old newspaper. On impulse, Mendoza lifted a corner of this sheet. "*¡Vaya!*" he said, pleased. "Little things do tend to slide under linings." He picked up a small something which had lain under the paper. Blew dust from it carefully. "The one thing he missed. Maybe the important thing . . . That little scrap of paper, yes. A snapshot. Maybe he didn't know she had this. And maybe it's nothing to do with all this at all." He held it up to the light from the front window.

It was a photographic negative, standard size—two and a quarter by three and a quarter.

"*Pares o nones,*" said Mendoza softly. "*¡Donde menos se piensa salta le liebre*— How unexpected! Is it? Can it be? I could swear—"

"Something, Lieutenant?" asked Palliser. "Something—usable?"

Mendoza lowered the negative. He looked at Hackett and Palliser with a rapt, withdrawn expression. He said, "But why did he have to murder her?"

Of course—motive, he thought. In one sense, you could say there could not be a motive strong enough to justify murder. On the other hand, Mendoza had come across just a few cases where he could understand why murder had been done. Not to feel that in the same circumstances he might have done murder himself—but why the motive was enough.

Usually going back to sex or money. Sometimes both.

Did you really have to ask, what motive is enough? Very properly, it was not necessary in law to show motive: only the tangible evidence. It was a good idea to show it, to spell it out to the jury, but it was not necessary. They made quite a thing of it in fiction, and that was where fiction veered off to the left from real life. The fiction writers wouldn't touch some motives Mendoza had known with a barge-pole.

He had had a front seat at the perennial production of crime for twenty years. Among other things it had taught him, rather dismayingly, that the human animal is very largely irrational. Ninety-nine percent of all the homicides he had seen (he reflected again as he often had) would not have happened if somebody had been a little less impatient, or greedy, or ignorant, or careless, or, of course, drunk or hopped-up. If somebody had had a little more self-control.

He could imagine, here, a motive of sorts. A dim outline was forming in his mind, pure hypothesis. It was not a strong motive, not at all. It looked as if somebody had just lost his temper. Yes. Unless, of course— But it was early to say. Find out more.

He knew, now, where to go to find out what would probably be one hell of a lot more. The key to the whole case.

It occurred to him, starting for that place with Palliser as a witness, that they'd been very lucky here. If they'd been even, perhaps, a day later— Dying, they'd said.

And that probably entered in too.

And he'd find out what unimaginative half-trained idiot had seen the woman before, and asked such routine, dull questions that a little something hadn't come out to suggest asking different questions. Because *something* must have been said— Of course, dying.

He hoped they were not too late already.

# 20

"**—S**uch a little fool," said the woman in the hospital-bed. "She couldn't—size up people. You know—what I mean. Took them—how they said and looked. Why, that cat—had more sense about people . . . It was silly, about that cat. But she had that good job then—at Mallow and Woodes. Big dress-manufacturers, they are, she ran—one of the cutting machines, got eighty a week—it's union. And—then—he wasn't around any more, take half her money . . . Said—always wanted a real thoroughbred Persian—gave fifty-five dollars for it, and it was an awful cute kitten . . . What?—that charm for her bracelet—yes, I know—she wanted it. I—got it—for her. Christmas before last. She showed it me—this big jewelry catalogue she had—she wanted it, and I saved up—I was still working then—and got it for her . . . It was thirty-seven-fifty and the tax . . ."

"You mustn't tire yourself, my dear," said the nurse. She shot a glance across the bed at Mendoza and Palliser: a troubled glance. She had set screens partially around the bed, in this twenty-bed ward.

Genevieve Walker's eyes were on the white screens. "Doesn't matter, does it? Maybe not—much time, and anything I can do to help—anything I can tell them— To help get him. Help get him—good . . . Please promise me something. Not the screens, nurse. Not ever. They make me feel—shut in. I'll be—shut in—long enough. Soon enough."

"All right, my dear. Would you like a drink of water?"

"Thanks . . . No sense about people. I guess—well, everybody spoiled her. So pretty—and kind—and always laughing. Didn't seem to matter—she didn't maybe have much common sense . . . And those trashy stories she read, True Romances. I told her he was a wrong one. She wouldn't listen . . . Because he was goodlooking and all—and of course she was only nineteen. Only nineteen . . . Why, I found out—nearly right away—lied to her about where he . . . Sorry, I'll try—speak up. Got to. Whitesville, Kansas," she said very clearly. "That's where. And I'll bet—good reason come away, too. Not like us coming—when Aunt Flo died, left me the house—" She stopped, gasping.

The nurse said, "Just try to take it easy and quiet, now."

They had been met by the nurse at the elevator. One of the two who had decided to call in. A pretty girl, maybe half white, who had warned them not to upset Miss Walker. "She's very weak, you know. This awful thing—I don't know whether she can even stand *knowing*. I see you've got to ask her things, but the super says I'd better be right there."

"How long has she got?" asked Mendoza.

"Nobody can tell, sir. God takes them at His own time. And her only twenty-nine, it seems a waste—but you've got to figure He's some reason, you know." She said that very simply.

But Genevieve Walker had taken it surprisingly well. When Mendoza told her who he was, she lay still for a long moment, looking up at him, and then she said, "Something bad's happened to Jenny, hasn't it? That's why she didn't come."

"Yes, Miss Walker, I'm afraid so."

"Jenny's dead, isn't she?" She would have been pretty, before she started to die. More character in her face than in Jennifer's. Her hair was darker, tawny blonde, and her eyes hazel. She was too thin, too flushed; and of course at the General they hadn't much time for cosmetics or hair-curlers, and perhaps she was past worrying about that. "Tell me," she said. "Please. It's all right, I can take it."

The nurse had kept a hand on her pulse all the same. But she just shut her eyes for a long moment and then she said flatly, "I wonder if it was Bob . . . My poor Jenny. No sense about people. Might be—I guess—almost anybody. She *trusted* people. You know?"

"You realize, Miss Walker, whatever you can tell us—"

"Yes," she said. And she'd been telling them painfully, now and then stopping to regain her breath, sip water.

She said again now, very clearly, "Whitesville, Kansas. It was on a letter he got. I saw it—I wouldn't snoop around like that usually, but—I felt he was—*wrong*. And it was signed—it was signed *Mother*. So you see. Putting on . . . And the man—that man, that day—said, Pierce. Hello, Pierce, nice to see you. It was—I didn't like it . . . he made up some story to tell Jenny, and she believed it, but I—didn't like it . . .

Moved right in, you see, after they were married—we had the house, and— But what it came to, just kind of a—place to stay—until he found something better, you know? . . . Living on her—said, so hard, break into writing for T.V. Wasn't any more a writer than me . . ."

Palliser, who had taken a course in shorthand, was getting it all down as accurately as he could; he was rusty, and her voice kept fading out. Mendoza just sat and watched her intently, now and then putting in a quiet prompting question. The nurse stood at the other side of the bed, watchful, alert.

Genevieve Walker passed a listless hand over her brow, smoothing back the tumbled tawny-blonde hair. "—On account of the winters," she said. "Said a nice warm climate like California be better for me. And—seemed kind of providential, Aunt Flo leaving me the house— you know. Peoria, we came from—I tell you that? Jenny was just out of high, it was seven years back . . . both got good jobs, I was at that big bakery, Helms', it was fine—until I got sicker and couldn't work—and Jenny met Bob. Right from the start I didn't like him, but you couldn't tell her . . ."

"When, exactly, Miss Walker?"

"You—have to know that, sure, yes . . . We came—in '56, May '56 it was. I guess it was—around next February, March, she met . . . They were married in July. Six years ago in July. She was too young . . . What? I'm sorry, I'll try . . . Yes, sir, I know. He had—a job, selling, a department store it was . . . I don't remember, it wasn't long before he quit—said he quit, I think he got fired—I think it was The Broadway. I seem to remember . . . Said he's going to break into the big money, writing for T.V., then . . . But, minute Jenny lost her job, he was off, sure, you bet! I *told* her what kind he was. No good. And crooked, too, you could tell. If he thought—he wouldn't get caught . . . She wouldn't listen. Funny, but that was Jenny, she never got mad at me for it—she never got mad—at anybody. Just, she'd say, I—didn't understand—him. Crazy about him, she was . . . Yes, sir. Yes. That was—it'd be about February, '59. When she lost the job. Just after her birthday . . . never saw him again, no—not likely! Until he came— wanting a divorce . . . It wasn't Jenny's fault about the job, she was real conscientious at any job, but they were laying off—she was at an assembly plant then, small parts like for airplanes, and they were laying off, was all. Then she got—this good job at Mallow and Woodes, see— good money . . . Funny idea I had—" she moved restlessly. "That cat.

A nice cat—pretty. But it was like—sort of—it was *instead* of Bob. Silly. Way she babied it, talked to it. You know?"

"Yes, Miss Walker," said Mendoza. "I don't want to tire you. But, about Margaret Chadwick. She came to see you?"

Genevieve Walker opened tired eyes on him. "There was this other man—came to ask about *her*. I don't know why, he didn't say. Only asked, had she—ever said anything much—about herself . . . I didn't like her much. I guess she meant—to be kind. But she—sort of, you know—like looking down her nose at me."

At anyone so improvident, so lower-class, as to be a charity patient in the General Hospital. Yes.

"What? . . . Well, yes, I seem to remember she was here twice when Jenny was, she met her . . . There was that picture. That was funny, Jenny and I wondered about it, afterward. I mean a snapshot . . . My poor Jenny. Always thought he'd come back. Only thing he came back for was, make her get a divorce. She wouldn't do *that.* Said, her own husband—still loved him, couldn't they be together again way it was. She always hoped—that. Telling herself crazy stories about it, like—you know—those trashy movies and romance magazines. Some silly misunderstanding—and he'd realize all of a sudden—he really loved just her, and—come back . . . Making up excuses for him . . . I *tried* tell her—"

"Miss Chadwick," said Mendoza softly. "The snapshot? She saw it?"

"Jenny—dropped her purse. It—she always carried that picture around, in her purse . . . this other man, asking about Miss Chadwick, but he didn't ask—anything about that. Why? It—was—funny . . . asked if she could—"

"Try to speak up a little, Miss Walker."

"—Sorry. Yes, sir. If she could have it, and of course—Jenny said no —it was funny, and then—"

"I'm sorry, I think you'd better go," said the nurse suddenly. "I don't like her pulse. I'm sorry, I do realize—but we have to—"

Mendoza stood up. "Yes, I know. I think we've got enough. Can she sign a statement, say in an hour?"

"I should think so, sir," said the nurse.

Genevieve Walker said strongly, "—Must help you, tell anything you want to know—catch him, whoever did it . . . I think—I think— maybe it was Bob. Because—she said—wait, please, I'm strong enough —tell you . . . Said he'd come back—see her again, that—Sunday.

Week ago last Sunday . . . That was—Wednesday, when—about the picture. She—my poor Jenny—"

"Please, you'd better go," said the nurse.

"What *is* this, Lieutenant?" asked Palliser. "The husband? I don't get the connection. Bob Hill?"

"No?" said Mendoza. "An hour. Until we see a print from that negative. Then, I think, very clear—just the tiresome mopping-up to do, tracking down all the details . . . And what a business. Yes, I think rather an offbeat business. One on impulse, and one very thoroughly planned . . . He lost his temper. I can see that. He must have, because to do it like that, still broad daylight, and his car probably sitting in front— He had luck there. Yes, I can see that happening, with Jenny Hill. The shallow, sentimental, rather stupid female, mouthing all the clichés about true love. Annoying. Beware of women who talk about True Love, John. Or, in fact, women who talk about love at all. I don't go even halfway down the road with the head-doctors, but I do agree with that—by experience, not theory—that the people who are at all voluble about sex are almost always those very under-par sexually themselves."

"Well, but I don't see—"

"We will see," said Mendoza. "It's all coming untangled. And what a stupid business it looks like. Our Margaret I can see, in a way. But why the hell kill her? She couldn't prevent it—only make a lot of trouble. And inoffensive little Jenny Hill—pampering her Silver Boy—" He shot the Ferrari into high almost viciously. "Oh, this one we'll get. This one I'll take pleasure pinning down . . . Because he knew about the cat. I think the cat was there when she was killed. But of course he never gave one damn about the cat—what might happen. One of those people—a cat can look after itself, oh, sure. This one—"

And Palliser said, "Well, excuse me, but that sounds as if you thought the cat was, er, more important than the women. I mean—"

Mendoza laughed sharply. He said, "Yes, in a way, John. The cat was the innocent bystander. Both the women had—as per usual—done a little something to put themselves in danger. Our Margaret asked for it, meddling. An unpleasant girl, Margaret. And a lot of stupid people like Jenny Hill—whatever her good qualities—invite murder . . . The detective-novels have a lot to say about the general earmarks of murderers. You want to know what the only common denominator is in real life? It's the complete blank to any other feelings but the killer's. The utter lack of empathy—like lacking an arm or a leg. For other people— for a cat . . . Our Margaret was small loss, and if Jenny Hill was a nice girl she was also silly. But I resent the random cruelty to the cat. If you want to know, I'll get him for the cat—I can't say I give one damn about Margaret or Jenny."

"But, Lieutenant—you know who?"

"I know who," said Mendoza. "We will now proceed to prove it. With bells on." He braked the Ferrari in the headquarters lot and got out. "You get that statement typed up and rush it back to the hospital for signing. No telling how long she's got."

"Yes, sir."

Upstairs, Mendoza called Sergeant Lake into his office and began to dictate a long telegram to the Police-Chief of Whitesville, Kansas.

They were busy, quite a few men, all the rest of that day, collecting the evidence. It was a little absurd how easy it was to collect, once they knew what they were looking for and where to look. The story unfolded before them as clear as print. Or almost.

The tangible evidence started with the short-handled spade in the garage of the house on Florentina Street. Its back still bore a few faint traces of blood and tissue; there were, of course, no fingerprints on it anywhere.

The charm-bracelet from which the gold charm had been suspended was in Jennifer Hill's handbag.

They went to Mallow and Woodes, where she had run one of the big cutting machines. Where a young man named Redding, a stock-clerk, led them to the foreman—and went white as a sheet, hearing about Jennifer Hill. Maybe Redding had hoped to make time with her; too late now. The foreman had been annoyed at her and now said, Poor kid. He produced—or caused the office to produce—a short letter received on Monday: a typed letter, signed *Jennifer Hill*, saying that urgent family business had come up and she had to quit her job.

"This was a rough and ready plot, all right," said Mendoza. "He never thought we'd look beyond the ends of our noses!" The D.A.'s office was going to like this one. They commandeered the letter. *How* the D.A. would like it! No typewriter in the Walker-Hill house, and very likely it would be easy to show that signature as a forgery. What family business would demand cessation of her salary? The only family she had was near death in the General.

They printed the negative, and of course the D.A. would like that too. Very much.

They got the foreman to identify the body formally. He did so mostly by the dress—and the charm-bracelet. Most of the girls she'd worked with could swear to the charm-bracelet; she'd worn it all the time. With just that one charm dangling from it. A pleasantly plump and pretty young woman who'd worked the next machine to hers could even describe the accident, when the charm fell off. It had happened at about four o'clock Saturday afternoon; and of course Jenny's bag was in her locker, and she'd just tied the charm in her handkerchief and tucked it into her bra for safekeeping. Had left the bracelet on then, but probably removed it later and put it into her bag.

Rather interestingly, the outside of the front door, the kitchen door and the kitchen table at the house were absolutely clean of prints. Places he remembered touching, so he'd polished them well.

About then a long wire arrived from Whitesville, Kansas—and that was extremely interesting. Part of its contents caused Mendoza to send a wire to the Chief of Police in San Francisco, asking questions and cooperation.

It was almost anticlimax when Palliser received a wire from the Crown Lapidary Company informing him that, after search, they had found the record of the order for the charm. It had been ordered on November 10th, the year before last, by a Miss Genevieve Walker, 2620 Florentina Street, Los Angeles, who had enclosed a postal money-order for the full amount. They had no record of Miss Walker as requesting one of their catalogues.

No, of course that had been Jennifer Hill. And you never knew what odd little points would be brought up by the defense at a trial; you automatically gathered in as many facts as possible. Crown Lapidary was requested to say whether Mrs. Jennifer Hill had ever sent for one of their catalogues.

Obvious questions were asked in obvious places.

(At the small-animal hospital the cat slept, in his temporary cage. His stomach was full, and a start had been made on combing out the snarls in his coat; the festering foxtail had been found, removed, and the place cleaned. He disliked this strange place, but at least humans were taking care of him again. He slept, philosophically.)

It was all in by the end of the working day. It had, in fact, said Hackett, been a little like getting olives out of a bottle: once the first one was pried out, no trouble at all about the rest. But of course the reason for that here was very obvious too: this one, underestimating the cops, hadn't thought they'd look beneath the surface. They had, but not knowing the direction to look. Once they knew that, they turned up the evidence automatically, easily.

"Of course it could be he had reason to think so," said Hackett. "Maybe the force in Whitesville isn't very bright. And as for San Francisco, well, they've got a lot of big dumb Micks up there . . . But why in hell did he, Luis? See it as the only way? Flying off the handle with the Hill girl, that I see. But Margaret—she could have been annoying, sure, made things a little difficult, but she couldn't have prevented—"

"No. But when you come to think of it, Art—all that nice money, you know. The rest of it. I guessed wrong. I thought the motive was sex, but it was money. As it so often is . . ."

In a way, that was an enjoyable day. Always so satisfying to clean something up nice and neat like this.

"When will you take him?" asked Hackett, coming into the office at five-thirty. "Here's the warrants."

Mendoza looked up from Genevieve Walker's statement. Suddenly he smiled. "I think," he said, "I'll do this the way they do in the detective-novels, Art. Just for a change. Maybe for my own amusement. *Tal vez, es el mejor modo de hacerlo*—best way to do it. Have somebody call them all and ask politely if they'll be in my office at ten tomorrow morning. Because—while we've got all this beautiful evidence—it's always nice to get a confession, isn't it? At least a few damaging admissions. And a couple of things that have turned up, well, I'm inclined to think our friend hasn't been quite—mmh—open with his—"

"I get you," said Hackett, grinning.

"I like an audience," said Mendoza, stretching. "A policewoman, please. A stenographer. A couple of witnesses—you and Palliser."

"Right."

"And I am now going home."

"So am I. Nothing much more to do here."

Hackett went home, to sample the new tournedos of beef at last, and afterward worried about all the probable calories in rich brown sauce, sautéed mushrooms, stuffed eggplant, and the rather exotic-tasting new salad dressing. Not to mention the special topping for baked potatoes.

He worried aloud to Angel, who said, "Don't be silly, Art, you're a big
man, you need lots of good food."

"Well, but the doctor did say— And you know, just a plain high-
protein diet—"

"Oh, dear, but it's so *dull,*" said Angel. "No scope at all."

"Yes," said Hackett humbly. "Oh, by the way, we've got this thing in
the bag. It seems—"

Mendoza went home and told Alison it was all cleaned up. "They
were linked, all right. Nice and tight—the blonde and our Margaret."

"Who?" He told her. After a moment Alison said, "But why? She
couldn't have actually prevented— Oh. Oh, I do see—in a way. The
rest of the money."

"Bright girl."

"But what a thing—just for money."

"It is," said Mendoza, "the hell of a nice thing to have lots of."

"Isn't it. And of course you can say glibly, anyone who grew up in
poverty, he's got a reason to do—almost anything—for money. But you
and I never had much as kids. My lord, about the first thing I remember
clearly at all is a ramshackle base-camp in the Sierra del Burro in Coa-
huila—Dad was building a dam there—and him giving me a bath in a
mountain stream. I can still feel how cold it was." She laughed. "And
one of the workmen coming by and apologizing so politely for having
unwittingly observed the little lady—I suppose I was four or five . . .
And you never had as much as I had. Hoarding soap. *We* didn't—build
it up as the most important thing."

"You don't need to be told, people come all sorts. The head-doctors,"
said Mendoza, "I don't go along with. You come equipped with this or
that personality—character. It can be modified, but only to a degree."
He laughed suddenly. And to her raised brows: "Nothing. I was thinking of a rather nice woman I once met, who'd say it all depends on the
stars in your horoscope. I'm the way I am because I was born at seven
A.M. on February twenty-eighth in a certain year, under the sign of
Pisces—"

"And maybe so," said Alison. "They say all Pisces people are strongly
intuitive. And goodness knows I suppose I'm a typical Scorpio."

"*¡Vaya despacio!*" said Mendoza. "I thought I had married a halfway
intelligent wife. Let's celebrate by going out to dinner."

"Hinting that I can't cook, again. To El Ralámpago on the Strip."

"No, *por favor*. No place with an orchestra and dance-floor. I'm too tired."

"You always are. All right. I'm not in the mood much either. What a thing . . . I'm sorry for Mr. Chadwick."

"I hope," said Mendoza, and he was quite serious, "this may be the impetus to stir him up to leave his wife and get a divorce. We'll see . . . One thing, if we haven't accomplished much else, we've got Arden and Darrell. Small fry, but helpful. Darrell handed us—inadvertently—the name of his marijuana supplier, which pleased Pat Callaghan because he's a new one they didn't know about."

# 21

He sat at his desk, at ten o'clock the next morning, and surveyed them pleasurably. The principals in the case. This very simple—once they had the key—case. The alert, slim, uniformed policewoman sitting apart, watchfully. Hackett in a straight chair near the door. Palliser in another nearby. Sergeant Lake with notebook and pen poised. Mendoza lit a cigarette.

"I do not understand," said Myra Chadwick, "why we were asked to come here. I do not—"

"To listen to me lecture," said Mendoza. Extra chairs had been brought in; they sat in them stiffly, well-dressed, upper-class people. "On homicide. I've had quite a lot of experience with homicide, Mrs. Chadwick. I hope you'll all find me—interesting. Most of them are remarkably dull, you know—because the kind of people who commit deliberate homicides are apt to underestimate the intelligence of the police. Once we had the key to this one, we found it—dull. In fact, rather a stupid business. I beg your pardon, I should have said these two. It was, of course, a double kill."

(One of them moved slightly.)

"I don't understand this either," said Charles Chadwick loudly. "I—"

"You will, Mr. Chadwick. Very shortly . . . I knew," said Mendoza, "that Miss Chadwick had not been killed by a hold-up pro choosing a random victim, at once. The set-up to convince us of that was—very crude, very obvious, you see. I knew it was a personal motive. Now. All of you are aware that Margaret Chadwick was—" he looked at his cigarette— "a busybody. A gossip. She was—mmh—inquisitive and suspicious. She pried. She interfered. She—" he inhaled—"found out things."

"What do you mean?" said Myra Chadwick. "I don't—that's like slandering—Margaret—"

"We're laying all the cards on the table," said Mendoza gently. "Being quite frank, here. That's the kind she was. You all know it. A good many people had reason to dislike Margaret—if nothing stronger. A number of people can testify to that—aspect of her character. Naturally, we wondered if perhaps her prying had turned up a dangerous secret. Dangerous to someone—and to herself. We looked. We found some interesting little things. Almost everybody," said Mendoza, "has some little secret he'd rather keep to himself. Innocent or not. Margaret found them out. And we had to follow along, and find out—what she had found out—looking for the one who might have had a motive, for that reason . . . Mr. Chadwick."

"Yes?" He had to clear his throat; he looked gray.

"She *had* told you she knew—your secret. Hadn't she?"

Chadwick lost what little color he had. "Yes, Lieutenant," he said steadily. "Yes." His wife's eyes rolled sideways toward him in ugly speculation, suspicion.

"But she hadn't yet talked to you, Mrs. Chadwick."

"I don't know what you mean. This is all outrageous. A waste of time. You're being extremely rude and stupid. Margaret was murdered by some dope-fiend—"

"There had been," said Mendoza, "a good deal of random malicious talk, Miss Chadwick. Always. Hadn't there? Margaret—your sister Margaret—disapproved of your fiancé, Mr. Lord, said he was marrying you for the money."

"I—it was jealousy!" cried Laura Chadwick. She clutched her handbag, leaning forward. "That was all it was, just jealousy! Yes, but— And *she* wasn't engaged, but right away she had to prove she could be, she started talking about being engaged to George Arden, but the times I met him, he didn't act as if— She was just jealous!"

"Laura, honey," said Lord quietly.

"And that's very possible," said Mendoza. "Mr. Chadwick—Mrs. Chadwick. Had Margaret ever said anything to either of you about that? Accusing Mr. Lord of being a fortune-hunter?"

"Yes," said Chadwick distastefully. "Yes, I'm afraid she had, Lieutenant. It was—I put it down to spiteful jealousy, as Laura says. It was nothing, I didn't— If we're being so frank, I'll say that—Margaret never had many dates with young men, wasn't popular. But I don't understand what—"

"Just clearing the air," said Mendoza. "That's all. Margaret had been —mmh—spiteful toward a number of people. Who might be supposed to have a reason, a little reason or a big one, to want her out of the way. We looked, and found them. These days, you know, we're pretty smart fellows. We like to think." He gestured casually with his cigarette. "Sergeant Hackett there, he was a psychology major up at Berkeley. Me, I never went to college, but I'm reasonably smart about people. But this boy didn't know that. He figured us for dumb cops, all right." He put out his cigarette, carefully.

"What do you *mean?*" cried Laura Chadwick.

"Well, for one thing," said Mendoza, "he never thought we'd make a connection between Jennifer Hill and Margaret Chadwick. He probably hoped we'd never identify Jennifer Hill at all—even if we found her."

"What—who is Jennifer Hill?" asked Chadwick.

"Was, Mr. Chadwick, was. She was a rather silly, pretty girl who also got herself murdered last Saturday night. For a very slim motive. Because somebody lost his temper with her silly sentimental talk. Just like Margaret, she was strangled. And awhile afterward, somebody took a spade and battered in her pretty face, because he didn't want her identified."

Laura Chadwick made a strangled, sick, wordless exclamation.

"Is it necessary to—really, Lieutenant—" Chadwick half rose.

"It is necessary. Sit down, Mr. Chadwick." Mendoza straightened in his chair. "But it is not necessary to play cat-and-mouse about this any longer. I have the warrants for arrest here before me. Mr. Lord—"

Lord sprang up, cat-quick. "What the *hell*—you can't mean—"

Mendoza smiled at him. "Sit down, Mr. Lord. You're jumping to conclusions. Maybe you have a reason?" Slowly he got out his cigarette-case, extracted a cigarette, tapped it on the desk, put it in his mouth, lit it with a flick of the desk-lighter. He said gently, "Why, you small-time, hick glamour-boy, did you think you'd get away with it? I know every move you made. Everything about you. Police-Chief Jensen of Whitesville was very forthcoming."

*"What the hell do you—I don't—"*

"You thought Genevieve Walker, who is going to die so soon, would die soon enough not to say anything. To stir up a fuss about Jenny's disappearance. That after she died, the hospital wouldn't look too far or too long for an only relative. It was a gamble. You took it. But you didn't know that, suspecting you, she had—in her own word—snooped, before. Had seen a letter postmarked Whitesville, Kansas."

"I don't know what you're talking about." Impassive. Stolid.

"And heard a man address you as Pierce. She's still alive, Lord, and she's made a statement. Would you like me to tell you all your movements on last Saturday night?"

"No!" cried Laura Chadwick. "No! I don't—I can't—"

"Laura, baby, this guy's been smoking opium. He can't—"

Charles Chadwick was on his feet. "No, you can't mean to accuse— Why? What reason—"

"Sit down, all of you. We are going back to last Saturday night," said Mendoza. "In detail." His voice was hard. "But first we're going to take a look at the background. Because we know it, make no mistake. The gentleman you know as Kenneth Lord, Mr. Chadwick, is in reality Mr. Robert Meredith Hill, and he comes from Whitesville, Kansas—not the deep south. His father had a small hardware store there, but he died when Robert was eight, and Mrs. Hill had rather a hard time as a widow. There were a couple of years when she was on public relief. Robert worked at a number of odd jobs, and before he was twelve he'd been in a little trouble. Involving the odd minor theft here and there— the rifling of the housewife's purse when he was washing windows for her, the picking up of anything small and portable to sell for what he could get. The odd thing was, everybody liked Robert, such a nice-looking, polite youngster, and nobody liked to turn him in. But finally somebody did—the local newspaper. Because he'd been selling papers, had a regular route, and got to pocketing the subscription-money and forgetting to turn it in. He was put on probation, that time. Very early he found out, did Robert, that his good looks and nice manners could— mmh—get him things very easy. Among other things, girls. When he was twenty, nine years ago, he was working as a clerk at a Whitesville drugstore. He was well-liked in spite of his little record—he always put up a good front, the likeable friendly fellow. He was going around with a nice girl named Mary Warren, and he got her in trouble. As the phrase goes. He—"

Laura Chadwick had been sitting frozen, white-faced. Now she cried out, "No! No! It's not—that's not so! You've got it all wrong! He comes from Virginia, he—"

"Please be quiet, Miss Chadwick." The policewoman went over to her. "To buy Mary Warren an abortion," Mendoza went on, "he robbed the drugstore till. In order to do that, he used a hammer on the proprietor of the drugstore, a Mr. Chester Adams, who happened to come in at the wrong moment. Mr. Adams didn't die, but it was a close thing for awhile. Mary Warren had her abortion—and died of it. And of course, he was rather easily found out—because Mr. Adams, when he was conscious, could name him. So he ran. Police-Chief Jensen missed him, unfortunately. Police-Chief Jensen thinks that Mrs. Hill has always known where Robert was, but refused to give any information, denying it. I think so too. We know where Robert ran. He ran as far as San Francisco, where he started calling himself Allen Pierce. He got a job as a salesman, he was again well-liked—until he fell for an easier way to make money and got to be an errand-boy for the numbers-racket fellows. But money was always such a temptation to him—he double-crossed one of them eventually and decamped with the whole take. So he had to run again. He ran down south, and he got another job as a salesman, at The Broadway. He was using his own name again. And in February or March of 1957 he met and eventually married a pretty girl called Jennifer Walker. She had a good job and his salary wasn't so much. She was a simple, sentimental little thing, loved and trusted him and gave him anything he asked for."

"*No!*" said Laura Chadwick. "No, it wasn't that way—"

"You shut up," said Lord. "Lot of nonsense. He can't prove— Just a lot of crap—"

"The easy way," said Mendoza. "The easy way to get money. Always. At one time he had some idea of breaking into T.V. But then, after awhile, he had another idea. Rich people, they have stocks and bonds. This hick ignoramus," and he laughed. "Like the double-talking modern economists. He just didn't know that about eighty percent of the people who own stocks and bonds, the capitalists, are small investors with less than five thousand bucks a year income. No. He got himself a job at a big brokerage. He figured he'd make contact with a wealthy widow or an heiress, no trouble at all. And no trouble for good-looking, well-brought-up, polite Robert to annex one like that. She'd jump at him, sure. Scion of a genteel old southern family. He gets the accent very well, doesn't he? So he left the sentimental little blonde wife, she was no use to him any more—she'd lost her job anyway—"

"*No!*" gasped Laura Chadwick. "No, it wasn't—she didn't either love him, she just wanted his money, she was a tramp and went with other—"

"*Laura, shut up!*" said Lord.

"So that was what he told you? Of course. She was quite a respectable girl. Only silly—no common sense. As her sister said. Her sister has made a statement, you know, Mr. Lord. Mr. Pierce. Mr. Hill . . . You will persist in underestimating us," said Mendoza, and smiled at him amusedly.

"You—!" said Lord, and moved. Hackett caught him, forced him back to the chair.

"Bullies," said Myra Chadwick coldly. "Liars—bullies! This is outrageous. Obviously—"

"Oh, yes, it was all very obvious, Mrs. Chadwick," said Mendoza. "Once we started to unravel it. His attempts to cover up were—laughable."

"This is— No," said Chadwick, shaking his head. "No, it can't be—because Laura was with him that night, she can say he didn't—"

"Why, yes, so she was, wasn't she?" said Mendoza. "I said the warrants for arrest, you know—plural."

"*Oh, my God, no!*" Chadwick sat down again as if his legs refused to hold him.

Myra Chadwick said coldly, lips pinched, "It's obvious the man is incompetent or dishonest. He's been bribed by the real murderer to—"

"That must be the way it is, all right. Or he's off his head. Now, Laura baby—"

"I'm afraid it isn't as simple as that, you know. We have so much evidence. Would you like to see the wire from Police-Chief Jensen, Mr. Chadwick? I might say," said Mendoza, "that one of the first suggestive little points was that Margaret Chadwick carried no snapshots of her family around at all. Only of Arden. And I think that was the conventional gesture. Yours can hardly be described as a close family." Chadwick put a hand over his face, dumbly. "You'd never really liked your sister much, had you, Miss Chadwick? No, she wasn't a very likeable person, I'm afraid. And on the other hand, Mr. Lord had become the center of your life. As for Mr. Lord, well, of course he had found his heiress at last, and he didn't mean to let go of her."

"No—no—I didn't—he didn't—"

"I know about ninety-nine percent of it, you know. I can tell you just how it went. Suppose you listen, both of you, and please don't hesitate to correct me if I go wrong."

"Just let him talk," said Lord. "Lot of crap."

"A week ago last Wednesday, Margaret was visiting Miss Genevieve Walker at the General Hospital, and Miss Walker's sister, Jenny Hill, was there too. She happened to drop her handbag, and things fell out of it. Among other things was a snapshot, and Margaret had a glimpse of it and recognized Mr. Lord's picture. She asked questions, and was told that it was a picture of Mrs. Hill's husband. Margaret had never liked you, Mr. Lord—I wouldn't doubt partly of jealousy, but also because—unlike Mrs. Hill—she had a little common sense. She suspected that you were marrying her sister for the money, and while there was nothing she could do about it, she hadn't hesitated to say so—to her family, not to outsiders. That would be bringing gossip a little too close to Margaret, and she also knew that talking outside would invite her friends to think that she *was* just jealous. But here was something to delight any busybody's heart! He was married—or had been—maybe there was a lot more to find out about him. A lot more unsavoury things, to take pleasure in telling Laura. Maybe some things so unsavoury that her parents would try to break the engagement—"

"They wouldn't—they couldn't! I'm of age, I—"

"Oh, yes," said Mendoza. "We'll come to that point later, Miss Chadwick. I don't know what happened next but I can make a good guess. Margaret wanted a copy of that snapshot, which showed Lord and Jenny Hill together in a—mmh—very loverly manner. I think she got the address and went to see Jenny Hill. I don't know whether she told her the whole story—I doubt it—or offered her money. But I think she got the snapshot, because Jenny either had another print or knew she could always get one, as she had the negative. We found the negative, by the way. You had quite a look for it, didn't you, Mr. Lord, and thought she'd lost it or destroyed it."

"Goddam—"

"Anyway, Margaret showed it to you, Miss Chadwick, and told you all this. You were in her car at the time. You snatched for the snapshot and tore a corner off, didn't you?" She was shaking her head numbly. "You ran to Lord. I think, because he knew that nothing would make you break with him, he had already told you about Jenny. Not, of course, revealing that she knew him by a different name. You knew nothing of his real past—nothing but the nice story he'd made up to go

with his new name. He had told you that his wife was a tramp, no good
—that he'd been fooled by her, taken in. That he was trying to get her
to divorce him. So now you ran to tell him that Margaret knew about
her, and was threatening to tell her parents. You were probably a little
puzzled by the different name, but I expect he made up some plausible
tale to—"

"No, it's not—he was *acting* then, he'd used another—"

*"Laura, for God's sake shut up!"* said Lord.

Mendoza laughed. "No, not a very satisfactory accomplice, is she? I
see. You told him that Margaret said she was going to hire a private
detective to check up on him. I think—how right am I?—that Margaret
had used Thursday and Friday trying a little amateur detective work
herself, hoping for more ammunition before she sprang this on Laura,
and it was either Friday or Saturday that she decided to hire Mr. Hogg
instead. Well, of course she couldn't be allowed to do that, as you saw
instantly, Mr. Lord. You—"

"I refuse to stay here any longer," said Myra Chadwick, "to listen to
this nonsense! Come, Laura. We—"

"Sit down, Mrs. Chadwick. You will all stay and listen." The policewoman went to her, put a hand on her arm. "You had already told
Laura, or then told her, some plausible tale about your past record
looking bad—because of corrupt police in your home town?—because
you'd, maybe, nobly taken the rap for a pal? If the Chadwicks learned of
it, they wouldn't any longer approve of your marriage to Mr. Lord, Miss
Chadwick. And of course, no, they couldn't have prevented you from
marrying him. But, as I've no doubt he pointed out, there was all the
rest of the money. Your mother's money. If Mrs. Chadwick knew your
husband to be a crook with a record, who had married you just for the
money—"

"No! He loves me, we love each—"

"I really don't think she'd have left money to you without a few
strings attached. Without tying it up in a trust. Would you, Mrs. Chadwick? And that, Mr. Lord would find very inconvenient. Possibly it
would be a trust prohibiting Miss Chadwick from willing the capital
herself. Very awkward indeed. There was also the fact that—well, I
suppose you can all subtract as well as I can. The bulk of the money
would be left to the two sisters. If there was only one— *Sit down, Mrs.
Chadwick.* I hadn't finished. Just how long do you think you might have

lived, after making that will? He has one attempted homicide and two completed ones to his credit."

"No," she said. "You're not—saying—" Her eyes moved to Laura, wide, incredulous.

"I don't think you had much trouble persuading Laura, Mr. Lord. She has some elementary common sense too. You thought of a good way to do it—make it look like a random kill, by a smalltime pro hopping her car. Strangling, because of avoiding bloodstains. You set it up for Saturday night—before she had a chance to see the detective, to tell her parents. You knew she'd be out alone, coming home fairly late.

"It was really Jenny who was the bigger problem. I don't suppose Mr. Lord would have any moral scruples about becoming a bigamist, but that could be very awkward too. It would very likely be a large wedding, reported in the society columns, and Jenny might see the pictures and come forward, all injured innocence, to say, but that's *my* husband. And there might also, some day, arise the legal question of inheritance—from his wife—"

"No!" screamed Laura.

"Well, you never know," said Mendoza. "Getting rid of inconvenient people can get to be a habit. Mr. Lord had been trying to persuade Jenny to slip over to Reno for a quiet divorce. But she still loved him, hoped he'd come back to her—she refused. Even, I think, when she was offered a bribe—of your money, Miss Chadwick. Mr. Lord went to see her again that Saturday, to argue with her. I think he went there directly after work, and arrived between six and six-thirty. He argued with her, and she simply went on refusing. I have it on good authority that she 'never got mad' at anybody—and that can be very annoying. Her silly sentimental chatter made him so mad that before he could stop himself he found he'd killed her. It doesn't take long to strangle someone, you know . . . Well, he hadn't meant to go that far, and it put him in a little spot. His car was outside for anyone to see. And it was broad daylight. But he did a little thinking, and saw how he could—with luck—get away with it. He knew that her only relative was dying. With luck, Jenny would never be found—if she was, she might never be identified. It meant a little risk, carrying the body around in the car for a few hours, but there was every chance he'd get away with it. There are apartments on both sides of the house—transient people probably taking little interest in neighbors. He could hope that nobody had seen him come. He went out and drove his car into the garage, out of sight. It was the hour when a lot of people are having dinner, aren't looking out windows. Only one person saw him. Unfortunately, she knew Mrs. Hill and remembered the incident. A Mrs. Whipley who lives in the same block. She said she thought maybe Mrs. Hill had found a nice young man to go around with." Mendoza smiled. "He had to wait for dark, or at least dusk. He spent the time looking through the house for anything which might lead to him. He abstracted a few letters from a pile she'd kept, and perhaps other things—but he didn't find that negative. Somewhere around seven-thirty, when it was almost dark, he wrapped the body in a blanket—Miss Walker says there should be an extra blanket for each bed, and we noticed that one brown one was missing—and carried it out to the car. It's only ten feet or so from the back door to the garage, and there's a trellis partially screening it from the street. In the garage, he used a handy spade to batter in the face—"

"No, he didn't, he never did such a—"

"No, I don't suppose he mentioned that to you, Miss Chadwick. He locked the body in the trunk of the car, wrapped in the blanket. It was long enough after death for the bleeding to have stopped. And he drove up to Hollywood to pick you up. Now all he had to do was get rid of the body, and he had an idea about that . . . On Sunday, when he had more leisure, he wrote—typed—a nice little letter of resignation to Jenny's employers, and forged her signature. He thought that would take care of everything." Mendoza looked around at them, lighting a new cigarette. "Well, that's Part One. We now go on to Part Two—Margaret."

# 22

"**I** can't listen to this," said Chadwick. "I can't believe—"

Myra Chadwick sat stiff in her chair, staring remotely before her, absolutely expressionless. Fleetingly Mendoza wondered whether she was capable of any honest emotion at all. Even fear. Even hate. He said, "You have to know it all, Mr. Chadwick. We all do . . . Jenny hadn't been planned. Margaret was planned. You had to tell Laura about Jenny, Mr. Lord, but I think she was probably more relieved than otherwise. Two birds with one stone. Now the way would be clear. I wonder if you told her that Jenny had attacked you in some way, that it was really self-defense? Well, it doesn't matter. You went and had dinner at Frascati's—with Jenny's body slowly stiffening in the trunk of your car—"

"Don't," said Chadwick. "Not—Laura, not—"

"And you went on to the Club Afrique, just as you said," Mendoza went on remorselessly. "But from there, at a little after ten o'clock, the two of you made a phone-call. The waiter noticed that you were both absent from the table, and made the logical deduction—the dance-floor. Laura dialed the Hacketts' house in Highland Park—because of course she'd taken care to find out where Margaret was going—and handed the phone to you. You asked for Miss Chadwick and handed the phone back. That established that the call was from a man. When Margaret came, Laura told her a pretty story. I don't know what the story was, but again I can guess. I think she said she'd had a quarrel with Lord, that she'd found out more about him, and was ready to admit that dear Margaret was so right. And that he'd gone off and left her stranded here, and would Margaret please come and take her home, because she hadn't any money for a cab? No need to leave her own party right away,

Laura'd be all right here until she came, but if she just *would*. And she
told Margaret she was at Giuseppi's. Am I right, Miss Chadwick?"

"You *devil!*" she screamed at him.

"And wouldn't Margaret be pleased to hear that! Yes, but you had a
few anxious moments, I think. You got Margaret to say approximately
what time she'd leave, and you could estimate about what time she'd be
turning into Giuseppi's parking-lot. That nice, dark, unattended lot.
I've had a look at it. I think you parked round at the side, where there's
room for only a few cars—and it's darker there. You left the Club
Afrique at about eleven, went to Giuseppi's and waited in the lot. She
was a little late. She finally came at about eleven-twenty-five. You were
on the lookout for her Buick, Miss Chadwick, and you stepped out and
beckoned her, as she got out of her car. Margaret came over to you—
probably assuming that you'd met friends after Mr. Lord left you, and
were waiting in their car, having had enough of the—mmh—gaiety
inside. You asked her to get in for a moment—maybe you were sobbing
into a handkerchief, incoherent—and she did. And Mr. Lord, from the
back seat, reached out and took her by the throat."

Chadwick made an inarticulate sound. He said something that
sounded like, "Her own sister—"

"Within three minutes, you were sure she was dead. You pulled her
over the seat, Mr. Lord, and put her on the floor, with a coat or something laid over her. And you both went into Giuseppi's to listen to your
favorite pianist. Only, of course, you didn't. You had too much else to
do. There are a couple of entrances and exits. You took a table and
ordered drinks to establish your presence. But as soon as the place
darkened for the floor-show, you left a bill on the table and got out. I
don't suppose you were in the place ten minutes. I'm frank to say I
don't know why you took the trouble to transfer both bodies to the
Buick, but I know you did—probably on one of those dark little streets
above Sunset. Because while you were doing it, that tiny piece of the
ring that had held Jenny's charm to her bracelet fell out in the Buick.
You didn't know about the charm, no. I can imagine a reason for the
transfer. The Buick was much newer, in better condition—maybe you'd
been having some trouble with your car, Mr. Lord, and had visions of
getting stalled on the freeway with two bodies. Anyway, you did that. It
was then about a quarter to twelve. You went straight downtown to drop
Jenny first. That construction job is just across the street from where
Lord parks his car every day, he'd noticed it. Bury a body there, let

them build an office-building over it, nobody the wiser. A good idea—
only the bulldozers weren't finished, you see. You took the freeway, you
were there by twelve-ten or even a little earlier—with Miss Chadwick
trailing you in your car. Naturally, nobody around the business area at
that hour. It took you maybe ten minutes to dig the body in as deep as it
was—I think with one of the tools in your trunk. You then drove out
North Broadway and dumped Margaret, having first rifled her wallet
and taken the snapshot. The yards are only about a mile from where you
left Jenny. You parked the Buick on a dark side-street, and took over
your own car again, and drove Miss Chadwick home. You dropped her
at between a quarter of one and one o'clock. I may say that I think Miss
Chadwick waited until the house was quiet and she knew her parents
would be asleep, and searched Margaret's room for any incriminating
evidence she might have found, or written down. It had all gone smooth
and easy—just as you'd planned it. You thought we'd take it for what it
looked like." Mendoza glanced at Lord and shook his head. "We have
slightly higher I.Q's than that, Mr. Lord. The car-hopper wouldn't have
missed her wrist-watch or that fourteen-karat cigarette-case. Wouldn't
have dropped her handbag with her, to tell us who she was and that
she'd been driving. Wouldn't, above all, have abandoned the car . . . I
think you most probably dropped the blanket into the river-bed on your
way back to Hollywood. A lot of funny things find their way into the
wash, and of course there's no water in it this time of year, we're having
a look. I think—"

"Goddam you! No! No, you can't—prove all that, you—"

"I think we can, Mr. Lord," said Mendoza. "I really think we can.
Quite a lot of nice evidence."

And Myra Chadwick said suddenly, in her thin sharp voice, *"Me?* He
would have thought of killing *me? They* would have—Laura—"

Oh, yes, thought Mendoza. *Me.* Just reaching her, and that was the
first aspect of it that she reacted to. A threat to *me.* And you could say
that the wheel had come full circle, because that was where it had
started, all those years ago. She was a woman like that—her daughters
had been like her—and she had brought them up that way.

"Oh, my God," said Charles Chadwick. "Oh, my God. Let me out of
here, I can't—I can't—" He half-rose, tugging at his shirt-collar, and
slumped back into the chair and slid off to the floor. The policewoman
and Palliser were beside him in an instant.

"He's just fainted, sir, he'll be all right . . . loosen his collar—"

Mendoza stood up. "Robert Meredith Hill, I am arresting you on a charge of homicide—"

He said nothing at all, as Hackett came up to lead him out. They wouldn't get a confession here. His eyes were blank. But as Hackett took his arm, he said one word, viciously, to Mendoza. It was Laura Chadwick who screamed and struggled and went into hysterics.

The court calendars were always full, and the case didn't come to trial until September. They were tried jointly, which was a break for Lord because Myra Chadwick was paying the lawyers. Mendoza went on to other cases, and half forgot Margaret Chadwick and poor silly Jenny Hill. And Alison's house on Rayo Grande Avenue (now beginning to be paved, as promised, by Woodes Bros.) started to go up. And the great smoke-silver cat had other, new hands to stroke him, new voices to praise and soothe him; and after a few uneasy days he settled down to his new place.

Lord was the more voluble during the trial, claiming that the whole idea had been Laura's, that he'd dragged his heels from the start— claiming that Jenny Hill had threatened him with the poker, that that had been self-defense. Laura Chadwick (whose newspaper pictures hardly justified the headlines calling her *Lovely Blonde Heiress)* was docile, quiet, and remarkably unconvincing. Her lawyer painted a heart-rending picture of a young, inexperienced girl in love, completely under the thumb of her murderous lover.

The trial was slightly delayed during its second day when Detective-Sergeant Arthur Hackett, called to give evidence for the prosecution, was found to be absent from the courtroom. Sergeant Hackett was subsequently not held for contempt only because he was able to plead that he had been, since three A.M. that morning, at the Highland Park Memorial Hospital awaiting the arrival of his and his wife's first child. (The newspapers reported with glee that it turned out to be a nine-pound boy, christened Mark Christopher.)

Neither Lord (Hill) nor Laura got away with it. But the jury evidently felt that Laura was a little less guilty. They gave her life. Lord was sentenced to the gas-chamber.

Happening on an account of the verdict in the *Times,* Mendoza said, "Well, juries. Ask me, she was more—culpable—than he was in a way, her own sister. But they never like to send a woman to the chamber. You can understand it."

"What? Oh, yes," said Alison absently. Alison, these days, was more often than not present only in body, her mind being up on Rayo Grande Avenue deciding on the exact shade of paint for the master bedroom, the tile-pattern for the master bathroom, and worrying as to whether the big window in her studio, designed to admit desirable north light, was really big enough. "Luis, I was just wondering. Would you think that twin b—"

"*¡Jesus, Santa Maria y José—pare—no hay tal!* What the hell, *querida?* I would not! One of those kingsized things, I've no objection at all to having the recommended forty inches' width sleeping-space per person, but—*¡por Dios!* This is sabotage."

"Why on earth the fuss? Oh—you idiot, I meant for the guest-room, of course. I was just trying to decide between Danish walnut and mahogany. *Amado,* would I think of—"

And of course there was an appeal. And on the last day of November (with the painters imminent in Alison's house) Mendoza was summoned up to San Francisco to give evidence. Kenneth Lord (Robert Hill) was claiming insanity, to save himself from the gas-chamber. Apparently he was clever enough to have faked some plausible symptoms, and he also had a smart lawyer.

Mendoza did some swearing. He was in the middle of a little teaser of a case; but you couldn't argue with a subpoena. He went home to pack a bag. Alison drove him to the airport. "You won't know I'm gone," he said, kissing her goodbye.

"Liar. I'm bound to notice now and then. Nobody to wake me up all night—"

"*¡Mujer falso!* I do not snore."

"Oh, I never said *that,*" said Alison. "Take care, love."

Lord had either put up a nice show as a lunatic, or the board was very thorough. They kept Mendoza two days. He saw Lord only once. Tiresomely, he had to go over the evidence again, and describe Lord's demeanour at the time of arrest and so on, and give them his personal opinion as an experienced investigator. He gave them that in one sentence: "The man's as sane as you or me, he was sane when he committed the crimes, it was deliberate homicide for personal gain."

That was the only time he saw Lord. And Lord met his eyes across the room with cold hatred, and his lips formed a name for Mendoza.

Lord didn't get away with it.

Mendoza landed back at Burbank at two-fifty of an unreasonably

warm December afternoon, and took a cab home. He found Alison
lying on the couch with three cats on and around her, and El Señor
detached on top of the phonograph.

"*Mi amor solamente,* did you miss me? . . . That's a lie. You've
been up there twelve hours a day, standing around straw-bossing the
job."

"I have. But I found a few stray moments to miss you, *novio.* Just
here and there. Did he get off? . . . Good. He deserved it. Oh, there
was something in the morning's paper, I saved it to show you—about
Mr. Chadwick. Here."

The brief article, on a back page, said that Charles Chadwick, father
of Laura Chadwick recently tried and convicted, etcetera, had filed suit
for divorce against, etcetera. "Poor man," said Alison. "Maybe he'll
have some happiness now. You said the Ross woman was about forty?
Still young enough to have children, maybe. Maybe they—"

"*¡Porvida!* You're getting a complex about children. And I thought
they were going to start painting the kitchen today—why aren't you up
there supervising the job?"

"Well—" said Alison. She moved closer and reached up to smooth
his moustache. "Well, I was. It's going to look very nice. But then the
smell of the paint began to make me feel sort of queer—and I got to
wondering—I mean, it's only a couple of days, and I haven't seen a
doctor yet, of course—"

"*¡No, zape, no me diga, despacio!* Don't tell me—"

"And I've been wondering," said Alison, "how to break it to you
gently—because you'd better be warned—but there are twins on both
sides of my family."

"*¡Atrocidad!*" said Mendoza violently. "No! *¡Absolutamente,* I for-
bid it!"